Patents AND Trademarks
Plain&Simple

Michael H. Jester
Registered Patent Attorney

CAREER
PRESS

THE CAREER PRESS, INC.
Franklin Lakes, NJ

Copyright © 2004 by Michael H. Jester

PATENTS AND TRADEMARKS PLAIN & SIMPLE
EDITED AND TYPESET BY KRISTEN PARKES
Cover design by Foster & Foster, Inc.
Printed in the U.S.A. by Book-mart Press
Please note: All trademarks and service marks appear capitalized.

To order this title, please call toll-free 1-800-CAREER-1 (NJ and Canada: 201-848-0310) to order using VISA or MasterCard, or for further information on books from Career Press.

The Career Press, Inc., 3 Tice Road, PO Box 687,
Franklin Lakes, NJ 07417
www.careerpress.com

Library of Congress Cataloging-in-Publication Data

Jester, Michael H., 1964-
    Patents and trademarks plain & simple / by Michael H. Jester.
        p. cm.
    Includes bibliographical references and index.
    ISBN 1-56414-728-2 (paper)
        1. Patents--United States. 2. Trademarks--United States. I. Title.

T339.J47 2004
608.773--dc22

2003069605

I dedicate this book to my wife, Dorothy, and my three children, John, James, and Julia, whose love and support allowed me to successfully pursue an intriguing profession that combines law and science.

Acknowledgments

I wish to acknowledge all my mentors who helped me during the early part of my patent law career. I especially want to thank patent attorneys Paul Vapnek of San Francisco, California, and Ken Klarquist of Portland, Oregon. Through their kindness, wisdom, and patience, they inspired me to master the difficult field of patent law. I also wish to acknowledge and thank patent attorney Walter Duft of Clarence, New York, for his insightful editorial contributions to this book.

Contents

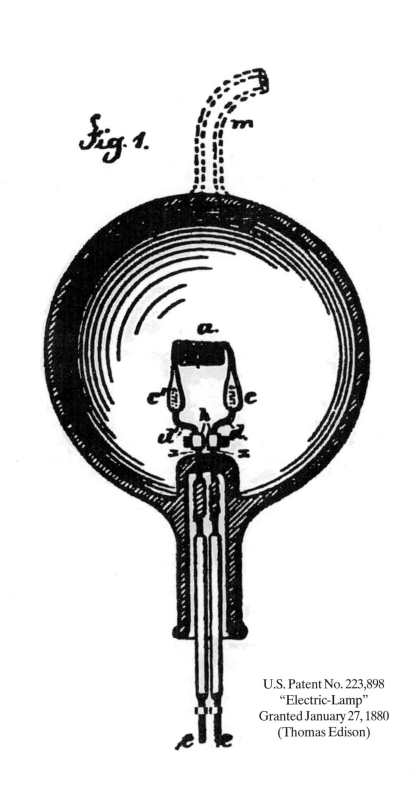

Fig. 1.

U.S. Patent No. 223,898
"Electric-Lamp"
Granted January 27, 1880
(Thomas Edison)

Preface

I t was the straw that broke the camel's back. I read a feature article on patents published in the *USA Today* newspaper that explained that in order to get a U.S. patent "[t]he invention must be new and useful or be an improvement on an existing device" (April 11, 2001). Because it misstated the legal requirements for obtaining a patent, the article was terribly misleading. In the United States, an invention, as claimed at the end of the patent after the description, must be useful, novel, and nonobvious in order to be patentable. *USA Today* had confidently misinformed millions of novices that all they have to do to get a U.S. patent is to make an improvement to an existing device. With that misinformation in hand, the starry-eyed inventor begins his or her search for the Holy Grail, wasting countless hours and dollars along the way. To add insult to injury, the article had nothing to do with trademarks, yet it featured a huge blowup of the trademark registration symbol (®). *USA Today*'s patent bombast finally prompted me to write this book to help fill the information gap that the public faces when it comes to patents.

Large businesses, and public companies in particular, have ready access to sophisticated patent legal advice. They regularly take advantage of this advice to secure exclusive rights to their new products and the results of their research and development. However, individual inventors and small business owners are not so fortunate. Chances are they do not even know that there is a significant difference between a regular attorney and a patent attorney. Usually their personal attorney is not much help when it comes to patent law.

Individuals and small business owners might want to read a short, easily understood book about patents to see if they even need a patent attorney or to enable them to better communicate with the patent attorney they have retained. Not surprisingly, most books on patents are very complex works written for patent attorneys, by patent attorneys. There are a few patent-related books aimed at the average person, but they are usually written by non-attorneys and deal primarily with how to sell an invention: a daunting task, to say the least. Frankly, all of the "how to" patent-related books that I reviewed were full of bad advice stemming from the authors' limited personal experiences and lack of formal training in patent law.

Trademarks are also extremely important to the success of any business. Because the United States Patent and Trademark Office (USPTO) handles both patents and trademarks, the subjects naturally go hand in hand. There is a great deal of misunderstanding in the general public regarding the nature of trademarks, how to select a good one, how to search a trademark, the relationship of Internet domain names, and what you need to do in order to police your valuable trademark rights. Therefore, Chapters 22–26 address these subjects.

The USPTO has a fine Website, but most people do not know it exists. The portions of the USPTO Website dedicated to telling the general public about patents and trademarks are necessarily very general and written in the same vanilla style as the IRS 1040 form instructions; that is, they don't explain how to best take advantage of the system, which, after all, is not their purpose.

This book is intended to help regular folks learn something about our wonderful U.S. patent and trademark legal system that is the bedrock of our world-dominant economy. I tried to dispel myths, give helpful anecdotes, avoid using legalese, and keep my discussions *plain and simple*. Above all, practical advice is given to help people cut through some of the red tape.

Disclaimer

This publication is intended to provide accurate general information in regard to U.S. patent and trademark law. It is sold or otherwise disseminated with the understanding that neither the author, nor the publisher, is providing legal advice to any particular person or entity through this book. Intellectual property law is an extremely complex subject. Therefore, this short text cannot possibly fully explain all the intricacies of patent and trademark law and how it might apply to various fact situations. In addition, patent and trademark law, like all areas of the law, is constantly changing and evolving. Readers should seek legal advice from a competent patent and/or trademark attorney regarding their specific fact situations.

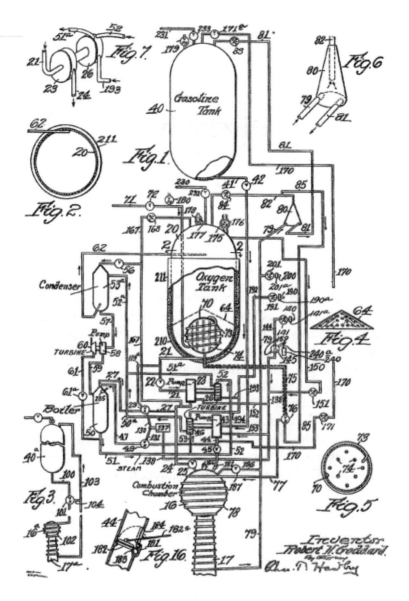

U.S. Patent No. 2,395,113
"Mechanism for Feeding Combustion
Liquids to Rocket Apparatus"
Granted February 19, 1946

(pioneer patent of Robert H. Goddard
on liquid-fueled rocket design)

Introduction

T he English Parliament enacted the first patent law in 1624. The concept was simple, but revolutionary. In return for disclosing an invention to the public, a subject of the crown was *granted* the exclusive right to commercialize his invention for a limited number of years. This kept the king from arbitrarily granting monopolies to his cronies and spurred the development of more inventions to benefit mankind. At the time, many innovations were processes that would otherwise have been kept secret, such as methods of dyeing fabric. The invention couldn't be trivial, such as colored doorknobs, but, in general, had to solve a real problem in a beneficial way.

The name "letters patent" reflects the fact that the document granting the exclusive rights is open to public view. Ever since Parliament's adoption of the Statute of Monopolies, it has been the custom in letters patents to set forth both the legal grant and an official description of the invention. Thus, every patent is a hybrid legal/scientific document.

History of Patent Law

When the founding fathers drafted the U.S. Constitution, they recognized that England's patent system was partly responsible for its considerable industrial and economic might. It was self-evident that people were encouraged to innovate and invest when they knew they would receive the exclusive rights to the fruits of their labors for a significant number of years. Article 1, Section 8, Clause 8 of the U.S. Constitution, as originally ratified, provides: "[t]he Congress shall have power...to promote the progress of science and useful arts, by securing for limited times to authors and inventors the exclusive right to their respective writings and discoveries."

The U.S. Congress passed the first patent law in 1790 and it has periodically amended the laws pertaining to patents, most recently in the American Inventors Protection Act (AIPA) of 1999. The bulk of the U.S. laws relating to patents are found in Title 35 of the U.S. Code. The manner in which those laws are interpreted and applied in particular fact situations is determined in the federal district courts with a right of appeal all the way to the U.S. Supreme Court.

What a Patent Does and Does Not Entail

A U.S. patent grants the right to *exclude* others from making, using, selling, or offering for sale the invention covered by the claims of the patent. It is *not* an affirmative right to make what is defined by the claims. Many patents are dominated by earlier granted patents that have broader claims. For example, let us presume that Jack was the first to invent the pencil and that he received a patent having a claim that calls for a wooden shaft with a graphite core. Jill later invents an improvement and gets a patent on a pencil that has a claim calling for a wooden shaft, a graphite core, and an eraser on the end of the pencil. Jill cannot sell eraser-equipped pencils without Jack's permission because they fall within the broad claim of Jack's earlier patent. She would infringe Jack's patent if she proceeded without a license under his patent. However, Jack cannot sell eraser-equipped pencils without Jill's permission because they are covered by the claim of her later patent. Because the public mostly wants to buy eraser-equipped pencils, one solution in the real world would be for Jack and Jill to grant each other royalty-free cross-licenses under their patents. This would allow both inventors to sell regular wooden pencils *and* eraser-equipped pencils. They might also legally agree not to license any other parties, thus foreclosing competition from anyone else.

Much has been written comparing patents to monopolies. In truth, the exclusive right afforded by a patent is not a monopoly, but a government grant of exclusive rights in return for teaching the public. A valid patent bestows upon the public a benefit it did not previously have in the form of knowledge that will help advance the useful arts. The antitrust laws were enacted many years after the U.S. patent law to restrain abuses of the marketplace, such as the oil and steel monopolies, that artificially control supply, limit competition, and keep prices high. It is therefore inappropriate to describe a patent as an exception to the rule against monopolies, as this denigrates the important contribution that inventors make to society.

It is still possible to violate the antitrust laws by improperly using the patent system. For example, it would be an antitrust violation to fraudulently procure a patent through concealment of an earlier publication disclosing the same invention, and then sue competitors for infringement of the patent. It would also be an antitrust violation to condition the sale of patented articles on the purchase of nonpatented articles. It would also be a violation of antitrust laws to create and use anti-competitively a so-called patent pool, by purchasing every unexpired patent in a particular market with the intent of restraining competition in that market.

Historical Inventors

Thomas Jefferson was the first patent examiner. In 1802, Congress established the U.S. Patent Office as the sole federal agency responsible for examining patent applications and granting patents. For many years, it was located near the White House. During the War of 1812, the English burned down much of Washington D.C. Legend has it that a British army officer holding a torch spared the U.S. Patent Office. He had been told by a defiant government employee that the small wooden building held knowledge for all mankind and that no educated Englishman would destroy it.

Thomas Edison is the number-one all time U.S. inventor, having personally been granted more than 1,000 U.S. patents, a record that is likely never to be broken. To put his achievement into perspective, consider that it is rare to see an engineer or scientist who has been granted more than 10 U.S. patents in an entire lifetime. In nearly 30 years in the patent law business, I can only remember three inventors that I personally had contact with that have been granted more than 20 U.S. patents during their lifetimes. Just to tie Edison's record you would have to be granted more than 20 patents per year, every year, for more than 50 years!

George Eastman, the founder of the Kodak Company, is reported to have been granted more than 600 U.S. patents in his lifetime relating to film and photography. In the early 1880s, he invented rolled photographic film as we know it today and cameras that could use his new film. In 1888, he introduced the small box-like Kodak camera, priced at $25, that used a roll of film and could take 100 pictures.

Robert Goddard is perhaps the most prolific yet underappreciated U.S. inventor, having been granted 214 patents. He pioneered the liquid-fueled rocket, making major advancements in launch control, tracking, engine design, stabilization, and recovery. Much of his work would later be incorporated into the German V-2 rocket, and still later, into the U.S. and Russian space programs. Goddard was a visionary who also patented magnetically levitated and powered passenger trains, and vacuum tube oscillators, among other groundbreaking advancements. In 1960, years after his death, NASA and the U.S. military paid $1 million for past infringement and for a license under Goddard's patents. At the time, this was the largest sum of money ever paid by the U.S. Government for patent infringement.

When World War II ended, the United States and Russia scrambled to divide up the German rocket scientists and remaining supply of V-2 rockets. After intense interrogation in New Mexico, one of the leading German rocket experts allegedly complained, "Why are you asking me all these questions about the V-2 rocket technology? Why don't you ask your own Dr. Goddard?" The U.S. military not only failed to recognize the tremendous military potential of Dr. Goddard's research and development in rocketry, but also failed to classify the same, thereby allowing the Germans and Russians to perfect Goddard's breakthroughs and gain an early lead in ballistic missiles and space exploration.

Historical Patents

The first several thousand U.S. patents were unnumbered. To date, more than 6 million U.S. patents have been granted and the number granted annually continues to increase. U.S. Pat. No. 1,000,000 was granted in 1911 for an invention titled "Vehicle Tire." U.S. Pat. No. 5,000,000 was granted in 1991 for an invention titled "Ethanol Production By *Escherichia coli* Strains Co-expressing Zymomonas PDC and ADH Genes." Amazingly, less than 10 years later, U.S. Pat. No. 6,000,000 was granted in 1999 for an invention titled "Extendible Method and Apparatus for Synchronizing Multiple Files on Two Different Computer Systems."

Approximately 80 percent of U.S. patents are granted to companies, 15 percent are granted to individuals, and 5 percent are granted to non-profit institutions such as the University of California. About half of U.S. patents are granted to foreign-based companies and citizens of foreign countries. The bulk of the foreign companies and individuals obtaining

U.S. patents are from Canada, Germany, France, Italy, Japan, South Korea, Taiwan, and the United Kingdom. Every year a list is published ranking the top 50 recipients of U.S. patents for the prior calendar year. IBM annually leads the list, having been granted nearly 3,000 patents in the year 2000 alone, further supporting its annual patent royalty income of more than $1 billion.

History of the USPTO

In the 20th century, the U.S. Patent Office was renamed the U.S. Patent and Trademark Office (USPTO) in recognition of its other primary function of examining trademark applications and granting trademark registrations. Today, the USPTO has thousands of employees, its own zip code, and roughly a billion-dollar annual budget, all financed by user fees. The USPTO has recently consolidated its operations in a new campus in Alexandria, Virginia.

The director of the USPTO heads the office. He also has the title of assistant secretary of commerce, is nominated by the president, must be confirmed by the U.S. Senate, and usually has to resign as soon as a new administration takes over the White House. For much of the 20th century, the so-called commissioner of patents was usually a former chief patent counsel of a major U.S. company such as Phillips Petroleum. More recently, the commissioner (now called the director) has typically been a career government attorney with related government experience, or many years experience with the USPTO itself. At the time of the writing of this book, the director of the USPTO is a former congressman from California.

Intellectual Property

Patents are one type of so-called *intellectual property*, which also includes trademarks, service marks, copyrights, mask works, and trade secrets.

A trademark is a word or a group of words, letters, numbers, and/or symbols that identify a unique source (for example, manufacturer) of particular goods, such as Kraft for cheese, Microsoft for software, and WD-40 for household lubricant. A service mark is a similar unique designation for services, such as Merrill Lynch and Charles Schwab for stock brokerage services. The federal law of trademarks and service marks allows companies to protect the valuable goodwill they build up around the words and symbols under which they sell their products. The primary focus of this book is on patents; however, trademarks can be extremely valuable to a business as well. You may invent a new product and need to patent it and register a trademark for your new product. Or you may simply build a business around unpatentable goods and services and still need to market them under exclusive names and/or logos.

A copyright is an exclusive right to make and distribute copies of works such as books, videos, sound recordings, software, and the like. A copyright arises under federal law and only protects the expression of an idea, not the idea itself. Copyright registration is handled by the U.S. Copyright Office, which operates as part of the Library of Congress and not the Patent and Trademark Office. Unlike a patent, a copyright cannot protect a function, concept, structure, process, or any other utilitarian subject matter. In general, mask work protection addresses exclusive rights in the photolithographic layouts of integrated circuits, and is only of real interest to chip manufacturers such as Intel and Advanced Micro Devices.

A trade secret comprises any information maintained in confidence that is valuable to a business and not known to its competitors, such as formulas, blueprints, financial data, and source code for computer programs. The most famous example of a trade secret is the formula for the Coca-Cola soft drink. Unlike patents, the law of trade secrets provides no protection against competitors who buy your product, reverse engineer the same to figure out how it is built and how it operates, and then manufacture a similar product. Most states have laws that prohibit the misappropriation of trade secrets and allow private parties to bring civil suits to obtain injunctions and money damages. Federal law does not permit civil suits for trade secret misappropriation.

Copyright and trade secret law falls outside the scope of this book. Unfortunately, it also is difficult to find helpful books on these subjects written for individuals and small business owners. Should you engage a patent and trademark attorney at some stage, he or she will usually be fairly knowledgeable about other forms of intellectual property protection besides patents and trademarks.

Why Get a Patent?

I conclude this Introduction with a discussion of reasons for bothering to get a patent at all:

1. A patent enables you to stop competitors from using your invention. In the absence of patent protection for your product or process, you don't have exclusive rights and usually will have to compete on the basis of price and other factors.

If you develop a new product and don't patent it, your competitor can simply copy the product without incurring any research and development costs. Your competitor can then sell the same product for less money and maintain the same profit margin.

2. A patent can be sold or licensed. Either way, you can receive a substantial amount of money for your invention rights if your invention is patented. Without a patent or at least a pending patent application, virtually no company will buy or license your invention rights. Why should they? As soon as it goes into the public domain, they can copy it with impunity. In addition, most companies will not even consider unsolicited invention proposals unless the invention is either already patented or the subject of a pending patent application, and even then only if the inventor will waive all rights except patent rights. They don't want to be sued for stealing someone's idea.

3. If you patent your product or process, this means that nobody else can patent it and hold you up for royalties, or worse yet, prevent you from making your product. The U.S. patent system is a first-to-invent system. In other words, the first person to make the claimed invention gets the U.S. patent so long as a patent application is timely filed. If you don't file, you run the risk that someone else will independently invent the same thing, file a patent application, and later assert the resulting patent against you.

4. If you obtain a U.S. patent, you may be able to settle an infringement claim by cross-licensing with your competitor. You may need a license under a particular patent owned by your competitor, and it may similarly need a license under your patent. Rather than pay each other royalties, you can simply agree to grant each other a royalty-free license.

5. A patent becomes a valuable asset of your company if you successfully commercialize the invention. This helps build the value of your company if you ever seek venture capital or bank financing if you decide to sell shares of stock in your company to the public, or if you wish to sell your business.

6. Patents increase the prestige of your employees and your company. If your company keeps getting more and more valuable patents in a given field, it will gain notoriety for being innovative and on the cutting edge.

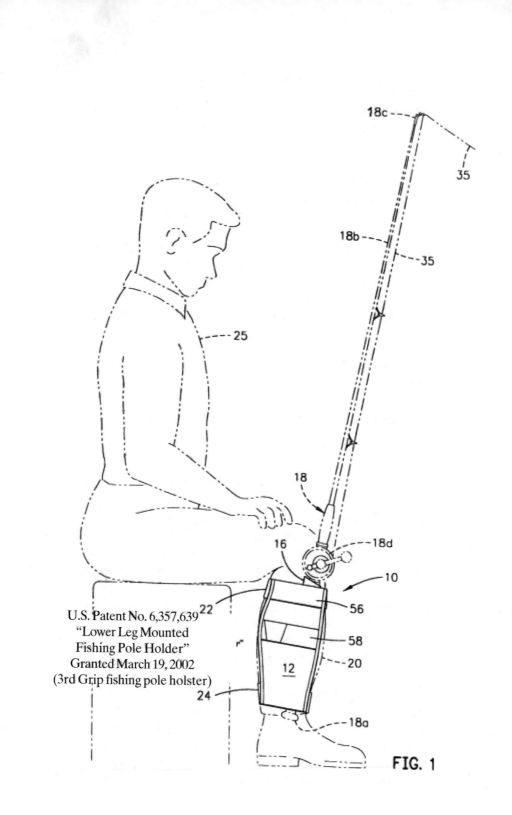

U.S. Patent No. 6,357,639
"Lower Leg Mounted
Fishing Pole Holder"
Granted March 19, 2002
(3rd Grip fishing pole holster)

FIG. 1

CHAPTER 1

The Process of Inventing

I
t has been observed that innovation is always invention, perhaps just not always *patentable* invention. Chapter 2 discusses what the U.S. patent laws require in order for an invention to be patentable. But before discussing those principles, it is helpful to consider the manner in which inventions are made. It is only through understanding the process of inventing that one can begin to appreciate what kinds of innovative efforts might lead to valuable patent protection in the United States.

From time to time I hear people say, "I wish I could invent something." Usually, they are dreaming about a financial windfall that they would expect to flow naturally from such activity. However, they misperceive the inventive process. It is first and foremost, problem-solving. In the vast majority of cases, valuable inventions are made by individuals in a particular field of endeavor who are frustrated with the shortcomings of the devices, processes, or materials available to them, and so they develop something better. It should come as no surprise, then, that the most worthwhile inventions are developed by people with experience in the field to which the inventions pertain. A plumber working in the field is more likely to come up with a valuable plumbing invention than a mechanical engineer merely working as a designer. The most the latter can do is to consult with plumbers in the field to define the problem. But the engineer's solutions may not take into account ease of use, durability, and so forth, from the same viewpoint as the experienced plumber who must employ the solution in the field.

Individuals with little or no technical training can still come up with valuable inventions; however, they are unlikely to come up with valuable inventions in highly technical fields. A good example of a nontechnical but highly serviceable and marketable invention is the patented 3rd Grip fishing pole holster illustrated at the beginning of this chapter. This device can be readily manufactured in high volume at relatively low cost from Nylon fabric and ABS plastic pipe. The pole holster allows fishermen to use both hands to bait hooks and remove fish, and to eat or drink while fishing. The fishing pole does not have to be held awkwardly between the legs, leaned precariously against a railing, or laid on the ground where it can be stepped on. Literally hundreds of U.S. patents have been granted on fishing pole holders since at least as early as 1819, yet it wasn't until 2002 that a low-cost, serviceable body-mounted version was patented.

Starting the Inventing Process

The inventing process, therefore, starts with recognition of a particular problem. Next, all of the existing solutions to the problem should be carefully considered, assuming they exist. Are the prior efforts to solve the problem practical? What are their shortcomings? Returning to the 3rd Grip fishing pole holster as an example, the prior fishing pole holders fell into several basic categories. The first consisted of brackets mounted to a boat or railing with screws or bolts. Clearly these fishing pole holders were not portable. There were also spikes that were driven into the sand and had cups for holding the fishing pole handle. Complex folding stands and bucket supports also existed. Finally, there was a whole family of body-mounted fishing pole holders. Only the latter category offered the promise of easy portability and ready accessibility sought by the inventor. However, prior art body-mounted fishing pole holders were mostly Rube Goldberg contraptions. (The term "prior art" means inventions publicly known, offered for sale, or used publicly in the United States, and inventions published anywhere, before you made your invention, subject to complicated time limitations). Many were uncomfortable chest harnesses. Only a few examples of leg- or thigh-mounted fishing pole holders had been developed, but they were so complex in construction and/or uncomfortable to wear that they had never been successfully commercialized.

The inventor of the 3rd Grip fishing pole holster did not do a patent search before he made his invention. He was generally familiar with all of the foregoing types of fishing pole holders except for the leg-mounted variety, which had never been successfully commercialized. The inventor discovered on his own that the best location for a body-mounted fishing pole holder is the lower leg because it places the tip of the fishing rod at the best height for baiting and removal of fish and also keeps the angle of the rod undisturbed regardless of whether the fisherman is standing or sitting. At first, the inventor fashioned a leather holster, like a gun holster. But it turned out to be too stiff, too heavy, and too uncomfortable. It would also have been too expensive to manufacture. A leather fishing pole holster would not hold up well when subjected to seawater. Eventually, after a series of different embodiments evolved, he came up with his Nylon fabric holster with a plastic pipe in its pocket for receiving and supporting the rod handle simply by sliding it in the pipe. This fishing pole holster is readily secured around the leg with wide Velcro straps. The inventing process for the 3rd Grip fishing pole holster took about one year. Early on, the inventor had functionality, manufacturability, durability, cost, comfort, and potential market size well in mind. Successful inventions satisfy a demand where the market is crying out for something better. The converse approach of conceiving an invention in a vacuum, and then trying to get the marketplace to accept it rarely succeeds. The marketplace has enthusiastically received the 3rd Grip fishing pole holster, whose use and benefits can be seen at *www.3rdgrip.com.*

In retrospect, the process of inventing an improved fishing pole holder might have been aided by performing a patent search as soon as the problem was defined in the inventor's mind. The patent search results would have allowed the inventor to weigh the prior attempts by other inventors to solve the same problem in deciding how best to design his own fishing pole holder that would hopefully work better and be manufacturable at a reasonable cost. Many impractical approaches would have been readily recognized and discarded, and the best bits and pieces of others combined into the new combination. As a result, the inventor would have saved weeks, if not months, in the design process that ultimately led to the development of the 3rd Grip fishing pole holster. After all, the very function of the patent system is to teach the public what others have proposed as solutions in the hope that the information gleaned will spur inventors to develop improvements. Techniques for patent searching are discussed in detail in Chapter 3.

Conception and Reduction to Practice

Thomas Edison supposedly said that inventing is 1 percent inspiration and 99 percent perspiration. In other words, once you have a concept in your mind for solving a particular problem, the real work comes in trying to make it work. The U.S. patent law breaks down invention into a two-step process. The first step is called *conception*. This is the inventor's idea of a complete and operable invention. The second step is called *reduction to practice*. An *actual* reduction to practice occurs when the invention has been physically constructed and demonstrated to be fully operable for its intended purpose. The invention need not be in refined commercial form in order for there to have been an actual reduction to practice. A *constructive* reduction to practice occurs when a U.S. patent application has been filed. Under the U.S. patent laws, the dates of conception and reduction to practice, along with any diligence that takes place between them, are pivotal in determining priority between competing inventors. Accordingly, inventors are well advised to keep written dated records of their inventing efforts and to have them witnessed by others should they hope to win an interference proceeding in the USPTO that decides priority of inventorship. Records of your invention need not be notarized. The United States is a first-to-invent country, not a first-to-file country. In other words, the first inventor is entitled to the award of a patent, not the first to file an application on the invention, provided that the first inventor timely files a patent application in the USPTO, that is, within the one-year grace period under U.S. patent law.

Inventing is quite often a joint or collaborative effort between several people. This frequently occurs through many brainstorming sessions. It may take place over many months or even years. It may be difficult, and indeed impossible, to pinpoint the exact contributions of several coinventors. However, in order to achieve coinventor status, each person must have been involved in the conception of the invention. One who merely constructs a prototype of an invention conceived by another does not rise to the level of inventor status under the U.S. patent laws.

Attempts have been made to at least partially automate the inventing process. Software can be purchased that will run on personal computers that is designed to stimulate creative thinking. This software employs an interactive question-and-answer dialogue designed to focus the user on solutions to problems that the user has defined. I do not know of any examples of valuable inventions that can be attributed to the use of such invention stimulation software, but I have heard that these computer programs can be helpful at an early stage.

Would-be inventors should bear in mind that the vast majority of patentable inventions are results of recombined and rearranged earlier devices and methods. Technology and product development move in small increments, and there are rarely any radical breakthroughs. Consider that the vaunted cruise missile developed during the Cold War was fundamentally a modern version of the V-1 buzz bomb developed during World War II. The guidance, warhead, and engine of the cruise missile were each substantially improved, but the basic functional elements, their combination, and the result were all old.

More often than not, inventors conceive their inventions and then run into difficulties reducing them to practice. Frequently, the way that they overcome unforeseen difficulties turns out to be the valuable invention. The Russians put Sputnik into orbit, but Hughes Corporation figured out the method of using gyroscopic precession and small bursts of tiny rocket engines to maintain proper orbit and altitude that are so critical to a functioning telecommunications satellite.

Serendipitous Inventions

The U.S. patent law has no litmus test that equates patentability with the manner in which a device, method, or composition of matter was invented. In the U.S., a patentable invention can result from a so-called flash of genius or it can result from years of trial and error. Indeed, it is recognized that some patentable inventions are the result of serendipity. In one famous example, a person afflicted with epilepsy noticed that he had no seizures when he pursued his hobby of taking and developing photographs. He later realized that vapor from a particular developing compound that he was inhaling was safe and effective in averting his seizures. This compound was then successfully commercialized as a pharmaceutical. In another case, an inventor struggling to make a water-activated battery for military use accidentally had his cigarette ash drop into a batch of chemicals he was mixing. The added carbon was the final ingredient that made the composition work for its intended purpose.

Perhaps the most striking example of a different manner of inventing is the way that genomic companies crunch out newly identified pieces of the human genetic code via computer. These pieces of genetic code are then plugged into canned patent applications that are filed at the USPTO. Both the value and validity of this assembly-line, shotgun approach to inventing and filing patent applications have yet to be determined. Who is the actual inventor? Isn't the genetic code something that was already in nature and, therefore, old?

Age Limits for Inventors

Finally, there is no age limit or qualification for inventing or patenting. U.S. patents have been granted to inventors as young as 5 years old. Patents are regularly granted to senior citizens, whose applications get expedited treatment if they file a Petition to Make Special stating that they are 65 years of age or older.

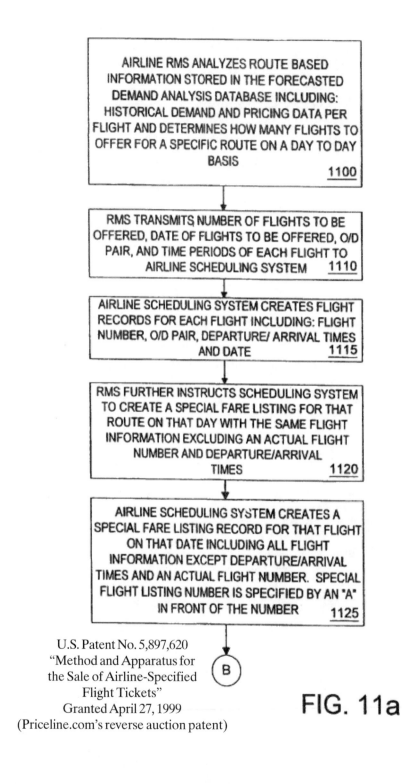

AIRLINE RMS ANALYZES ROUTE BASED INFORMATION STORED IN THE FORECASTED DEMAND ANALYSIS DATABASE INCLUDING: HISTORICAL DEMAND AND PRICING DATA PER FLIGHT AND DETERMINES HOW MANY FLIGHTS TO OFFER FOR A SPECIFIC ROUTE ON A DAY TO DAY BASIS   1100

RMS TRANSMITS NUMBER OF FLIGHTS TO BE OFFERED, DATE OF FLIGHTS TO BE OFFERED, O/D PAIR, AND TIME PERIODS OF EACH FLIGHT TO AIRLINE SCHEDULING SYSTEM   1110

AIRLINE SCHEDULING SYSTEM CREATES FLIGHT RECORDS FOR EACH FLIGHT INCLUDING: FLIGHT NUMBER, O/D PAIR, DEPARTURE/ ARRIVAL TIMES AND DATE   1115

RMS FURTHER INSTRUCTS SCHEDULING SYSTEM TO CREATE A SPECIAL FARE LISTING FOR THAT ROUTE ON THAT DAY WITH THE SAME FLIGHT INFORMATION EXCLUDING AN ACTUAL FLIGHT NUMBER AND DEPARTURE/ARRIVAL TIMES   1120

AIRLINE SCHEDULING SYSTEM CREATES A SPECIAL FARE LISTING RECORD FOR THAT FLIGHT ON THAT DATE INCLUDING ALL FLIGHT INFORMATION EXCEPT DEPARTURE/ARRIVAL TIMES AND AN ACTUAL FLIGHT NUMBER. SPECIAL FLIGHT LISTING NUMBER IS SPECIFIED BY AN "A" IN FRONT OF THE NUMBER   1125

B

U.S. Patent No. 5,897,620
"Method and Apparatus for
the Sale of Airline-Specified
Flight Tickets"
Granted April 27, 1999
(Priceline.com's reverse auction patent)

FIG. 11a

CHAPTER 2

What Can Be Patented?

I n the United States, there are three kinds of patents, namely, *utility patents*, *design patents*, and *plant patents*. A utility patent can cover a machine, article of manufacture (device), circuit, composition of matter (including pharmaceuticals, genes, and DNA), process, living organism, software, or method of doing business. More than 6 million utility patents have been granted in this country. Unless otherwise indicated, the entire focus of this book is on U.S. utility patents.

Types of Patents

A design patent covers the outer ornamental appearance of a manufactured article, frequently the shape of a plastic molded product such as a Motorola cell phone. Less than a half-million design patents have been granted in this country. They represent an inexpensive way to prevent "look-alike" knock-off products, but they are very narrow in terms of the scope of exclusive rights they provide. A design patent cannot cover structure, function, or composition. Infringement of a design patent is determined simply by comparing its drawings to the shape of the accused product to determine if the ordinary observer would be deceived; a test similar to that used in determining trademark infringement.

A plant patent can cover a new variety of any asexually reproduced plant (not grown from seeds) such as a fruit tree, a rose bush, or a strawberry plant.

Tuber propagated plants such as potatoes are ineligible. Only a few thousand plant patents have been granted. To some extent, plant patents are being supplanted by utility patents on genetically engineered plant-related inventions such as disease resistant corn.

Some subject matter is not patentable in this country. Laws of nature and physical phenomena cannot be patented. Nor is it possible to patent abstract ideas. Literary, dramatic, musical, and artistic works cannot be patented, but can be protected by copyright laws. Theoretically, subject matter that is offensive to public morality cannot be patented, although this prohibition is rarely applied.

In the United States, patents are issued every Tuesday. A short abstract of each patent is published by the USPTO in a thick weekly paperback journal called the *Official Gazette for Patents*. Anyone can subscribe to this journal. The patents are broken down into three broad categories, namely, mechanical, electrical, and chemical. A perusal of the *Gazette* shows that many patents in the mechanical category claim industrial processing machines or tools, such as oil drill bits, plywood veneer driers, power tool improvements, ventilating equipment, irrigation equipment, recreational vehicle improvements, and so forth. Most of the patents obtained by individuals, as opposed to companies, claim inventions that fall into the broad mechanical area. These include lots of gadgets such as fishing pole holders, luggage carriers, flashlights, toys, exercise machines, computer keyboard supports, and so forth. The electrical category is dominated by patents obtained by large integrated circuit manufacturers such as Micron Technologies, computer companies such as IBM and Sun, telecommunications equipment manufacturers such as Lucent and Nortel, and software companies such as Microsoft. The chemical area is dominated by patents obtained by large manufacturers of industrial chemicals such as DuPont, Union Carbide, and BASF; large oil companies such as ExxonMobil, ChevronTexaco, and Shell; pharmaceutical companies such as Eli Lilly, Novartis, and American Home Products; and biotech companies from large to small, such as Amgen and Ligand.

Business Methods

A 1998 decision by the U.S. Court of Appeals for the Federal Circuit (CAFC) expressly overruled the long-standing prohibition against the patenting of methods of doing business. Legal commentators, companies in the software business, and the cyberspace community at large both hailed and condemned the decision. Much of the e-business world was soon in a dither. How many more patents like the Amazon.com "one-click" patent and the Priceline.com reverse auction patent were going to hamstring the new Internet-based economy? In reality, any patent attorney worth his or her salt had long known how to describe and claim such inventions as computer systems and software-implemented processes in a manner that avoided the old rule that business methods were not patentable subject matter.

In response to relentless public outcries, the USPTO implemented a heightened scrutiny examination policy for patent applications claiming business methods. This policy involves more searching for nonpatent published prior art, a second review of any allowed application by another patent examiner, and random quality checks. I suspect that patent applications on e-business methods will now face much more aggressive obviousness rejections. This will have the practical effect of substantially reducing the percentage of such applications that result in patents, and significantly narrowing the scope of claims of any patents that are granted on e-business methods. In many cases, patents will be wrongly denied to individual inventors and small businesses that cannot afford protracted examination proceedings at the USPTO and/or appeals. Many patent attorneys feel that it is improper to single out patent applications in one area of technology for super-duper examination. All inventions must meet the same statutory criteria for patentability.

At the height of the dot-com craze, I prepared and filed a U.S. patent application on a very clever and potentially lucrative e-business invention in return for the promise of a small equity stake. The business failed to get off the ground before the world of dot-com companies collapsed. I learned firsthand why patent attorneys usually don't take equity in lieu of legal fees. The USPTO issued two consecutive Office Actions with ridiculous rejections. For example, the first Office Action contained an anticipation (lack of novelty) rejection based on a publication that took place after the filing of my client's application. I overcame that rejection, but the second Office Action contained another absurd rejection. My client gave up and allowed the application to go abandoned.

Inventorship

At the most fundamental level, one must be an inventor or a coinventor to apply for a U.S. patent. If you saw a cool kitchen gadget in Europe, you cannot patent it in the United States. Only the European inventor of that gadget can apply for a U.S. patent, and then only if he or she does it within a year of the first publication of the invention anywhere, and within one year of its first use or sale in the United States.

In the United States, patents are applied for in the name or names of the true inventors, not in the name of the employers or their managers, as in some foreign patent systems. The concepts of sole and joint inventorship are very esoteric. It is sufficient to say here that a person is properly listed as a coinventor if he or she was part of the conception process (the mental part of coming up with the invention) with respect to at least one claim in the patent application. Those who merely reduce a conception to practice under the direction of another are generally not inventors. For example, if Cathy conceives of a new lawn mower that uses a rotating laser beam instead of a steel blade, and Bob merely builds the prototype to her specifications, Bob is not a coinventor.

Criteria for a Patentable Invention

In the United States, an invention as claimed must be useful, novel, and nonobvious in order to be patentable. The USPTO examines applications to determine if a claimed invention satisfies all three criteria in accordance with court decisions interpreting the patent laws, as well as regulations promulgated by the commissioner. Patent examiners follow procedures laid out in two enormous three-ring binders titled the Manual of Patent Examining Procedure (MPEP). You would have to be a true glutton for punishment to actually read the MPEP unless you were a patent examiner or a practicing patent attorney. Indeed, its sheer volume and extreme complexity are often enough to dissuade attorneys from even attempting to pass the federal patent bar examination.

Utility

Usefulness, or utility, as it is also known, is rarely an issue when it comes to mechanical or electrical inventions. Utility should not be equated with practicality, manufacturability, or marketability. An invention has utility if it performs some function useful to mankind. Thus, a door-lock set faceplate lined with animal fur so that its keyhole can be located in the dark by feeling along the door would satisfy the utility requirement. This is true even though the fur-lined keyhole would have almost no chance of ever being used by the public, let alone achieving commercial success. Utility also requires operativeness; that is, a machine that will not operate to perform its intended purpose cannot be patented. The USPTO has retained the authority to require a working model, and from time to time it uses this power to dispense with patent applications claiming perpetual motion machines. The utility of a mechanical or electrical invention claimed in a patent application is normally demonstrated by some threshold level of operability that is readily discernable from the detailed description portion of the patent application. In one interesting case, the USPTO was upheld, in rejecting for inoperativeness, an invention directed to improving the flavor of liquids by subjecting them to a magnetic field.

In the case of chemical inventions, utility can be a serious problem. Even if a chemical compound is new and nonobvious, it must still perform some useful function. Practitioners sometimes joke that, if nothing else, a blob of new material can function as a paperweight. However, if, for example, the material is purportedly a desiccant (moisture absorber), test data should be included in the patent application to support this utility. The real problem regarding utility arises with pharmaceutical inventions. A patent application on a method of treating a particular disease in humans or a medicinal compound for treating the same often includes substantial clinical test data on animals because of restrictions on human testing. In general, it is impermissible to equate satisfaction of the utility requirement under U.S. patent law with Food and Drug Administration (FDA) approved efficacy, but even so, problems in this area frequently arise.

Novelty

Novelty is the second requirement of the three-pronged test for patentability of a claimed invention. In the most general terms, to be patentable in the United States, the invention must not be old at the time you made it. More specifically, the invention must be different from that which constitutes prior art, namely, inventions that were previously known or sold or used in this country, or that others have previously patented or described in a printed publication anywhere in the world, or described in a U.S. patent application filed before your filing date, or invented prior to your date of invention and which have not been abandoned, suppressed, or canceled. There are also certain loss of rights provisions that can defeat those who delay in filing a patent application even though their invention is technically novel. In particular, in order to be patentable, the invention must not have been offered for sale or placed in public use in the United States, or patented or described in a printed publication anywhere in the world, by the inventor or anyone else, for more than a year prior to the filing date of the application. Typically, this "statutory bar," as it is called, is triggered by the inventor's own commercial activity. The bar affords a "one-year grace period," but no longer, to allow the inventor to perfect his or her invention and determine if it is commercially feasible before expending the money required to file a patent application. Most foreign countries do not have a one-year grace period and instead require filing before any nonconfidential disclosure of the invention. Effectively, a U.S. inventor interested in foreign patents must file in the USPTO before the first nonconfidential disclosure of the invention. The inventor then has one year under the Paris Convention Treaty to file corresponding foreign patent applications claiming the priority benefit of the earlier U.S. filing date.

Publications that can be prior art against a claimed invention include prior patents, published patent applications, books, magazines, articles, and product brochures. These publications do not have to be in the English language, as the U.S. patent law presumes that any inventor could have any publication translated. An in-house patent counsel for a large U.S. company once told me that if his client decided against seeking patent protection for a potentially valuable invention, it would arrange to publish that invention in one of the former Soviet Republics in an obscure (non-Russian) language. No competitor was likely to ever find the publication. Later on, if the competitor made the invention independently, and got it patented, the obscure publication could be cited to invalidate the patent claims. This method troubles me, but I cannot say there is anything illegal about it.

Nonobviousness

Nonobviousness is the third and final requirement of the three-pronged test for patentability of a claimed invention in the United States. At the time the invention was made, even if it was useful and novel, it must have been nonobvious to one of ordinary skill in the art (field of invention) to which it pertains. As a practical matter, in the first instance, nonobviousness is a subjective determination made by a USPTO patent examiner who supposedly follows the holdings of legions of court decisions that spell out how obviousness should be determined. Many individual inventors become distressed when the examiner initially rejects their claimed invention for obviousness. They almost universally proclaim, "If it was so obvious, how come nobody did it before me?" Such an argument carries no legal weight whatsoever.

The proper test for obviousness, as enunciated by the U.S. Supreme Court, involves determining the scope and content of the relevant prior art, the differences between the claimed invention and the prior art, and the level of ordinary skill in the prior art. The inquiry then focuses on whether the *differences* would have been obvious to a mythical person of ordinary skill in the relevant art who is presumed to have the closest prior art references before him or her. However, court decisions repeatedly emphasize that the *invention as a whole* must be considered in determining obviousness. The USPTO examiner is permitted to, and often does, combine the teachings of more than one prior art reference. However, this is permissible only if there is an express teaching, suggestion, or motivation in the references to do so. In order for there to be an express teaching, suggestion, or motivation, the reference must literally set forth those concepts in words that clearly convey the concept(s). Hindsight reconstruction is prohibited. The manner of making the invention cannot be used to deny nonobviousness. The old "flash of genius" requirement promulgated by Justice Douglas of the U.S. Supreme Court was legislatively overruled by the U.S. Congress when it passed the landmark revision of the U.S. patent law in 1952. The obviousness statute specifically states "[p]atentability shall not be negatived by the manner in which the invention was made."

In making the obviousness determination, the patent examiner, judge, or jury is allowed to consider so-called "objective evidence" of nonobviousness. This objective evidence, which is sometimes referred to as "secondary considerations," includes evidence of commercial success of the claimed invention, long-felt need, skepticism of experts, copying of the invention in preference to the prior art, and the failure of others. Unexpected results are also indicia of nonobviousness.

In the early 1980s, I represented the original inventor of the first commercially successful thermometer for taking human body temperature by inserting an infrared-sensitive probe in the external ear canal. Unfortunately, the USPTO examiner cited an old patent granted in 1966 that showed the basic concept; however, it did not teach or suggest the calibration process that made the thermometer clinically accurate to FDA standards and, therefore, commercially feasible. As a result, my client was able to obtain valuable patent protection on its revolutionary tympanic thermometer. An interesting sidelight to that story was that it soon became apparent to my start-up client that it made good business sense to essentially give away the thermometers, because each one used in a hospital or a doctor's office required hundreds of disposable sanitary probe covers per day. I also was able to patent the disposable covers, and, therefore, they could be sold at hefty profit margins. My client's ear thermometer business and patents were ultimately acquired by American Home Products, and then Tyco International. Hundreds of millions of dollars were made. More importantly, however, the quality of healthcare was significantly enhanced by providing a novel, rapid, and accurate way of taking human body temperature. Without the patents, this would not have happened nearly as early as it did because investors would not have risked their capital without the promise of exclusivity in the marketplace.

The fact that a mechanical or electrical invention is merely a new combination of existing parts or components does not automatically lead to a legal conclusion of obviousness. Indeed, outside the chemical field, nearly all patented inventions are new combinations of old elements, old combinations of newly modified elements, or hybrids of the two. Technical progress is almost invariably made in small increments. People mistakenly think that progress is regularly made in great leaps. When Thomas Edison invented the incandescent lightbulb, it was an old practice to make a filament glow by encasing the filament in a glass vessel and passing an electrical current through the filament. Edison's patent claim to an electrical lamp was limited to making the filament out of a "carbon of high resistance, made as described, and secured to metallic wires."

In the late 1980s, I filed a patent application for a visionary client on a system that integrated a video display into a gas station pump. The concept was very practical in that it combined various elements of existing, readily available electronic hardware. The concept was also potentially very lucrative in that a driver is a captive audience for viewing advertising while pumping gas. The price per gallon and gallons pumped were overlaid onto the video images. The USPTO repeatedly rejected the claimed invention for alleged obviousness even though the prior art it relied upon did not disclose, or even remotely suggest, such a combination. On appeal, the CAFC, in a two to one decision, upheld the USPTO, essentially buying into its reasoning that the claimed invention was inherently obvious. The client decided it wasn't worthwhile to petition the U.S. Supreme Court to review the CAFC's decision. The highest court in the land has almost complete discretion to hear only those cases it chooses, and it typically selects one in about 3,000 civil cases that it is annually asked to review. Recently, I noticed that large oil companies have begun installing gas pumps with video screens in their gas stations in the United States. However, because my client never got a patent, he could never build a company around his idea, license his patent rights, or sell his invention.

In the end analysis, only a patent attorney or patent agent should provide an opinion about whether a particular invention is nonobvious. He or she may recommend a patent search to provide a basis for formulating such an opinion. Patent searching is discussed in the next chapter. Be careful about engineers and scientists forming their own opinions about obviousness. To many of them, lots of things are obvious. But valuable patent rights can be lost where nonpatent attorneys express lay opinions based upon a misunderstanding of the proper legal test for obviousness.

The fate of the inventor of the first computerized spreadsheet program, sold for a short time under the trademark VisiCalc, illustrates the severe costs of misunderstanding what can be patented in the United States. Rumor has it that he thought that his invention couldn't be patented because it was a computer program or b cause it was an obvious computerized version of the existing manual proce ss. Perhaps he waited too long to file based on these mistaken beliefs. In truth, a clever patent attorney could have presented the invention as a novel system and process, and probably obtained the allowance of some very valuable patent claims. This didn't happen, and instead, the basic invention went into the public domain. Another company made a sexier version of the computerized spreadsheet program, and with better marketing, made billions of dollars selling it under the Lotus trademark. Today, Microsoft licenses its Excel spreadsheet program to tens of millions of personal computer users. The company that made the VisiCalc program disappeared into obscurity.

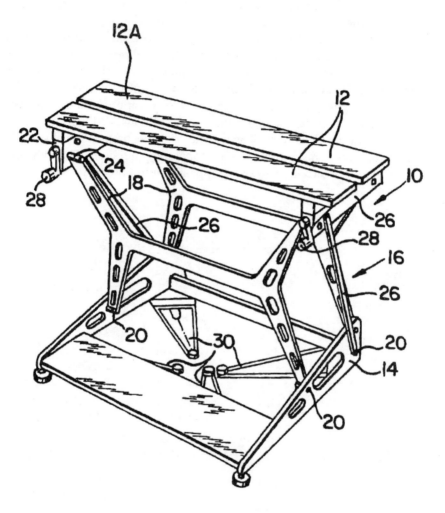

U.S. Patent No. 4,034,684
"Workbench and Foldable Leg Assembly Therefor"
Granted July 12, 1977
(Black & Decker Workmate bench)

CHAPTER 3

Patent Searching

atent searches are often performed to ensure that the inventor is not simply reinventing the wheel. You may run into a so-called "silver bullet" prior art reference that fully anticipates all of the principal features of your invention and thereby evidences a lack of novelty. In other words, a single patent or article verbally describes and/or shows in drawings all of the features of your invention. Alternatively, a search may uncover most of the features of your invention, indicating that you probably will face an obviousness rejection from the USPTO. This may lead you to rethink your position. Many times an inventor can significantly enhance his or her own design by incorporating features shown in patents located in a search. Patent searches can also be conducted in order to determine if a proposed product might infringe an already granted patent owned by someone else. Such "right-to-use" searches are usually only conducted by very large companies, and the special way they are conducted, and their potential benefits, are outside the scope of this book.

Ways to Conduct Patentability Searches

There used to be three basic ways to conduct a so-called patentability search in the United States for prior art that is potentially relevant to the novelty and/or obviousness of an invention. The first (traditional "manual search" way) employed a searcher who physically combed through the "shoes" at the Public Search Room at the USPTO after determining the appropriate USPTO classes and subclasses from the USPTO Manual of Classification and/or consulting with USPTO patent examiners. Believe it or not, these shoes were actually wooden boxes stored in metal racks, each holding paper copies of all the prior art patents classified in a given sub-class. The paper copies were generally removed from a shoe and laid vertically in a metal stand that allowed a searcher to flip through them, quickly scanning their front pages. As of the writing of this book, the USPTO has announced its intention to discontinue maintaining the shoes at the Public Search Room in order to save money. Thus, traditional manual patent searching has been discontinued.

The second way of searching involves performing a computerized key-word search on one or more of the databases of U.S. patents. The third way is to search technical literature such as magazines, journals, and product manuals. The computerized search can be performed by the inventor and/or the patent attorney. The literature search is usually performed by the inventors, as they are typically aware of, and have access to, the leading nonpatent scientific publications (often obscure) pertaining to the field of interest.

Reliability of Patent Searches

Patent searches are limited in their reliability based on several factors. First, only so much time can be spent searching from a cost standpoint. Second, the USPTO classification system is imperfect. Third, patents are frequently misclassified and/or are missing from the shoes.

Computerized Searches

Computerized keyword searches, particularly those of patent data-bases, also are problematic. First, the full text of U.S. patents is only keyword searchable on the free USPTO Webpage for patents issued commencing in 1976. In many non-high-tech areas, relevant prior art patents could have been granted in the 1940s or 1950s, or even in the 19th century. If you know the number of the patent of interest, you can look at an image of the same on the USPTO Webpage, but you have no way of searching the text of any patent granted prior to 1976 with this technique unless you have access to a very expensive proprietary patent database. Second, the accuracy of a computerized patent search is highly dependent upon the structure of the so-called "Boolean" search commands. For example, in searching for an optical switch with a built-in memory chip, one might ask for all patents based on the Boolean search command "optical" and "switch" and "memory" appearing in the specification of the patent. This would undoubtedly turn up thousands of patents, most of which would be only marginally relevant to the particular invention being searched. Also, patents using alternate terms (for example, "CMOS RAM" instead of "memory," would be missed) and could be highly relevant. No matter how carefully and exhaustively a Boolean search command is constructed, relevant patents can still be missed. This is simply due to the fact that outside of chemistry, there are no rigorous universally accepted definitions for terms used to describe structures, circuits, and processes.

Classification Searches

The USPTO generally separates patent applications and patents into three broad classifications—mechanical, electrical, and chemical. The USPTO Manual of Classification further breaks down this subject matter into hundreds of classes, many having dozens of subclasses. Therefore, U.S. patents can be searched by class and subclass. Certain examining groups or art units in the USPTO (now called "Technology Centers") are responsible for examining patent applications claiming subject matter in particular classes. The classification system is very cumbersome indeed. The classes and subclasses are listed in an enormously large and complex three-ring binder whose contents remind one of the way all living organisms are classified by phylum, genus, species, etc. The USPTO classes and subclasses are constantly being reorganized. Issued U.S. patents indicate their class and subclass on their face, but they are frequently misclassified. Furthermore, classification is based on what is being claimed in an issued patent, not by what is disclosed. As will be explained in Chapter 5, a patent contains a set of claims at the end that are one-sentence definitions of the exclusive rights. Much haggling occurs between the USPTO examiner and the patent attorney over the wording in these claims. Sometimes a patent will disclose important information that may potentially prevent you from obtaining a patent, but claim other subject matter that also is disclosed. Therefore, the patent gets classified in a manner that prevents you from locating it if you do a patent search strictly by class and subclass. Generally, only patent examiners and patent attorneys should make any attempt to use class and subclass information in patent searching.

Every U.S. patent lists the closest (most relevant) prior art considered by the examiner on the face of the patent. Usually this is a list of U.S. patents by number that the examiner found in his or her own search, along with those referenced by the patent attorney. The patents that are listed can be individually reviewed to see what patents they cite as being pertinent.

When searching for relevant U.S. patents, whether manually or via computer, it is important to bear in mind that most U.S. patent applications filed prior to November 29, 2000, are secret, and not published, until they are granted. As a result, several years' worth of pending applications cannot be inspected. In fast-moving high-tech fields, there may be little point in knowing that nobody else had thought up the invention as of two or three years ago. It is possible to do a very exhaustive search, file a patent application, and then have it rejected due to a very pertinent patent that issued after the search was completed. Under U.S. patent law, U.S. patents are effective as prior art as of their filing dates, which are usually several years before their issue dates.

Literature Searches

Literature searches are even less reliable because technical literature, by and large, is not fully cataloged and available for searching on any one single computer database. Product literature and manuals may be obscure, and there may be no formal collections or archives of the same. If a company handed out 50 brochures at a trade show in Las Vegas in 1981, the brochure technically constitutes published prior art. The brochure could be used in patent litigation to invalidate a patent claim, provided that an original copy of the brochure could be properly authenticated, dated, and its dissemination corroborated by at least one testifying witness with personal knowledge of the critical events.

A patentability search can still be a useful tool. It is sometimes possible to get as high as an 80-percent reliability factor. That is to say, with a comprehensive search in a technical field that is not rapidly evolving, there may be only a 20-percent chance that the examiner will find a more pertinent reference than any uncovered in the patentability search. A patentability search is somewhat like insurance in that it can reduce the chances that a great deal of time and money will be spent on preparing and filing a patent application only to have it rejected due to an extremely close prior art reference. It also can help the patent attorney focus the claims of the application, as initially drafted, on the novel features of the invention.

In some cases, potential investors may wish to know whether a patentability search has been conducted and may be more willing to invest if they are convinced that the invention is, in fact, novel. Generally, the more money that is spent on a patentability search, the higher its reliability, but the principle of diminishing returns is applicable. In the end analysis, a client must decide whether the cost, time, potential risk, and potential reward justify performing a patentability search, taking into consideration his or her particular circumstances.

Each way of searching for prior art has certain drawbacks and advantages. I personally have performed more than 1,000 hours of searches on the free USPTO patent database accessible at *www.uspto.gov*. Even with my many years of experience in the field, use of the advanced search engine, and knowledge of the prior art, it is amazing how difficult it can actually be to perform a reliable patentability search. My recommendation for individuals who feel very comfortable with computers and the Internet is as follows: Do some searching to get familiar with other patents granted in your area of interest, but do not assume that you have found the closest prior art. From time to time I engage foreign patent attorneys in Germany and Japan to search the records of the European Patent Office (EPO) and Japanese Patent Office (JPO). Searches of foreign prior art, which can be cited by a USPTO examiner as the basis for a prior art rejection, are very expensive and usually done only under special circumstances; for example, when investigating the risk of infringing a competitor's patent in a key foreign market.

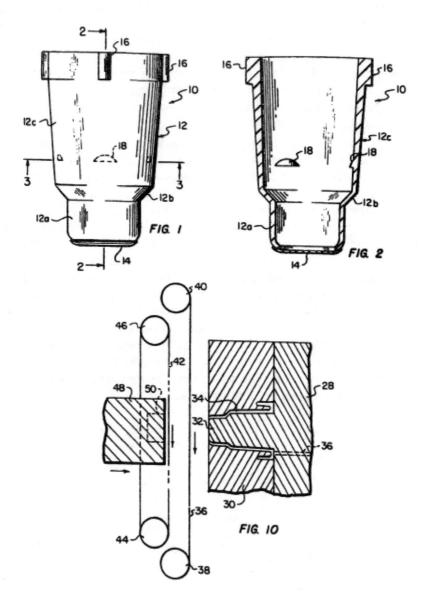

U.S. Patent No. 4,662,360
"Disposable Speculum"
Granted May 5, 1987
(Ear Thermometer Probe Cover)

CHAPTER 4

When to File a Patent Application

T There is a legal answer and a practical answer for when to file a U.S. patent application.

Legal Answer to When to File a Patent Application

The legal answer is that the United States has a one-year grace period for filing a patent application. The one year commences from the earliest to occur of the first offer for sale in the United States of a product embodying the invention, the first public use in the United States on a nonexperimental basis, or the first publication of the invention anywhere. Only if the offer for sale or use occurred in the United States does the one-year grace period commence. In contrast, a publication anywhere in the world starts the one-year time period . If you want to preserve your foreign patent rights, you have to file the U.S. patent application prior to the first nonconfidential disclosure of your invention. So if you need to disclose the invention ahead of time to potential investors, designers, consultants, and customers, you had better get them to sign a confidentiality agreement.

An offer to license an invention, as opposed to an offer to sell products embodying the invention, does not trigger the one-year grace period under U.S. patent law.

Practical Answer to
When to File a Patent Application

The practical answer to the question of when to file is more difficult. Essentially, one should file the U.S. patent application as soon as feasible, but definitely soon enough to avoid a statutory bar date (the one year anniversary of earliest offer for sale, public use, or publication).

As you might expect, complications arise in determining exactly when the one-year grace period commences. One of the most frequent bases for successfully challenging the validity of a U.S. patent in federal court is that the claimed invention was offered for sale or in public use in this country more than a year prior to the application filing date by reason of the patent owner's activities. What if the product embodying the invention is still in development and one of your salespeople "pitches" the forthcoming product at a trade show? The U.S. Supreme Court has held that the one year commences when: (1) there has been an offer for sale; and (2) the invention is "ready for patenting." As to the first part of the two-pronged test, the U.S. CAFC has held that the offer for sale must be a formal commercial offer in the sense that a binding contract would be created if the offer were accepted. So the offer must be specific as to terms; that is, price, delivery, and identification of the product. As to the second part of the test, to be on the safe side, one must equate "ready for patenting" with conception because an experienced patent attorney is often capable of drafting an elaborate patent application in a familiar subject area based merely on the proverbial "sketch on a cocktail napkin." Public use also is problematic. Public use in the patent law sense means that the inventor or others derive some benefit from unrestricted use of the invention. Even secret use can be "public use." In an old court case, a woman's corset made of whalebone was held to be in public use even though it was hidden beneath her skirt during her trips outside the home. The sale of Krispy Kreme doughnuts in North Carolina for more than a year made in secret with a one-of-a-kind fryer would bar seeking a U.S. patent on the fryer.

As already mentioned, the United States has a first-to-invent system. The first inventor is awarded the patent provided he or she files within the one-year grace period and provided that the invention, as claimed, is useful, novel, and nonobvious. As between competing inventors, in the United States, the patent is not necessarily awarded to the first to file as it is in most foreign countries. If two or more applications that claim substantially the same invention are co-pending in the USPTO, and if their filing dates are close enough, the USPTO will declare an interference to determine who is the first inventor. This is a rare, complex, and lengthy legal proceeding conducted before three administrative law judges. Taking appeals into account, an interference typically lasts three to five years. In the case of the original laser patent, the interference proceedings took more than 20 years to be decided. It is important to keep a bound engineering notebook with contemporaneous entries regarding your original conception and the various additional work you perform in reducing your invention to practice. An actual reduction to practice involves the physical carrying out of the invention, such as the construction of a working prototype. A coworker or trusted friend who is familiar with the technology involved should read, sign, and date each entry contemporaneously with its creation. Notarization is not required. The reason for keeping these entries is that you will need to have corroborated evidence of your conception, diligence, and reduction to practice if you want to win an interference or a priority defense in federal court. Such record-keeping is mandatory for engineers employed by major companies such as Hewlett-Packard and IBM.

Poor Man's Patent and the Invention Disclosure Document

What if I mail a description of the invention to myself and keep it sealed so that the postmark will validate when I first came up with my invention? This is the so-called poor man's patent, and it is utterly worthless. It is inadmissible in an interference proceeding for the simple reason that it is not corroborated and it is therefore untrustworthy. Think about it. Anyone could mail themselves an empty envelope to get a postmark, and many years later, steam open the envelope, insert a new undated invention description, and then reseal the envelope.

What about filing an Invention Disclosure Document with the USPTO for $10? Well, it is certainly better than a poor man's patent because it can be cited in a later filed patent application and also entered into evidence in an interference proceeding. However, the USPTO will only save it for two years.

Neither a poor man's patent nor a USPTO Invention Disclosure Document will toll a statutory bar. That is to say, the meter on the one-year grace period keeps ticking, so you will lose your patent rights if you don't timely file a patent application in the USPTO.

Filing in a Foreign Country

It is very important to maintain the confidentiality of your invention until you have filed a U.S. patent application that fully discloses and claims the invention. As explained in detail in Chapter 15, this will help maintain your foreign patent rights. It also will substantially reduce the risk that someone will steal your invention. Have any designers, consultants, potential financial backers, etc., sign confidentiality agreements before you show them your invention. Most established companies will be very reluctant to sign confidentiality agreements, so you need to file a U.S. patent application before you seek to sell or license your rights.

It is a serious violation of U.S. law, with possible criminal penalties, for a U.S. citizen to file a patent application in a foreign country before filing in the USPTO. This is, in effect, an unauthorized export of technical data if not done pursuant to a previously granted foreign filing license. Congress allows the U.S. Department of Defense (DOD) to review each and every U.S. patent application shortly after it is filed in order to have the opportunity to classify it as "secret" because of national security concerns. While all U.S. patent applications are initially maintained in secret, until publication or grant, the DOD can place a high-level restriction on the inventor and his patent attorney not to disclose anything about an invention. Even if you file on a lasagna maker, you cannot file overseas first without risking criminal sanctions. Naturally, the DOD is most concerned with weaponry and atomic energy inventions. If the DOD slaps a secrecy order on your patent application, you still get to prosecute it under very strict confidentiality controls, but publication and issuance are held up indefinitely. Secrecy orders are reviewed annually. I remember filing a patent application in the USPTO on a method of remotely piloting a drone aircraft. It had a secrecy order placed on it, and the application finally issued as a patent 13 years later.

Provisional Patent Applications

A few years ago, Congress amended the U.S. patent law to provide for the filing of a provisional patent application, and inventors got all excited. While a regular U.S. utility application must meet very strict individual standards as to format, a provisional application can be little more than an invention disclosure. No claims are required. The filing of a provisional application does stop the regular one year time limit from continuing to run. However, you still must file a regular utility patent application within one year of the filing date of the provisional patent application in order to obtain the priority benefit of its filing date. Even then, you only get the provisional's filing date if the provisional patent application is detailed enough to fully disclose the subject matter covered by the claims of the regular utility application. Thus, the provisional patent application is best suited for professors and research scientists who have written scholarly detailed papers about their discoveries that they cannot delay publishing. Rather than lose their foreign patent rights, they can file the paper in the USPTO as a provisional patent application.

Provisional patent applications have many shortcomings. They are not examined on their merits by the USPTO. They seem to be used almost exclusively by individual inventors representing themselves, and rarely by patent attorneys, except for the previous situation regarding the professor or scientist who is anxious to publish. The reasons will become more apparent after reading the next chapter about the content of a U.S. utility patent application. The problems with provisional patent applications can best be illustrated by one of my own experiences.

A defense contractor client of mine called me on a Monday and told me that the company planned to disclose a key modification to a jet fighter weapons system to a foreign air force by Thursday. Representatives of that air force, which was one of the United State's allies, refused to sign a confidentiality agreement. This meant that the foreign patent rights to the invention, which my client dearly wanted to preserve, would have been forfeited unless my client filed some sort of a U.S. patent application. There wasn't time to prepare and file a utility patent application on this complex electronic invention. But my client did have a thick engineering specification. So I slapped a cover sheet on it and filed the engineering specification as a provisional patent application in the USPTO. That's when the odyssey officially began. When it came time to file the regular utility patent application, I was faced with the mammoth task of trying to recast the engineering specification into the formal background, summary, detailed description, claims, and abstract required, while at the same time avoiding the prohibition against adding "new matter" to a patent application after its filing date. No new language could be inserted or else it might be considered new matter, and subsequent foreign filing could be very problematic. I had too much disclosure. Surprisingly, the USPTO frequently takes the position that eliminating text or drawings constitutes impermissible introduction of new matter.

The principal problem with the provisional patent application that I filed in the USPTO for my defense contractor client was that the engineering specification was never written to support claims with particular generic nomenclature. This presented the danger of indefiniteness in the claims and undue narrowness in their scope. Because none of the drawing figures could be cut out, they all had to be formalized at great expense. In addition, many engineering details that did not need to be in a regular utility patent application couldn't be excised, and when the U.S. patent was granted, they got published for all the competitors to see when the U.S. patent was granted. On top of all of this, some of the data in the engineering specification was military sensitive, and a special petition had to be filed to allow the same to be withdrawn from the USPTO file before its entire contents were made publicly available upon issuance of the patent.

Undoubtedly, provisional patent applications filed by the inventors themselves (so-called "pro se" applicants) will have too little disclosure, inadequate drawings, and will be missing the proper nomenclature basis for drafting broad claims. If these inventors even remember the one-year time limit to file the regular utility patent application, they will have to take the provisional application to an experienced patent attorney who will: a) have to charge more to try to fix the problem than it would have cost to file a proper utility patent application in the first place; and b) have little chance of obtaining the allowance of best claims possible because the new matter prohibition will prevent adding anything that looks or smells like new description or drawing figures. In many cases, the disclosure of the pro se provisional patent application will be entirely inadequate to support the claims the client truly deserves by comparing his or her invention to the closest prior art. If products embodying the invention have already been on the market in the U.S. for more than one year, it will be too late to correct the situation with a properly prepared patent application. So unless you have less than a week to file and cannot otherwise delay filing due to a filing bar deadline, it is highly advisable to file a regular utility patent application instead of a provisional patent application. Of course, in the end analysis, if at the end of the one-year grace period you can only afford to file a provisional patent application, this is a better alternative than forfeiting your U.S. patent rights.

Let us return to the practical answer about when to file a U.S. patent application. You should first try to build a prototype or test the invention. Frequently, I have observed that the inventor encounters unforeseen problems in reducing the invention to practice. Often it is the way that the inventor overcomes these unforeseen problems that turns out to be the valuable, patentable invention. This was true in the case of my client who invented the disposable probe covers for ear thermometers. His early conception of the invention required a transverse polymer film window, preferably less than 1 millimeter in thickness, extending across the end of a longitudinally extending tubular mounting body. The window had to be very thin so that the attenuation of infrared radiation emitted from the patient's ear canal would be minimized. The trouble was, after many months of trying, the covers could not be injection molded as airtight one-piece items with such a thin film window. The patentable solution was to injection mold the thicker tubular mounting body and, at the same time, press an advancing web of polymer film against the molten body. This allowed the film window to be simultaneously severed from the web of polymer film and thermally bonded to the tubular body around its entire circumference. (See the figure on page 44.)

Usually, it is advantageous to file the U.S. patent application at a time when the preferred embodiment that you disclose looks as much like your planned commercial product as possible. This improves the chances that your patent claims will cover your commercial product, and gives you a big psychological advantage with a jury in a patent infringement lawsuit. Where you can afford to do so, the best strategy is to file a U.S. utility patent application as soon as possible and then file a continuation-in-part (CIP) application in the USPTO while the former application is still pending in order to include any later developments. You then have the best of both worlds, namely, early priority and the preservation of both U.S. and foreign patent rights, while ensuring maximum coverage of all embodiments and features. If you follow this strategy, you should file the CIP in the USPTO as a Patent Cooperation Treaty (PCT) application designating the United States and claiming benefit of the earliest filing date in order to avoid so-called "self collision" in foreign patent systems. This is a situation in which the inventor's earlier case is used as prior art against the later case by foreign patent examiners—an oddity not permitted by U.S. patent law where the second patent application has the same inventorship and is filed within a year of the grant date of the earlier U.S. application when it turns into a U.S. patent.

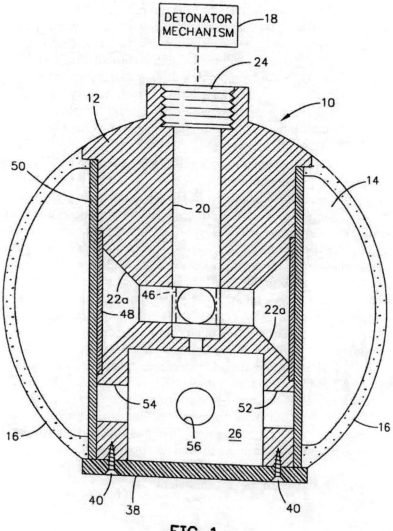

DETONATOR
MECHANISM   —18

12

50

10

14

20

22a   46
48

22a

54   52

56   26

16   16

40   40

38

FIG. 1

U.S. Patent No. 6,065,404
"Training Grenade for Multiple Integrated
Laser Engagement System"
Granted May 23, 2000

CHAPTER 5

What's in a Patent Application?

(M) any people think that a patent application is a form filled out by the inventor, like an application for employment. This is certainly not the case. A utility patent application is a uniquely written narrative document that must satisfy very stringent standards as to form and content. While it is true that the value of a patent depends on the underlying commercial value of the invention, the manner in which it originally is written and later amended during negotiations with the patent examiner is crucial to obtaining the maximum exclusive rights to which the inventor is legally entitled. Indeed, the U.S. Supreme Court has indicated that a patent is the single most difficult legal document to draft correctly. It typically comprises a written portion and drawings. The written portion of a patent application comprises the specification, claims, and abstract, which are discussed in detail in this chapter. Patent applications on certain process and chemical inventions need not include drawings, although one frequently sees molecular diagrams, charts of data, and flow diagrams in issued chemical patents.

Specification of a U.S. Patent Application

The specification of a U.S. patent application is divided into a background section, a summary of the invention, a brief description of the drawings, and a detailed description of the preferred embodiments. The specification of a patent application typically has much repetition, owing to the peculiar legal requirements for U.S. patents. It begins with a title of the invention, which should be short and technically accurate. Try to avoid use of the word "improved" in the title, as all inventions for which patents are sought are theoretically improvements. The background section of the specification describes the general field to which the invention relates and the problems faced by the inventor. For example, the problem could be dispensing small amounts of lubricating oil onto cramped or inaccessible parts of household machinery, such as door hinges. The discussion of the background would normally include a general description of existing devices or methods and how they do not adequately address or solve the problem. (For example, it is difficult to apply oil around the crevices in the hinge pin sleeves of a door butt-hinge with a conventional oil can that has a fixed rigid dispensing spout.) Prior art patents are often discussed in the background section of a patent application. However, this discussion should normally be limited to quoting directly from the patents themselves. Any comments interpreting or characterizing prior art references in your own words could come back to haunt you during later patent litigation.

Background

The background portion of the patent application should tell a story about unsolved problems and needs that the inventor has addressed. One approach is to set up a series of "straw men" that can each be knocked down; that is, problems in the prior art, each of which is overcome by the inventor's solution later described in the summary and detailed description sections. It is important to bear in mind that any patent granted on your application may later be scrutinized in detail in front of a federal judge and jury who are likely to have very little, if any, technical education or experience. Therefore, it should be written with this audience in mind. The first part of the background section is often a short tutorial on the products and technology involved. Many patent attorneys include a preceding section titled "Field of the Invention," which is merely a broad sentence describing the technical area to which the invention pertains. The USPTO may deem statements made in the background section to be admitted prior art. Thus, you should be careful not to describe novel aspects of your invention in this section.

Summary of the Invention

The summary of the invention is supposed to be a brief narrative description of the applicant's invention. It should naturally flow as an answer to the problems and shortcomings of the prior art discussed in the preceding background section. Patent attorneys disagree as to whether the summary should include objects and advantages. They are not legally required, but some practitioners find them invaluable in a patent jury trial because they can point out that the defendant's accused device achieves the same objectives. Even though this has absolutely no legal bearing on whether a particular claim reads on the accused device, they believe that they can subtly influence the jury into finding infringement by showing that the patented device and the accused device are both directed to overcoming the same exact problems. Any object recited should be that of the invention as claimed. If the summary is overly narrow, the defendant's counsel may try to persuade the judge or jury that claims should be construed narrowly consistent with the summary of the invention section. Therefore, most experienced patent attorneys have adopted the practice of rewriting the broadest claim of the application in multisentence format and using this text as the summary of the invention.

Brief Description of Drawings

The next section of the patent application, namely, the brief description of the drawings, is just that. Each figure of the patent drawings is described in a single sentence, for reference purposes.

Here are the figure descriptions from U.S. Patent No. 6,065,404 on a simulated grenade used in military training exercises:

Fig. 1 is a vertical sectional view of a first embodiment of our training grenade.
Fig. 2 is a vertical sectional view of the central core of the first embodiment of our training grenade.
Fig. 3 is an elevational view of a second embodiment of our training grenade with portions broken to illustrate details thereof.
Fig. 4 is an enlarged sectional view illustrating a portion of a third embodiment of our training grenade.
Fig. 5 is an elevation view illustrating a portion of the third embodiment of our training grenade.
Fig. 6 is a view similar to Fig. 4 illustrating a fourth embodiment which employs snap rings.

Fig. 7 is a schematic diagram illustrating the programming of a player identification code (PID) into the first embodiment of our training grenade with a player's vest.

Fig. 8 is a schematic diagram illustrating the location of the first embodiment of our training grenade with a MILES flashlight.

Brief Description of the Preferred Embodiments

The detailed description of the preferred embodiments is, next to the claims, the most crucial part of the written portion of the patent application. A utility patent application need only describe an invention in sufficient detail to enable one skilled in the art to practice the same. However, the best mode for carrying out the invention known to the inventor(s) at the time of filing must be disclosed. The application must also sufficiently disclose and enable the invention, that is to say, sufficiently describe it so that one skilled in the art can practice the same without undue experimentation. If possible, it is best to describe the maximum number of alternate embodiments to support broader claims. The embodiment preferred by the inventor must be clearly indicated to ensure compliance with the best mode requirement. As to each embodiment, it is helpful to describe alternate structures. For example, a sports garment may use mating Velcro fabric strips to affix a removable fabric sleeve around a person's leg. However, it is best to describe other fastening structures that could be used, such as buttons, snaps, clips, or a zipper. Patent applications on electronic and software inventions usually contain block diagrams, flow diagrams, and a detailed description that tend to be at a level readily understood by others with experience in the same technical field.

Here are two paragraphs from the detailed description of the training grenade patent:

Referring to Fig. 1, a first embodiment of our training grenade 10 comprises a generally cylindrical metal core 12 surrounded by a biodegradable filler 14 such as talcum powder and a generally spherical outer frangible casing or shell 16 made of papier-mâché or paper treated with a fire retardant agent. The training grenade 10 has the approximate weight, size and configuration of an actual lethal hand grenade such as an M67 delay fragmentation hand grenade utilized by the armed forces of the United States. For example, the outer diameter of the spherical casing 16 may be approximately sixty-three and one-half millimeters, the overall vertical height of the training grenade 10 may be approximately eighty-nine and seven-tenths millimeters. The weight of the training grenade 10 may be approximately three hundred ninety grams. The training grenade 10 (Fig. 1) has a manually actuatable detonator mechanism, illustrated diagrammatically as box 18, similar to that utilized in the M67 grenade. The fuse portion of the detonator mechanism 18 is preferably a Model M228 fuse that is activated by a conventional striker which is held down by a safety lever. The safety lever is held down by a split pin which must be pulled out before throwing the grenade. The detonator 18 mechanism also includes a quantity of conventional primer compound and a quantity of a conventional detonator material.

The claims at the end of the written portion of a patent application are its most important part. They must find adequate support in the specification and particularly define subject matter that is both new and nonobvious over the prior art. Words and phrases used in the claims must find clear support or "antecedent basis" in the specification. As a result, the meaning of terms used in the claims is ascertainable by reference to the detailed description. Therefore, patent attorneys usually write a patent application by first drafting the claims. Then they draft the background and the detailed description of the preferred embodiments in order to ensure that the "story" of the invention supports the invention as claimed and that the essential features that are to be protected are fully described.

In the United States, infringement of a utility patent is determined in accordance with the so-called "all elements rule." Each and every element and limitation of at least one claim must be present literally or equivalently in the accused product in order for there to be infringement. According to U.S. Supreme Court precedent, the meaning of terms in a claim and its scope are legal issues decided by a judge based on the plain meaning of the words in the claim, their usage in other claims in the patent, their usage in the specification, and their usage in the prosecution history of the patent. More recently, the CAFC has announced a more liberal policy toward resorting to dictionaries to ascertain the meaning of terms in a patent claim.

Each patent claim is a single sentence. The introductory part of the claim is known as the preamble. It usually recites the name of the invention, such as a laser printer. The preamble typically concludes with a transitional phrase, usually the word "comprising," although claims to chemical inventions may use "consisting of." The transitional phrase is followed by the body of the claim, which consists of a number of separate paragraphs, each usually calling out a separate element, any limitations associated with that element, and its relationship to the other elements in the claim. On occasion, a claim may end with another transitional word, namely, "whereby," followed by a statement of some result achieved by the foregoing combination of elements. Generally, although not always, the preamble and the whereby clause are not counted in determining if the claim recites patentable subject matter or if it is being infringed. A field of use limitation recited in the preamble is generally given no patentable weight unless the claim is a method or process claim.

Claims are either independent (that is, they stand alone) or they are dependent, in which case they refer to and incorporate a prior claim. Patent applications normally have multiple independent claims and dependent claims. The reason for varying the wording of independent claims is to attempt to maximize the exclusive rights afforded by the patent. The broader the claims, the more difficult it will be for a competitor to knock off the claimed invention. In order to infringe a patent claim, a competitor's product or process must have each and every element or step recited in that claim. The omission of any single element or limitation, even if all others are present in the competitor's product or process, is normally enough to avoid infringement, unless an equivalent element or step is substituted in its place. However, the claim must recite new and nonobvious subject matter, compared to the prior art, in order to be allowed. This paradox, along with the rule that each claim must be in single-sentence format, makes claim drafting a very difficult task.

A dependent claim (that is, a patent claim that refers to and incorporates the elements and limitations of another claim) can only be infringed if the accused product or process has all the elements or steps of the base (parent) claim along with those added by the dependent claim. Therefore, dependent claims are narrower than independent claims. If a product or process doesn't infringe an independent claim, it is self-evident that it cannot infringe any claim that depends from it. You might then ask, why even bother to include dependent claims? The answer is twofold. First, Claim 1, for example, might later turn out to be invalidated in litigation over prior art that the patentee was not aware of during the prosecution of the application before the USPTO. However, Claim 2, depending from and adding further limitations to Claim 1, might still be valid and infringed. Second, dependent claims serve to give breadth to their parent independent claims. For example, under the doctrine of claim differentiation, if Claim 2 specifies a lightbulb as the source of illumination recited in Claim 1, the source of illumination element of Claim 1, alone, might be satisfied by a variety of light sources such as an incandescent lightbulb, a fluorescent lamp, a light emitting diode, etc.

The U.S. patent law permits an element in a claim to be expressed as a "means for" performing a specified function. Such an element is interpreted as being the structures disclosed in the specification and equivalents thereof. Thus, in a claim to a sports garment, one element could be "means for fastening opposing edges of a fabric sleeve after the sleeve has been wrapped around a person's leg." In infringement litigation, this so-called "means-plus-function" claim element would be satisfied if the accused infringer's product used Velcro fabric sections, buttons, snaps, clips, or a zipper, and mechanical equivalents of these structures, to fasten the opposing edges of the fabric sleeve. This assumes, of course, that the five specific examples of the fastening means were expressly or impliedly described in the specification. A claim consisting of only a single means-plus-function element is impermissible due to its indefiniteness.

The following is an example of Claim 1 of U.S. Patent No. 6,065,404, which discloses a reusable simulated grenade lobbed by soldiers in war games similar to laser tag where soldiers wear detectors that sense laser hits to determine if they have been killed or injured. (See the figure on page 52.)

1.   A simulated grenade, comprising:
a core;
a quantity of an explosive contained in the core for providing a non-lethal explosion upon detonation;
a manually actuable detonator mechanism mounted to the core for detonating the explosive;
transducer means connected to the core for emitting signals detectable by a plurality of sensors worn by a player within a predetermined proximity; and
circuit means mounted to the core including a switch actuated by the force of the explosion created when the explosive is detonated, the circuit means being connected to the transducer means for energizing the same when the switch is actuated.

Many times patent attorneys will refer to the "point of novelty" or the "patentable feature" of the invention. They are usually referring to that element or functional limitation of a claim that led the USPTO examiner to allow the same; that is, the patentably distinguishing recitation. A good example is Claim 1 of U.S. Patent No. 3,487,800, the original sailboard patent, which is set forth in the following paragraph. But for the limitation "said joint having a plurality of axes of rotation," Claim 1 arguably read on prior art sailboats with masts that are pivotal about a single laterally extending axis for stowage or passing under a bridge. To say that a claim *reads* on the prior art is to indicate that the words of the claim literally describe or match the invention shown and/or described in an earlier patent or published article. Such a claim is said to be anticipated, or, stated another way, it lacks novelty.

    1.   Wind-propelled apparatus comprising:
body means adapted to support a user;
wind-propulsion means pivotally associated with said body means and adapted to receive wind for motive power for said apparatus, said propulsion means comprising:
a mast;
a joint for mounting said mast on said body means;
a sail and means for extending said sail laterally from said mast, the position of said propulsion means being controllable by said user, said propulsion means being substantially free from pivotal restraint in the absence of said user, said joint having a plurality of axes of rotation whereby said sail free-falls along any of a plurality of vertical planes upon release by said user.

Here is Claim 1 from Priceline.com's U.S. Patent No. 5,897,620 on its reverse auction method of selling airline tickets:

    1.   A method comprising the steps of:
viewing, using a computer, special fare listing information for air travel to a specified destination location from a specified departure location within a specified time range, said special fare listing information excluding a specified departure time;
transmitting, using a computer, a request to purchase a commitment for carriage corresponding to said special fare listing information;
receiving a commitment for carriage, including an obligation by an airline to provide a seat on a flight, that satisfies said request but does not specify a departure time;
accepting said commitment for carriage; and
receiving at a time subsequent to said accepting an identification of said departure time.

Here is Claim 1 from Amazon.com's U.S. Patent No. 5,960,411 on its so-called "one-click" method of making purchase orders via the Internet:

1. A method of placing an order for an item comprising:
under control of a client system, displaying information identifying the item; and
in response to only a single action being performed, sending a request to order the item along with an identifier of a purchaser of the item to a server system;
under control of a single-action ordering component of the server system, receiving the request;
retrieving additional information previously stored for the purchaser identified by the identifier in the received request; and
generating an order to purchase the requested item for the purchaser identified by the identifier in the received request using the retrieved additional information; and
fulfilling the generated order to complete purchase of the item whereby the item is ordered without using a shopping cart ordering model.

Here is Claim 1 from Menusaver, Inc.'s U.S. Patent No. 6,004,596 on its manufactured peanut butter and jelly sandwich:

1. A sealed crustless sandwich, comprising:
a first bread layer having a first perimeter surface coplanar to a contact surface;
at least one filling of an edible food juxtaposed to said contact surface;
a second bread layer juxtaposed to said at least one filling opposite of said first bread layer, wherein said second bread layer includes a second perimeter surface similar to said first perimeter surface;
a crimped edge directly between said first perimeter surface and said second perimeter surface for sealing said at least one filling between said first bread layer and said second bread layer;
wherein a crust portion of said first bread layer and said second bread layer has been removed.

The CAFC has repeatedly said that limitations from the specification are not to be read into the claims. However, in infringement cases, the

CAFC often does this under the guise of interpreting the claims in light of the specification or of addressing enablement. In response, many patent attorneys have adopted the practice of not using any language in the title, field of the invention, summary, or abstract, that is not in the broadest claim.

One of my clients won a multimillion-dollar patent infringement jury verdict in San Francisco, California, that turned on the interpretation of a means-plus-function element. My client owned a patent on a tape drive used with personal computers to back up the data on the hard disk. The claims in dispute called for "means for opening the access door of the cartridge when the cartridge is inserted in the slot." The structure disclosed in the specification for performing this function comprised a pin and a linkage mounted on a sliding cartridge support tray so that movement of the tray to its retracted position would cause the pin to engage the rearward end of the tape cartridge access door to pivot the door open. The defendant's technical expert testified on a Friday that a fixed cam in the accused tape drive was not structurally equivalent to the pin and linkage. The prospects of winning the case looked very bleak for my client.

Over the weekend, my client's in-house counsel worked furiously to modify the plaintiff's commercial product, which looked exactly like that illustrated in its patent, to use the fixed cam from the defendant's device in place of the pin. During cross-examination on Monday, the defendant's technical expert was asked whether interchangeability was an indication of structural equivalence. After he replied affirmatively, which is consistent with the case law, the plaintiff's counsel showed him the modified version of the plaintiff's tape drive. The defendant's counsel vehemently objected. After a long conference between the judge and both trial counsel at the side of the judge's bench, the judge agreed to allow the plaintiff's counsel to continue to question the defendant's technical expert about the exhibit and to allow the defense counsel to expose any alleged inaccuracies during cross-examination. Shortly after the jury went into deliberation, they sent a note to the judge asking to see the plaintiff's modified tape drive, which had been marked as an exhibit and introduced into evidence. In a matter of hours, the jury returned a verdict of infringement. My client had won a very close patent infringement case, on which it subsequently collected many millions of dollars in damages and royalties. The defendant's trial counsel had made a tactical mistake in objecting so strenuously to the exhibit because it drew enormous attention to that piece of evidence and got the interest of an otherwise bored jury. This bit of trial strategy swung the case completely around in my client's favor.

Abstract

The abstract of the patent application is one paragraph on a separate page at the end of the application. It is limited to 150 words in length and is printed on the face of the patent to aid searchers and others in rapidly assessing the scope of its disclosure. Legal phraseology such as "means" and "comprising" should not be used in the abstract. Some patent attorneys merely use the same text as that appearing in the summary of the invention, shortening it if necessary. Others prefer to give a more specific description of the preferred embodiment or a narrative summary of several disclosed embodiments. The abstract is not a very critical portion of the application, and, if properly drafted, there is little risk that it will be successfully used to narrowly interpret the scope of the claims in patent litigation.

Here is the abstract for U.S. Patent No. 6,065,404 for the training grenade illustrated at the beginning of this chapter:

A re-useable simulated grenade is provided that may be utilized by soldiers training with a multiple integrated laser engagement system (MILES). The simulated grenade includes a central core having a blast chamber that contains a non-lethal quantity of an explosive detonated by a manually actuatable detonator mechanism. The core has a plurality of omni-directional passages containing a filler which is ejected to simulate the blast pattern of an actual grenade. A plurality of transducers such as infrared LED's, acoustic transducers or RF transducers are located on the core for emitting signals detectable by a plurality of sensors worn by a player within a predetermined proximity of the simulated grenade. A circuit including a pressure sensitive switch is located in the core and is connected to the transducers for energizing the same when the explosive is detonated. A player identification code (PID) is encoded onto the signals emitted by the transducers. Signal intensity levels are varied in a timed sequence upon the detonation to create kill and near miss (wounded) zones. After creating the kill and near miss zones, the circuit causes the transducers to emit an intermittent pulse to thereby facilitate location and recovery of the training grenade for recharging with explosive and filler and subsequent re-use.

Drawings

Patent drawings are required under U.S. patent law for all but chemical and process inventions. The drawings must illustrate every feature of the invention specified in the claims. They must conform to exceedingly strict standards as to form, margins, line thickness, shading, sectioning, schematic symbols, and so forth. The reason for specifying these standards is to ensure that patent drawings are published in a uniform style when the patent is granted. This allows the public to more readily understand the drawings and the invention disclosed in the patent. Throughout this book, drawings from various U.S. patents have been reproduced to give you an idea of what they look like. Individual parts and elements in the patent drawings are called out by separate reference numerals with lead lines pointing to the corresponding structure. These reference numerals are referred to in the detailed description. The USPTO requirements for formal patent drawings are so demanding that, as a practical matter, only an experienced patent draftsperson can properly prepare formal patent drawings. In the "olden days," they used to be drawn with India ink on a special type of cardboard called bristol board. Today, they are most often drawn with the aid of computer automated drawing (CAD) software that runs on a personal computer, and are printed on standard paper with a laser printer. One example of such software is sold under the AutoCAD trademark. CAD drawings produced during the design and manufacture of a product are often imported into the patent draftsperson's CAD software and then translated into USPTO format. This saves lots of effort and expense, and also ensures accuracy.

In patent applications disclosing mechanical inventions, the drawings are usually a series of perspective, side elevation, cross-sectional, and/or exploded views, and are sometimes fragmentary or broken. These different views are used to illustrate the important structure of the preferred embodiments described in the specification. Electrical and software inventions are normally illustrated with functional block diagrams and flow diagrams. It is rare that one still sees schematic diagrams of specific electronic circuitry. Chemical inventions, including pharmaceuticals and biotech inventions, often do not have any drawings, although they sometimes have elaborate charts and tables of data that appear in drawing form, molecular diagrams, DNA sequences, or process flow diagrams.

In the United States, informal patent drawings can be filed with the application and will suffice for purposes of obtaining an official U.S. filing date. Informal drawings may comprise, for example, sketches, conceptual drawings, or blueprints marked with reference numerals. Formal patent drawings have to be supplied on or before the deadline for paying the USPTO issue fee. The formal drawings must not introduce any new matter into the patent application. They are typically a "cleaned up" version of the informal drawings redrawn to meet USPTO guidelines, with no additional structure or features added. Most U.S. patent applications are now published 18 months after filing, and the USPTO may send a drawing objection early on if the drawings are deemed too informal for publication. A reasonable amount of time is then given to file corrected drawings.

The USPTO will permit a copyright notice or a mask work notice to be included in patent drawings, provided the specification of the application includes the following notice: "[t]he (copyright or mask work) owner has no objection to the facsimile reproduction by anyone of the patent document or the patent disclosure, as it appears in the Patent and Trademark Office patent files or records, but otherwise reserves all (copyright or mask work) rights whatsoever." I can only recall one U.S. patent with a copyright notice in the drawings. Those drawings were plans for a toy kite. However, both during the term of the patent and after its expiration, the copyright could not be used to prevent the public from making the claimed kite because copyright cannot extend to utilitarian articles. At most, the copyright could be used to prevent the copying of the kite plans *other than those appearing in the patent itself.* While I can't recall a specific court case involving the issue, it is clear that in the absence of a copyright notice, anyone is free to copy and disseminate the drawings of an issued patent for any purpose.

Taken together, the detailed description and the drawings of a patent application form the disclosure of the invention that must support the claimed subject matter. Once an application has been filed, it is not permissible to add new description or drawings that add any new features to the original disclosure, as this would violate the prohibition against the introduction of new matter. The reason is simple; namely, the priority of the application is based on what was disclosed at the time of filing. This date determines what is, and what is not, prior art. New disclosure can only be added by filing a continuation-in-part (CIP) patent application, which takes a new filing date with respect to the newly disclosed subject matter.

Sometimes, important information in a patent application will be illustrated in the originally filed drawings, but not described in the written portion of the patent application, and vice versa. In general, the application can be later amended if necessary to put these features into the missing part. For example, if it turns out that the oval cross-section of a sprinkler nozzle is an important patentable feature, it may be possible to amend the description and claims to include this feature even if it only is illustrated in the original drawings, and not described in any originally filed text.

Inventorship Oath

An inventorship oath or declaration must accompany the application, which can be executed by the inventor(s) prior to filing the application or after that. In this document, each inventor's name, residence address, and citizenship are set forth. Each inventor must execute the inventorship oath or declaration, under penalty of perjury, to confirm that he or she has reviewed the application and understands its contents and that the inventor believes he or she is an original inventor of what is being claimed. The inventor also must acknowledge the duty to disclose material information (prior art and best mode) during the prosecution of the application before the USPTO. The oath or declaration usually gives a power of attorney to one or more registered patent attorneys or patent agents to conduct all business before the USPTO on behalf of the inventor. It may also recite the serial number and filing dates of certain pending U.S. applications or foreign applications on which priority is claimed. An inventorship oath must be sworn to by the inventor before a notary public or other officer authorized to administer oaths. An inventorship declaration does not need to be notarized, so the declaration, as opposed to the oath, is used most of the time.

Assignments

Assignments usually are executed by the inventors at the same time they execute the inventorship oath or declaration. They usually convey the U.S. and foreign patent rights in the invention to the inventor's employer. The assignee will normally be indicated on the face of the granted patent. In general, there must be a written contract between the employer and the employee requiring the assignment; otherwise, the employee owns the patent rights, even if the invention was made in the course of the employment relationship utilizing company resources, but this rule may vary in different states. Assignments should be recorded in the USPTO to establish a proper chain of title. Patent licenses, on the other hand, should not normally be recorded. In its own handbook, the USPTO states:

[i]f an assignment, grant, or conveyance of a patent or an interest in a patent (or an application for a patent) is not recorded in the office within three months from its date, it is void against a subsequent purchaser for a valuable consideration without notice, unless it is recorded prior to the subsequent purchase.

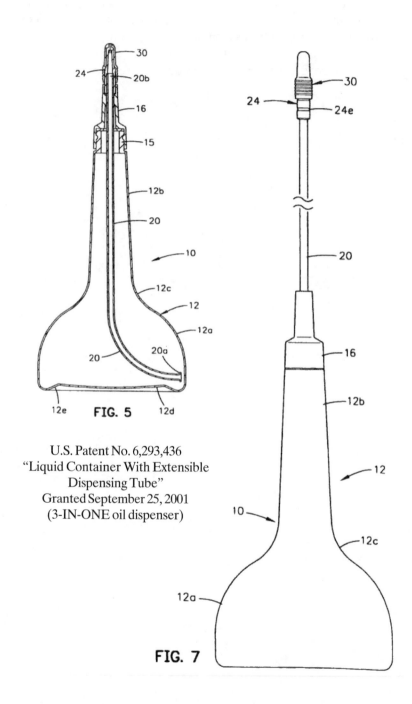

U.S. Patent No. 6,293,436
"Liquid Container With Extensible
Dispensing Tube"
Granted September 25, 2001
(3-IN-ONE oil dispenser)

FIG. 5

FIG. 7

CHAPTER 6

Patent Prosecution

T he term "patent prosecution" generally refers to the examination proceedings that take place in the USPTO with regard to all U.S. patent applications. Once the application is filed, there is a series of back-and-forth communications between the applicant's patent attorney or agent and the patent examiner to determine whether the application is proper as to form and meets all the legal criteria for the granting of a patent. No determination is made as to whether the invention sought to be patented infringes any prior patent. The length of the patent prosecution process depends largely on the subject matter being claimed, as different examining groups at the USPTO have application backlogs of different sizes. This has to do with the volume of applications filed in particular technical areas, the number of USPTO examiners available in particular fields, and the examiner turnover rate. In the past, patent applications on mechanical inventions typically issued about two years after filing, and on electronic or software inventions about three years after filing. It has frequently taken four or more years to obtain a patent on a pharmaceutical or biotech invention.

Patent prosecutions that are long in duration are disadvantageous to inventors for many reasons, not the least of which is that they cut into the period of exclusive rights afforded by the patent. This is because the term of a patent is measured from its earliest filing date if based upon an application filed on or after June 8, 1995. As part of the AIPA of 1999, the USPTO now has some rather ambitious goals to reduce the average pendency time of patent applications. Patent owners are eligible for patent term adjustment (PTA) in the form of a predetermined number of additional days of patent term calculated on the basis of certain delays in the administrative handling of applications. In addition, under the AIPA of 1999, there are certain rights to demand a royalty based on the pregrant publication of the application. However, this will only infrequently be of any benefit to the patent owner. This is because the invention claimed in the issued patent must be substantially identical to that claimed in the pregrant publication. It is usually necessary to significantly amend the claims during prosecution in order to overcome prior art.

Prosecution History

The USPTO will normally only correspond with the inventor's patent attorney or agent. Usually this is done in writing, although there may be telephone conferences and personal interviews at the USPTO. Interviews are most helpful where a model or prototype of the invention can be demonstrated. The substance of any oral communications is made of record in the file of the application for good reason. The collection of all the papers that lead to the allowance of a patent application is referred to as the prosecution history. This history is available to the public once any U.S. patent issues. Surprisingly, the public can now have access to the prosecution history of a published U.S. patent application while it is still pending and before it issues.

The prosecution history is a key piece of information upon which an interpretation of the scope of the claims is based. For example, during the prosecution, the applicant's attorney might argue that an element of a pending claim that calls for a drive assembly is different from certain structure shown in a cited prior art patent. In infringement litigation involving any subsequently granted patent, the patent owner would be barred or "estopped" from contending that the drive assembly element encompassed structure in the accused product similar to that distinguished during the prosecution of the patent.

Pregrant Publication

Applications filed in the USPTO are initially kept secret. However, applications filed on or after November 29, 2000, are automatically published after 18 months. A pregrant publication can be prevented by timely filing a request for nonpublication, which is not allowed if the application has already been, or will be, foreign filed. A nonpublication request can be later rescinded at any time. If an application based on the U.S. application is filed overseas after the filing of a nonpublication request in the USPTO, the applicant must notify the USPTO within 45 days or else the U.S. application will become automatically abandoned. This pregrant publication of U.S. patent applications was placed into the U.S. patent law to conform to the General Agreement of Tariffs and Trade (GATT) treaty earlier ratified by the United States. Most foreign patent systems have a 20-year patent term measured from the date of filing and automatically publish all applications regardless of whether they result in granted patents. Foreigners had been badly burned by submarine patents granted in the United States and wanted a patent term limited to 20 years from filing date, and pregrant publication to counter the perceived abuses of such delayed issuances.

Method of Submission

Patent applications should be filed in the USPTO via the Express Mail procedure so that the date of deposit with the U.S. postal system becomes the official U.S. filing date for priority purposes. The USPTO has recently implemented a system for permitting applications to be filed electronically over the Internet. So far, only the most adventuresome patent attorneys have attempted electronic patent application filing. My impression from viewing a USPTO-sponsored demonstration is that it takes a highly dedicated computer nerd to figure out the complex protocols, encryption keys, interface software, graphics conversion, and so forth. Eventually, the USPTO will undoubtedly make such electronic filing mandatory for all registered patent attorneys. I am personally sticking with filing by mail until all of the bugs are worked out of the electronic filing system. Applications also can be hand delivered to the USPTO in Arlington, Virginia, but virtually nobody files this way. It is prudent to include a return postcard listing all of the papers being filed. The USPTO will date stamp the postcard and apply a serial number. You will get this return postcard back weeks before you get the official USPTO filing receipt, and you can use it to prove your filing date should the need arise.

One of my colleagues filed a U.S. patent application via the Express Mail procedure, following all the requirements to the letter. His secretary deposited the envelope in the Express Mail box well before the final pick-up deadline. Much to his horror, the U.S. Postal Service Express Mail receipt that was later returned showed the next day as the date of deposit. This was apparently a potential disaster as it would make the U.S. application ineligible for its foreign priority date. This was because the date his secretary deposited the U.S. application was the one-year anniversary of its original filing in a foreign country by a non-U.S. citizen. Under the Paris Convention Treaty, the U.S. application had to be filed within that one-year period. The USPTO assigns filing dates to applications deposited via the Express Mail procedure based on the date of receipt written by the postman. So it gave the application an official filing date one day after its date of deposit. The USPTO regulations governing Express Mail filing had been fully complied with. Nevertheless, a Petition to the Commissioner and many declarations had to be filed to rectify the situation. It turned out that the postman never made a pickup at that Express Mail mailbox the day the application was deposited. The moral of the story is that if you really need the filing date, carry the Express Mail package containing the patent application into a U.S. post office branch and have a postal employee manually date stamp your Express Mail receipt.

An even more bizarre Express Mail patent application filing happened to another of my colleagues. He had his paralegal take the envelope to the local U.S. post office because he was filing on the last day of the one-year grace period. Surprisingly, filing on the last day is very common in patent law practice, in part due to many factors beyond the control of the patent attorney. Anyway, the paralegal called and told my colleague that the U.S. post office clerk was refusing to accept the package because it was more than 10 ounces, and emergency regulations had just been issued that morning to deny mailing of such packages because of a fear that they might be letter bombs mailed by the so-called "Unibomber." My colleague engaged the local office of one of our U.S. senators, and they finally convinced the manager of the U.S. post office branch to keep the package in a bombproof depository and to issue a receipt. It took about a year for the USPTO to implement a whole raft of regulations to award filing dates to patent applications that had suddenly been refused by U.S. post offices around the country.

Fees

Patent applicants who qualify for small entity status are entitled to a 50-percent reduction on all USPTO fees, including application filing fees, issue fees, and maintenance fees. This can amount to thousands of dollars over the life of a patent. A small entity, in general, is either an individual or a business with not more than 500 employees. Small entity status cannot be claimed where the invention is licensed to a non-small entity. Also, if a small business is a subsidiary of a large company with more than 500 employees, small entity status is not available. The improper payment of a USPTO fee at the small entity level, either through fraud or gross negligence, can lead to unenforceability of the patent in patent litigation. If you should discover that you have inadvertently paid a USPTO fee at the small entity rate when it should have been paid at the non-small entity rate, the deficiency should be remitted to the USPTO as soon as possible and a statement made on the record setting forth facts explaining the oversight.

Art Unit/Technology Center

Once a utility patent application is filed in the USPTO, it is assigned to an Art Unit or a Technology Center with examiners knowledgeable in the relevant technology. Most applications rest unattended in the USPTO for at least one year before an examiner acts on it due to the backlog of applications. A Petition to Make Special can be filed if you want expedited examination of your application, but your application must qualify. Grounds for a Petition to Make Special include the inventor's age (over 65) or health, the fact that the invention promotes conservation of the environment, the fact that a patent search has been done, the fact that a patent is needed to obtain investment financing, the fact that the invention thwarts terrorism, or that there is a prospective infringer. Stay away from filing a Petition to Make Special based on prospective infringement. An examiner will be very reluctant to allow broad claims knowing that the patent is likely to be litigated and his or her actions scrutinized by the accused infringer's counsel, a judge, and a jury.

When an examiner picks up an application and commences work on it, he or she performs a patent search. Examiners often have their own hard copy patent collections so they can do searches without having to resort to the USPTO patent database. Even if the inventor has filed an Information Disclosure Statement (IDS) making a record of the most pertinent prior art that he or she is aware of, the examiner will still do a search. Patent applicants and their patent attorneys are under a strict obligation to disclose the closest prior art they are aware of to the USPTO. Failure to do so can render any resulting patent invalid and/or unenforceable and could subject the patent owner to significant financial liability. The closest prior art also should be disclosed to the examiner for the practical reason that the claims of any patent that is obtained will have a presumption of validity over that prior art, which can only be overcome by clear and convincing evidence in federal court litigation.

Office Actions

After the examiner conducts a search, a first Office Action will be rendered, typically rejecting all of the claims of the application for lack of novelty and/or obviousness over specific U.S. and/or foreign patents or published applications. Often the examiner will not rely upon those prior art references uncovered in the applicant's own search, which inventors are generally obligated to cite. The first Office Action also may contain rejections of the specification and/or claims for indefiniteness or lack of adequate disclosure to support the claimed subject matter. Frequently, there are objections to the patent drawings, usually as a result of initially filing informal drawings.

The initial rejections contained in the first Office Action do not mean that a patent will not ultimately be granted. The prior art rejections are the examiner's way of forcing the applicant's patent attorney to file a response setting forth sound legal argument as to why the claims are patentable over the references, or forcing the patent attorney to amend the claims to insert additional limitations that serve to distinguish the claimed subject matter over the references. The patent examiner should initial each prior art reference listed on the inventor's information disclosure statement to confirm that they have been considered. Only references listed on the official USPTO prior art citation form and initialed on the inventor's information disclosure statement will be printed on the face of any patent. The patent claims are entitled to a presumption of validity over these prior art references.

Anticipation rejections, that is, rejections of claims as not being new (lack of novelty), must be limited to a single reference. In making a rejection for anticipation of a claim over a prior art patent or publication, the examiner is essentially taking the position that each and every element and limitation found in that claim is identically disclosed in the prior art reference, in the exact combination and relationship recited in the claim. If there are any differences between what is recited in the claim and what is disclosed in the cited prior art reference, the anticipation rejection is legally improper. Instead, the examiner would have to cite an additional prior art reference or references to supply the missing elements or limitations and reject the claim for alleged obviousness. But this is only legally proper if there is some express teaching or suggestion in the references themselves to combine them and/or modify them as proposed by the examiner.

Overcoming a rejection of a claim for lack of novelty is usually fairly straightforward. Either the patent attorney points out the distinguishing element or limitation in the claim as originally filed, or inserts such an element or limitation. Overcoming an obviousness rejection is much more involved. There are different strategies depending upon what references are combined and how the examiner states that it would have been obvious to make such a combination.

Inventor's Response

An inventor's response to a USPTO Office Action must be made within a prescribed time limit, which is usually three months. Extensions of time of up to three months can usually be obtained retroactively, upon payment of the prescribed U.S. Government fee. The maximum time allowed for response, by statute, is six months. If no response is timely received, the application will be held abandoned (no longer pending). However, it can be revived if it can be shown that the failure to timely respond was unintentional or unavoidable.

Responses to USPTO Office Actions must be in writing. Personal interviews with USPTO examiners can be arranged in their offices in Arlington, Virginia. They allow a back-and-forth discourse and the demonstration of prototypes and products embodying the claimed invention. Proposed draft amendments are frequently discussed. Patent attorneys also frequently conduct telephone interviews with examiners. An interview at the USPTO or over the telephone does not remove the necessity of filing a formal written response to an Office Action. The actions taken by an examiner are based solely on the written records, which may include an Interview Summary of what was discussed. The best time to conduct a personal interview with an examiner is after the first Office Action.

Many years ago, I took an inventor to a personal interview at the USPTO with an examiner in order to demonstrate a prototype of the claimed invention. The inventor's financial backer also wanted to attend and I reluctantly agreed. The examiner kept stating that the claimed invention would have been obvious with a combination of several prior art references. Finally, the financial backer blurted out, "If it is so darn obvious, how come I spent $3 million trying to get it to work?" Of course, the amount of funds spent to create or commercially develop an invention has no legal bearing on the obviousness determination.

The examiner usually issues a second Office Action, and hopefully at that point, there is an indication of allowable subject matter. In a typical situation, the second Office Action is made final, so the options in filing an amendment after final rejection are normally limited to accepting the allowed, or allowable, claims, or placing the claims in better form for appeal. If no allowable subject matter has been indicated, the inventor's options are to abandon the application, file a request for continued examination (RCE) for purposes of seeking allowance of a broader amendment, or filing an appeal. The cost of an appeal varies greatly with the complexity of the case and how far up the ladder the appeal proceeds from the examiner: to the USPTO Board of Appeals, to the U.S. Court of Appeals for the Federal Circuit, and, ultimately, in extremely rare cases, all the way to the U.S. Supreme Court. Assuming the application is formally allowed at some stage, a formal Notice of Allowance will be sent by the USPTO. An issue fee must be paid, along with a fee for extra copies of the issued patent.

Continuation Patent Application

A continuation patent application can be filed that contains the identical disclosure of another pending application. So long as it is filed before the parent application issues as a patent or is abandoned, the continuation application will be entitled to the same filing date. The claims of a continuation application can be changed dramatically through the amendment process. So long as the subject matter being claimed is adequately supported and it is new and nonobvious over the prior art, it will be allowable, assuming there is also utility. Sometimes the USPTO will render an "obviousness-type" double patenting rejection, which means that the claims of the continuation application are obvious in view of the claims of the parent application. This can be overcome by filing a "terminal disclaimer," in which the patent owner agrees that both patents will expire on the same date. Therefore, it is possible to obtain several patents on the same invention with claims of varying scope. Often companies will keep a continuation application pending for purposes of trying to gain the allowance of new claims specifically drafted to read on a competitor's later-developed product. This is perfectly legal, and indeed a very sound business strategy if one can afford the substantial legal and USPTO fees involved. Continuation-in-part (CIP) applications are also frequently filed to add new features that are later developed. The new subject matter, however, takes a new filing date.

One Invention, One Patent

The U.S. patent law only allows the claiming of one invention per patent. Sometimes a patent application will disclose and claim more than one patentably distinct invention. If the patent issues in this form, its validity cannot be attacked on this basis, and the patentee has essentially gotten a bargain. Less filing fees, issue fees, and maintenance fees will be required than if multiple patent applications had been filed, prosecuted, and issued. However, more often than not, the examiner will make a restriction requirement and require the inventor to elect which invention he or she desires to initially prosecute. The others can be held in abeyance and pursued by the filing of divisional applications before the issuance date of the parent application.

A string of original, continuation, divisional, and CIP applications can be filed off a common parent, and each will be entitled to its original filing date so long as they are all filed before the patenting or abandonment of a predecessor application in the string of applications. However, the term of each patent will be measured from the earliest filing date if any of the applications in the string was filed on or after June 8, 1995.

The term of a U.S. utility patent is 20 years from the filing date. Maintenance fees must be paid no later than the three and one-half, seven and one-half, and 11 and one-half year anniversaries of the grant date or else the patent will lapse. USPTO fees are increased annually to reflect increases in the consumer price index (CPI).

Public Use Proceeding

There is a rather strange and bizarre proceeding in the USPTO called a public use proceeding. If any member of the public wishes to, they can file a petition in the USPTO in connection with a pending patent application of another, alleging that the claimed invention was in public use in this country more than a year prior to the application filing date. Such proceedings are extremely rare. There is no statute specifically authorizing them, and virtually no court cases dealing with appeals from decisions by the USPTO in public use proceedings. With regard to applications filed before November 29, 2000, it was very difficult for a third party to institute a public use proceeding because it would rarely know about a competitor's pending secret patent application. With respect to applications filed after that date, in many cases they will be automatically published.

The problems inherent with public use proceedings are best illustrated by my own personal experience with one in the early 1990s. My client was a licensed fumigator on the West Coast who had developed a rather ingenious labor-saving apparatus and method for fumigating large volumes of fruit imported from Chile during the winter. Previously, forklifts were used to stack rows and columns of pallets of crates of fresh fruit measuring 6 feet in height and occupying several thousands of square feet inside a dockside warehouse. A half dozen workers then laboriously laid out hoses between the pallets, placed fans on stands between the pallets, pulled tarpaulins across the crates, connected the tarpaulins together, and pulled the tarpaulins down to the floor. Then a state-approved fumigant was injected through the hoses to kill insects and other pests, and the tarpaulins were laboriously removed by hand. Then all of the hoses and fans had to be collected before the forklifts could take away the pallets.

My fumigator client developed a large lightweight metal framework covered with a giant tarp having vertical side curtain walls. It was suspended from the warehouse ceiling by a system of cables and automatically lowered over the pallets with electric winches. The framework supported a system of fumigant injection nozzles, circulation fans, and evacuation fans to speed the process of fumigating the fruit, and subsequently removing the fumigant through the roof of the warehouse. All of the time-consuming manual work associated with the prior art method was eliminated, and worker safety was greatly enhanced.

The fumigating system and apparatus invented by my client had been very successfully employed on a non-secret commercial basis on the West Coast. The inventor had me file a U.S. patent application on it within the one year grace period measured from his first use of the invention for which he had been paid by a customer. The broad claims of his patent application were allowed by the patent examiner with little difficulty, as the prior art patents located were not that close to the claimed invention. Here is where things began to go badly. We sent a letter to an East Coast fumigator who my client felt had seen his invention in operation and commercially adopted it. The letter included the patent drawings and indicated that the invention was the subject of an allowed U.S. patent application, and that the technology was available for licensing at reasonable terms. To add credibility, the letter enclosed a copy of the Notice of Allowance from the USPTO examiner, but the serial number and filing date were purposefully whited-out to prevent the recipient of the letter from filing a protest document of some sort that would then get associated with the pending application via the serial number and filing date.

Rather than proceeding with patent license negotiations, the East Coast fumigator filed a petition with the USPTO asking it to institute a public use proceeding based on the fact that a similar fumigating framework had allegedly been in public use on the East Coast for a number of years. The name of my inventor client, alone, and the subject matter described in the petition were sufficient for the USPTO to link the petition with my client's pending patent application. The allegations in the public use petition were supported by several declarations that fell woefully short of the guarantees of trustworthiness required to give them any weight or credibility. Simply stated, much of the testimony and photographs would not have been admissible as evidence in a federal court lawsuit challenging the validity of my client's patent, if he had been granted one. This is because the declarations contained mostly hearsay, lacked proper foundation, violated the best evidence rule, were uncorroborated, and so forth. However, despite numerous formal objections based on the Federal Rules of Evidence, the non-lawyer patent examiner gave the allegations full weight, and my client's patent never issued. The Manual of Patent Examining Procedure provides that a "statutory bar can only be established by testimony taken in accordance with normal rules of evidence, including the right of cross-examination." Unfortunately, my client was not afforded this safeguard.

The moral of this fumigator invention story is: don't say anything to a competitor or prospective licensee about licensing your invention until you actually have your patent in-hand. The allowed claims of a pending U.S. patent application are not entitled to any presumption of validity. Had my client waited to offer a license to the East Coast fumigator until after his patent was granted, then any case or controversy regarding its alleged invalidity would have to have been brought to federal district court for resolution. Legally, there can be no public use proceeding in the USPTO involving a granted U.S. patent. USPTO patent reexamination proceedings, discussed in Chapter 7, can only be based on prior art patents and publications. In federal district court, the East Coast fumigator would have had the burden of proving, by clearing and convincing evidence, that my client's claimed method and apparatus were invalid for anticipation. Moreover, much of the alleged evidence of prior public use of a similar apparatus and method on the East Coast would either have been excluded on the basis of various evidentiary objections, or the subject of rigorous cross-examination that would probably have led the jury to conclude that it fell far short of clear and convincing evidence of invalidity.

The USPTO regulation authorizing public use proceedings has since been amended so that the petition must be submitted prior to the date the application was published or the mailing date of a Notice of Allowance, whichever occurs first.

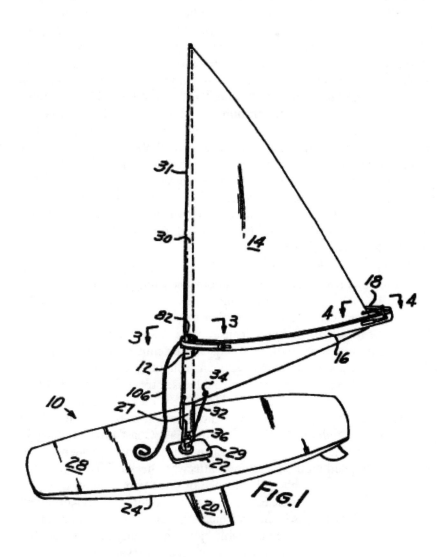

Fig. 1

U.S. Patent No. RE. 31,167
"Wind-Propelled Apparatus"
Granted March 8, 1983
(Windsurfer sailboard)

CHAPTER 7

Post Patent
Grant Procedures

N ow you have your U.S. patent. It is a beautiful printed document with a handsome cover including a gold seal and red ribbon. It bears a reproduction of the signature of the director of patents and trademarks. Make sure you safeguard this document, because if it is lost or destroyed, you can never get another original printed patent grant for the same patent number again. You can only get a certified copy, which has the same legal effect but isn't quite so regal looking. If you ever have to sue for patent infringement, the single most persuasive piece of evidence you can show the jury is the wonderful original patent grant. Imagine your attorney in closing argument holding that document and confidently speaking to the jury about the wisdom of our founding fathers in providing for the U.S. patent system that has helped the United States achieve its high standard of living. Picture in your mind jurors being asked by the accused infringer's attorney to find, by clear and convincing evidence, that your visually impressive patent is worthless after being duly examined and granted. I think you will agree that on this superficial level, the accused infringer has a tough job.

Once your patent has been granted, it is extremely important that all products that embody the patented invention be marked with the patent number. With a couple of exceptions, money damages for patent infringement do not begin to accumulate in the United States until the infringer has been formally notified of the infringement, unless goods embodying the patented invention have been marked with the patent number. This is the effect of the "marking" statute in the U.S. patent law. Where the goods are too small to display a visible patent number printed, screened, or otherwise applied to it, the patent number can be placed on a tag or label attached to the goods or on a container for the goods. There is an exception for method patents, because a method is not a tangible thing that can be marked with a patent number.

An infringer cannot be sued unless and until the patent is actually granted. Until that time, patent applicants should mark products embodying their invention with a notice indicating "patent pending" to ward off copiers. It is a violation of U.S. patent law to mark products with a patent pending notice when an application covering the product is not pending. It is similarly a violation to mark products "patented in the United States" or to apply a phony patent number when no U.S. patent covering the product has been granted. Apparently, it is not a violation of U.S. patent law to keep the patent number on the goods after the patent has expired. Many companies do this to deter copying on the theory that unsophisticated prospective competitors won't check the status of the patent. For example, the hinged staple remover jaws so frequently used in offices sometimes bear the number of a patent that expired before I was born!

Term of a Patent

The term of a U.S. utility patent is 20 years from its earliest filing date, a term that was only recently set by Congress when the United States ratified the GATT treaty in the mid-1990s in order to bring our patent term in line with the patent term of foreign countries. The term of a U.S. patent had been 17 years from the grant date for more than two centuries. The current patent term statute, which measures the term from the earliest filing date, means that if there were continuations, continuations-in-part, or divisional applications that led to the patent grant, any of which were filed on or after June 8, 1995, the 20-year period runs from the earliest of these filing dates. Any patent based solely on an application or applications filed before that date has a term that is automatically the longer of 17 years from its grant date or 20 years from its earliest filing date. Herein lies a trap. Many people miscalculate the expiration dates of older patents.

Where the prosecution took less than three years, and the patent is based solely upon an application filed prior to June 8, 1995, its term is longer under the 20-year calculation than the 17-year calculation. Significant infringement liability can result from companies that jump the gun and begin manufacturing products thinking a U.S. patent has already expired.

Under the provisions of the AIPA of 1999, U.S. patents are now subject to patent term adjustment (PTA). According to a hopelessly complex system that only an accountant could track, U.S. patents based on utility and plant applications filed on or after May 29, 2000, are entitled to a predetermined number of days of patent term extension based on certain administrative delays in the USPTO in processing a patent application. The number of days is printed on the Notice of Allowance, and there are procedures for challenging the USPTO's PTA calculation. In addition, certain patents on pharmaceuticals and other products that require Food and Drug Administration (FDA) approval before they can be marketed in the United States are eligible for up to five years of patent term extension commensurate with the length of time required for FDA premarketing regulatory procedures. Besides the foregoing, the only other way to extend a U.S. patent is to get a private bill approved by Congress and signed by the president. To my knowledge, this has occurred only once, and that was allegedly in the late 1940s in connection with the patent on the Nordon bomb sight used so successfully on B-17s during Allied bombing raids in Germany. What a great thing—you get a patent extended on a bomb sight that nobody needs anymore because World War II ended!

Maintenance Fees

If you look on the inside cover of an original U.S. patent grant, you will see a paragraph explaining that the patent is subject to maintenance fees. Maintenance fees are payable to the USPTO after the three, seven, and 11 year anniversaries from the grant date. The fees must be paid to the USPTO by the three and one-half, seven and one-half, and 11 and one-half year anniversaries from the grant date or else a surcharge must be paid in addition to the maintenance fee. If the maintenance fees are not paid by the fourth, eighth, and 12th anniversaries from the date of grant, the patent will lapse. The fees escalate from the first fee to the third fee, and a small entity discount is available. The USPTO uses the maintenance fees collected from patent owners as a primary source of its operating revenue, along with application filing fees and issue fees. Your patent attorney will docket the maintenance fee deadlines and send you reminders when it comes time to pay each maintenance fee. Make sure you keep your patent attorney advised of any change in your mailing address to ensure that you receive timely reminders.

As mentioned previously, if you and/or your patent attorney should fail to timely pay a maintenance fee by the fourth, eighth, or 12th anniversary deadline, the patent will lapse. However, a maintenance fee can still be paid within a two-year period, and the patent reinstated upon payment of an additional hefty late payment surcharge, provided a petition is filed to accept late payment based on unintentionally missing the payment deadline. Unintentional means that you and/or your patent attorney overlooked the deadline through some mistake or error. A conscious decision not to pay the maintenance fee because you couldn't afford it, or you briefly thought the patent wasn't worth much, or because its claims had been found invalid but the court judgment was later reversed, and so forth, bars a patent owner from having a late maintenance fee payment accepted on the "unintentional" basis.

After the sixth, 10th, and 14th anniversaries, a late payment of a maintenance fee can be accepted, and the patent reinstated, only if the failure to timely pay the maintenance fee is shown at any time to have been unavoidable. Reinstated patents are subject to intervening rights of third parties just the same as reissued patents, as described hereafter. The reinstatement of a U.S. patent on the basis that the failure to timely pay a maintenance fee was unavoidable requires the filing of a petition along with extensive documentary evidence to establish that the deadline was missed despite the patent attorney taking all steps that a reasonably prudent person would take. Let me give you an example from my own experience.

When I was a principal in my own midsize patent law boutique, I represented a manufacturer of electronic components for many years and obtained numerous patents for it. My firm had three separate docketing systems for keeping track of maintenance fee deadlines and a full-time docketing clerk. All three systems were regularly used, and clients were sent reminders well in advance to see if they wanted particular maintenance fees paid. If they replied affirmatively, payments were made immediately to the USPTO upon receipt of funds from the client. We made sure that no patent was allowed to lapse unless we received specific instructions from the client to allow it to lapse. On rare occasions, clients could not be located or had died, and we went to great lengths to contact them or their successors. Through circumstances too bizarre and complicated to recount here, all three systems failed with respect to one U.S. patent on an electronic component still being manufactured and sold by my client. We found this out, much to my horror, a few months after the two-year "unintentional" window had expired.

My heart sank, and I thought I would be subject to a malpractice lawsuit. I equated in my mind the "unavoidable" standard with so-called acts of God; that is, you could only reinstate the patent if a hurricane blew out your office or something like that. I promptly told my client that its patent had lapsed because the maintenance fee had not been timely paid and then set about researching if anything could be done to revive the patent. I soon found out about the "reasonably prudent man" standard. Not only did my law firm have a triple redundant docketing system—a main system and two backups—but it also had very experienced staff people working on sending out maintenance fee reminders and ensuring timely payment to the USPTO, with close attorney supervision. Over a period approaching 20 years we had not missed a single maintenance fee deadline. The USPTO will generally send maintenance fee reminders if it does not receive timely payment, but they are under no legal obligation to do so. Furthermore, the patent owner's failure to timely receive a USPTO maintenance fee reminder is not grounds for unavoidability. Shortly after my particular client's patent had been granted, my office had moved to a new building. The USPTO records showed that my firm had mailed a change of address form to the USPTO and it was duly noted by USPTO personnel in the official records of the USPTO in connection with the patent. Nevertheless, the USPTO mailed the maintenance fee reminder to our old office address, and it was never forwarded to our new office because the postal forwarding request had expired after six months.

I read many published court decisions where petitions to accept late payment of maintenance fees on the grounds of unavoidability were rejected by the commissioner of patents and trademarks (now called the director) and his decision was appealed. In court, the standard for overcoming the USPTO's denial of acceptance of late payment of a maintenance fee on the grounds of unavoidability is the abuse of discretion standard. The standard makes it exceedingly tough to get a director's denial overturned by a federal judge. Almost all of the unavoidability cases I reviewed were decided against the patent owner. It was incredible how harsh the decisions turned out to be. For example, in one case, the patent attorney was a solo practitioner who died, and his grieving wife took no timely steps to have his patent practice turned over to another patent attorney. The patent owner argued that its failure to timely receive a maintenance fee reminder from his dead attorney established that the failure to timely pay the maintenance fee was unavoidable. The commissioner denied the petition to reinstate the patent, indicating that the patent owner should have heeded the maintenance fee notice on the inside cover of the original patent grant and that, in effect, he should have picked a younger and/or healthier patent attorney in the beginning.

I spent a solid month doing virtually no billable legal work. Instead, I researched all of the unavoidability cases, consulted with other patent attorneys, and began writing a petition to accept late payment of the maintenance fee on the basis of unavoidability. I prepared an extensive legal argument, calling upon my many years of experience handling motions in patent litigation. I argued that my particular circumstances met the legal test for unavoidability. I also argued that even though the USPTO's mailing of the maintenance fee reminder to my old office address was not legal grounds for a finding of unavoidability, it should nevertheless be given some equitable consideration. Equity is a fancy legal term for giving relief outside the conventional avenues of statutes and legal precedents where it would serve the interests of fairness and justice. I prepared five extensive factual affidavits of the various attorneys and staff persons that had been involved. The petition, declarations, and evidentiary exhibits made up a stack of documents about 1-inch thick. I filed them in the USPTO and prayed.

Months went by and I didn't hear anything from the USPTO. I called the Petitions Office at the USPTO and had a clerk confirm that my petition was on file in the office that would decide the matter. Many more months went by. Finally, after one year had elapsed, I decided out of the blue to telephone the automated USPTO maintenance fee status line to hear the official status of the patent. Much to my shock and delight, a computerized voice recounted the filing date of my petition and then gave the date the late maintenance fee had been accepted upon grant of that petition nine months earlier. It turned out, amazingly, that the USPTO had mailed its formal decision granting my petition to my old office address, and that is why I never received it.

Corrections

Once your patent has been granted, read the claims very carefully, look over the specification, and review the drawings. If you find any typographical errors, or if the USPTO fails to include a drawing figure, or worse yet, included a drawing figure from someone else's application, you can file a request for a Certificate of Correction. If there are any minor inadvertent clerical errors in the patent that are not the USPTO's fault, these can also be corrected via the same process, upon payment of a fee. When a Certificate of Correction is issued, it has a gold seal and becomes part of the patent grant. Any changes of a substantive nature, such as those affecting the scope of a claim, can only be effectuated, if at all, through either reissue or reexamination.

Reissue

Reissue is a process whereby the original patent grant may be surrendered to the USPTO and the patent changed substantively by reason of it being wholly or partly inoperative. Patent owners typically use the reissue process to attempt to change the language of the claims in order to broaden them. They take the position that the claims were limited more than they needed to be in order to be patentable over the prior art, or conversely, that they are too broad and need to be narrowed in view of newly discovered prior art. An application seeking to broaden claims of an issued patent must be filed within two years of the grant date of the original patent. However, there is a prohibition against so-called "reissue recapture," which prevents broadening of the claims of an issued patent by removing a limitation specifically inserted during the original prosecution in order to overcome a prior art rejection.

Apparently, Claim 1 of the original sailboard patent discussed in Chapter 5 ran into rough waters. That patent was later reissued (No. Re. 31,167), with Claim 1 canceled and replaced with a similar claim adding two opposed booms providing hand-holds on either side of the sail.

Reissue applications can be filed after the two-year time limit, but only to narrow the claims or correct some other defect, such as failure to make a foreign priority claim, improper inventorship, and so forth. The term of the reissued patent remains the same as that of the original patent. The maintenance fee deadlines are calculated from the grant date of the original patent, not the grant date of the reissued patent. I ran across one court decision seeking to reinstate a patent that had lapsed on the basis that the failure to pay the maintenance fee on time was unavoidable. The story given was that the secretary misdocketed the maintenance fee deadline based on the reissue grant date, and the attorney in charge didn't catch it. Much to my surprise, the petition was granted. That error in judgment hardly sounds unavoidable to me, but hey, I'm glad the poor attorney and his client caught a break.

Reissued patents are subject to intervening rights. If a third person relies on the scope of the original claims of the patent and makes substantial investment in the manufacture of products that don't infringe those claims, the court may give that person relief if the claims are later broadened through reissue to read on those products. The court can provide that the person can continue to manufacture and sell those products subject to the payment of a prescribed royalty. I encountered exactly this situation in a patent infringement lawsuit discussed in Chapter 11 (page 122).

Reexamination

A second process in the USPTO for substantively changing issued patents is called reexamination. Congress changed the patent laws in the early 1980s to provide for reexamination as a cheaper, more expedient alternative to patent litigation. Essentially, any party, including the patent owner or a third party desiring to invalidate a patent, may file a petition in the USPTO seeking to reexamine any unexpired patent to determine whether the claims are patentable over published prior art references not previously considered by the USPTO in connection with any prior USPTO examination of the claims in issue. This can happen if a material reference surfaces after the grant of the patent that may potentially anticipate or render obvious any claim of the granted patent. Reexamination is limited to prior art patents and publications, and cannot be based on other information, such as an affidavit establishing that a particularly relevant product was sold by a third party in the United States more than a year prior to the filing date of the patent for which reexamination is sought. The new prior art must raise a substantial new question of patentability. The claims of an issued patent also can be narrowed through the reexamination process. A certificate is issued at the conclusion of the reexamination proceedings, setting forth the results of the supplemental prosecution.

The early promise of reexamination as an inexpensive alternative for invalidating claims of patents that should not have been granted soon dissipated in the mid-1980s. Practitioners found that in the overwhelming majority of reexaminations, the same USPTO examiner who granted the original patent confirmed the patentability of the claims in their original form, or slightly modified form, over the newly discovered prior art. The patent was then effectively stronger than before. Prospective defendants gave up trying to knock out patents in reexamination, and, instead, the process began to be used prophylactically by patent owners to defuse the challenger's best prior art and render it of little value to an accused infringer in a court validity challenge. The AIPA Act of 1999 created a new USPTO reexamination proceeding allowing greater participation by the challenger. It remains to be seen if this will achieve the goal of an effective, less expensive alternative to federal court patent litigation.

Interference Proceeding

There is yet another proceeding in the USPTO that can involve an issued patent. Namely, an issued patent can become subject to an interference proceeding with a pending application. That application must present a claim to the same or substantially the same subject matter as the issued patent prior to the one-year anniversary of the patent grant date. The purpose of an interference proceeding is to determine who is the first inventor entitled to the patent on the claim in question, usually referred to as the common count. The party with the earlier filing date is called the senior party. The party with the later filing date is called the junior party. In order to win an interference, the junior party must prove that he or she either reduced the invention to practice first, or conceived it first and was diligent from a time just prior to the senior party's conception to his or her own reduction to practice. The inventor's own testimony and documents are insufficient to win an interference. Corroborated evidence of conception, diligence, and reduction to practice must be produced.

Finally, at any time during the term of a patent, its owner may file in the USPTO a statutory disclaimer of one or more claims that have been determined to be invalid, usually because of previously unknown prior art. This is most often employed as a tactic during patent litigation to ensure that certain costs will be recoverable if the patent owner wins the lawsuit. If time and circumstances permit, it may be preferable for the patent owner to modify the claims of an issued patent through reissue or reexamination rather than by disclaiming claims of the patent.

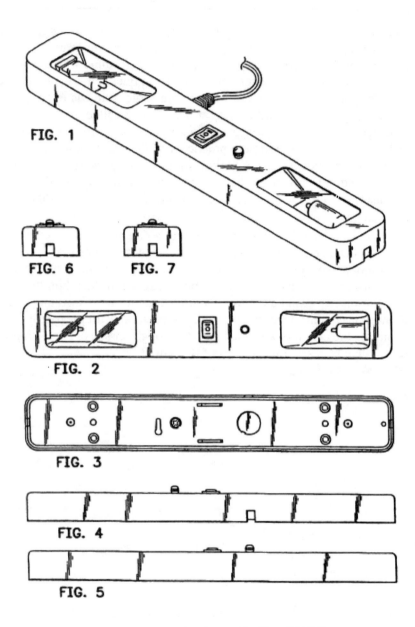

FIG. 1

FIG. 6   FIG. 7

FIG. 2

FIG. 3

FIG. 4

FIG. 5

U.S. Design Patent No. Des. 384,762
"Twin Lamp Low Profile Under Cabinet Light Bar"
Granted October 7, 1997
(Westec decorative halogen lighting for
mounting under kitchen cabinets)

CHAPTER 8

Design Patents-

(A) design patent covers the outer ornamental appearance of a manufactured article, frequently the shape of a molded plastic product such as a Sony Walkman portable audio player. Design patents are very narrow in terms of the scope of exclusive rights they provide. A design patent cannot cover structure, function, or composition. Infringement of a design patent is determined simply by comparing its drawings to the shape of the accused product to determine if the ordinary observer would be deceived into thinking that one is the other. The test for design patent infringement is similar to that used in determining trademark infringement.

Cost of a Design Patent

The cost of obtaining a design patent is only a fraction of what it costs to obtain a utility patent. Not only are the government filing and issue fees substantially lower, but so are the attorney's fees. This is because a design patent application has a very short text portion. There is only a minimal description of the drawing figures, followed by a single claim to the ornamental appearance of the article shown.

Unscrupulous invention promotion companies often arrange for their clients to obtain a cheaper design patent but not a utility patent as part of the services they provide for many thousands of dollars in fees. The inventors are later disappointed to learn that a competitor can easily avoid their design patent and produce a structurally equivalent, but visually slightly different, product.

Many years ago, I received as a promotional giveaway a molded plastic bottle opener. It consisted of a flat, disc-shaped octagonal handle that fit in the palm of your hand. A ring portion was formed in the center of the handle that precisely fit over the screw-off cap of a beer bottle. The ring had ribs that fit in between the sharp outer teeth on the bottle cap to provide a nonslip coupling. The octagonal handle provided leverage to unscrew the bottle cap without digging the teeth of the bottle cap into the fleshy portion of your palm. A tab extended from the octagonal handle with a hole in it for receiving a key chain. The handle had a thumb-sized opening for ejecting the bottle cap once unscrewed from the bottle. A company logo was printed on the octagonal handle for advertising purposes. The device was inexpensive and very functional, and I used it for many years. Unfortunately for the inventor, I could only find a design patent covering its particular ornamental configuration. That design patent could easily be avoided simply by changing the shape of the octagonal handle to, say, a hexagon, making it look different to an ordinary observer. A utility patent would have been far more valuable, assuming it had claims directed to the foregoing combination of structural elements without any limitation on the shape of the periphery of the handle. Infringement of a utility patent is determined by comparing the words of the claims to the accused product. In contrast, infringement of a design patent is determined by comparing the drawings of the design patent to the accused product to see if they have a dissimilar appearance.

Reasons to Obtain a Design Patent

Given the narrowness of the protection afforded by a design patent, you might ask why any inventor would even bother to obtain one. The reason is that design patents can, under certain circumstances, be a real price performer. Design patents prevent slavish copying, cost relatively little to obtain, and have no requirement for the periodic payment of maintenance fees. For example, it may cost a considerable amount to design the precise shape and dimensions of a bike-mounted flashlight holder. If a design patent is obtained on its configuration, a competitor cannot simply use your product as a master to make its own mold tooling.

Furthermore, while a design must still be novel and nonobvious over the prior art to be patentable, as a practical matter, the level of uniqueness or originality in the design required by a patent examiner in order to obtain a design patent is quite low. The bike-mounted flashlight holder might well be unpatentable from a utility patent standpoint, but still patentable from a design patent standpoint.

The mere filing of a design patent application on a product legally entitles the owner to mark all products embodying the design with the notation "Patent Pending." Competitors have no way of knowing, at least for the first 18 months, whether you filed a design patent application or a utility patent application. If you are granted a design patent, you can replace the patent marking notice with "U.S. Design Patent No. XXX." While this will indicate that the patent is in fact a design patent, many people are unaware of the narrowness of the exclusive rights afforded by a design patent. Either form of patent marking will, to some extent, act as a deterrent to those who might otherwise copy your product.

One of the costliest oversights in failing to obtain a design patent involved the wide-mouth bottle for Snapple fruit-flavored tea. Early on, the three New Yorkers who founded the Snapple Beverage Corporation began selling their drink in a very distinctive straight-walled cylindrical dimpled glass bottle with slightly curved shoulders and a wide-mouth opening. They created a whole new segment of the beverage industry, and Snapple tea drinkers readily sought out their distinctive bottles in beverage cases in delicatessens and supermarkets. Very soon, Lipton and Nestea fruit-flavored teas arrived to this new segment of the beverage market in wide-mouth bottles virtually indistinguishable in appearance from the Snapple bottles. This greatly facilitated the competitive introduction of similar fruit-flavored tea drinks, because Snapple drinkers automatically assumed, from the shape of the Lipton and Nestea bottles, that they were similar products made by the well-known instant-tea producers. Had the Snapple founders only spent a thousand dollars to obtain a design patent on the shape of their wide-mouth bottle within a year of its introduction, competitors would have had to use a different bottle shape. The current owner of the Snapple business has apparently realized the prior mistake, and has since patented its various sports bottle designs.

A design patent normally requires drawings that illustrate the front, left side, right side, top, bottom, and rear of the claimed design. In addition, there is usually a perspective view of the article. The drawings have no reference numerals and are shaded to show surface configuration and details. Examples of such views are illustrated at the beginning of this chapter for U.S. Design Patent No. Des. 384,762 titled "Twin Lamp Low Profile Under Cabinet Light Bar." Here is the lone claim of that patent:

> The ornamental design for a twin lamp low profile under cabinet light bar, as shown and described.

It is quite common to obtain both utility patent protection and design patent protection on the same article. For example, the disposable probe cover for tympanic thermometers claimed in U.S. Patent No. 4,662,360 (see drawing on page 52) also is covered by U.S. Design Patent No. Des. 303,008. The probe of the thermometer that was commercialized had a very particular curved frusto-conical shape; that is, the shape of a cone with the point lopped off. The probe cover had to mate precisely with the probe. The design patent would have protected against competitors wishing to make after-market disposable covers for its thermometers, even if the utility patent had never issued. The exclusive rights afforded by a design patent are theoretically limited to ornamental appearance. One could argue that a shape dictated by function cannot be protected by a design patent. As a practical matter, this is not a strong defense to a lawsuit for design patent infringement.

Furniture pieces such as chairs and tables are frequent subjects of design patents. Boat hull shapes also are well suited for protection via design patents. For example, considerable funds were undoubtedly expended to design the shape of the molded plastic Kiwi kayak. Unless protected by a design patent, a competitor need only purchase one of these kayaks and use it as a master to roto-mold duplicate kayaks, which could then be sold at lower cost because there would be little, if any, design engineering costs to amortize. Car companies such as Porsche obtain design patents on the shapes of their automobile bodies. They are not really concerned with other car companies making look-alike vehicles, but they can ensure that toy replicas of their vehicles are of high quality through design patent licensing programs. And certainly, there is little doubt about the value of the myriad design patents for the Rubbermaid line of resealable kitchenware and Little Tykes outdoor toys.

Design patents also can be very useful for nonmolded products. Shoe companies such as Nike and Reebok rely heavily on design patents to protect the configurations of their shoe soles and shoe uppers. This helps prevent the importation of cheap knockoffs of their latest shoe styles.

Term of a Design Patent

The term of a U.S. design patent is normally 14 years from its date of grant. This is different than the 20-year term of a U.S. utility patent. No maintenance fees need to be paid during the term of a design patent, unlike a utility patent, which requires three separate maintenance fees to be paid in order to enjoy its full term.

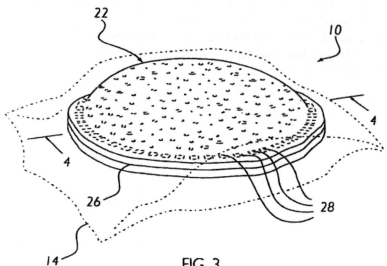

FIG. 3

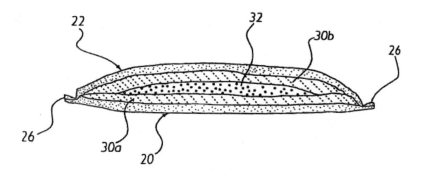

FIG. 4

U.S. Patent No. 6,004,596
"Sealed Crustless Sandwich"
Granted December 21, 1999
(manufactured peanut butter and jelly sandwich)

CHAPTER 9

Invention Marketing

F rom the outset, an inventor needs to decide if he or she wishes to develop an invention into a marketable product himself or herself, or try to sell or license the invention rights instead. Each alternative has its pluses and minuses. The former basically involves undertaking all the risk and effort associated with starting a business, and the latter depends upon finding someone else willing to assume these burdens. If you start your own business and successfully sell products embodying your own patented invention, you stand to make a great deal more money than if you merely sell or license your patent rights. However, I could invent the best hand tool in the last two decades and it would have far less chance of being widely commercialized than if I got Black & Decker to develop the design and market the resulting product through its distributors and tens of thousands of national retail outlets. The way in which you start and build a business around a single product is outside the scope of this book. Instead, I will discuss some of the hurdles that you face in trying to sell or license your invention rights.

Invention Promotion Firms

First and foremost, **avoid invention promotion firms**. Most of them are unscrupulous outfits that advertise on TV, on the radio, and in the yellow pages. For a flat fee (usually several thousand dollars), they purport to help you get a patent and sell or license your invention rights to a company. In reality, all you get is a design patent, or a very poorly drafted utility patent; a bunch of boilerplate binders; and a few letters to companies with names and addresses pulled out of readily available resources such as the Thomas Register directory of industrial products. (The Thomas Register Website address is listed in the Appendix.) Many states, including California, require invention promotion firms to disclose in written contracts with clients the number of individuals who have made more money from their invention rights than they paid the invention promotion firm in fees. Before they closed up and left the state, the leading invention promotion company in California could list only two or three clients out of the thousands it had bilked. The AIPA Act of 1999 created a process for the USPTO filing and publishing of complaints against invention promotion companies. The USPTO disciplinary rules also limit the circumstances under which patent attorneys and agents can accept work from invention development firms that have received a formal complaint from a federal or state agency. Anyone seriously interested in your invention would be willing to risk their own capital and efforts on its commercialization. The fact that invention promotion firms take all cash up front and risk none of their own money should be a dead giveaway that they do not seriously believe that your invention has strong market prospects.

Commercial Viability

It is important for an inventor to first determine whether a product is commercially viable before investing in expensive patenting or marketing services. A relatively inexpensive market evaluation of an invention is available through the University of Wisconsin's Innovation Service Center (WISC), whose telephone number is (414) 472-1365. The WISC employs a network of 300 experts in a variety of fields. Its evaluation costs approximately $225 and normally takes two or three months to complete. A similar market evaluation service also is available through the Wal-Mart Innovation Network. Its phone number is (417) 836-5667.

Marketing Your Product Ideas to Companies

There is a phenomenon in business known as the "not invented here" or "NIH" syndrome. Most established companies have research and development departments. Their job is to come up with new products and new product designs. If the company has to go outside for new ideas, it will normally have to pay for them, and this will increase its cost margins. If the president of the company sees that its best product ideas come from outside the company, then he or she may reduce or even completely do away with the internal research and development department, or at least substantially reduce its budget. Is it any wonder that engineers within a company reject ideas and technologies that do not originate with the company? A good example is the code division multiple access (CDMA) technology developed by Qualcomm for cell phones and high-speed wireless data transmission. By virtually any objective measure, CDMA is superior to the global system for mobile communications (GSM). CDMA permits many more calls to be squeezed into the same radio frequency (RF) spectrum allotment, allows much higher bandwidth data communications, and provides clearer voice quality. Nevertheless, Motorola, Nokia, and Ericsson stubbornly clung to GSM for many years because of NIH, much to their own financial detriment. This also has harmed global standardization of cell phone service access.

Most established companies have a formal policy of not considering unsolicited product ideas unless the idea is already the subject of an issued U.S. patent or a pending patent application. They are worried that if they look at an idea, reject it, and then later come out with a similar product, they will be sued for misappropriation, breach of confidential relationship, breach of trust, etc. As a practical matter, a company that reviews and then rejects an unsolicited invention proposal could be subject to a tort claim seeking a huge monetary judgment even if it already had a similar idea or if the idea is an old concept shown in expired patents. Therefore, most large companies require a person to sign a confidentiality waiver before they will consider an unsolicited idea for a new product. The waiver normally limits the legal rights of the submitter to whatever patent rights he or she may have. A sample Invention Disclosure Receipt Agreement is shown on page 100.

(Company Name)

(Address)
(City, State, Zip Code)

Invention Disclosure Receipt Agreement

NOTICE: This document sets forth policy and procedure regarding submission of ideas by persons not in the employ of the company.

It is the policy of (COMPANY NAME) to consider ideas relating to possible new products or manufacturing methods which might be useful in its _____ business.

(COMPANY NAME) does not accept or consider any ideas submitted to it on a confidential basis. Hence, (COMPANY NAME) prefers that whoever wishes to disclose an idea to it should first protect the idea under the patent laws either by obtaining a patent or at least filing an application for a patent. If this procedure is not feasible, then (COMPANY NAME) requires that a full written description of the idea, signed and dated, be submitted in lieu of a patent or patent application.

After submission of the written disclosure of the idea, (COMPANY NAME) will then be in a position to consider and evaluate the data submitted. Of necessity, (COMPANY NAME) reserves the right to conduct surveys and other investigations to determine the commercial worth of the idea, and to investigate whether the idea is subject to valid patent protection. (COMPANY NAME) will pay royalties or other compensation only for those ideas which, in the opinion of (COMPANY NAME), are patentable, and which are accepted in writing for commercial use by (COMPANY NAME) or its parent company. (COMPANY NAME) does not give reasons for rejecting an idea in view of the fact, among others, that (COMPANY NAME) cannot prematurely disclose its own development work.

(COMPANY NAME) is sincerely interested in improving its products and manufacturing practices. To that end, it welcomes and appreciates the opportunity of reviewing ideas that are submitted. Wherever warranted in the judgment of (COMPANY NAME), a license agreement or other contractual relationship will be negotiated for use of an idea that appears to have commercial and patentable merit.

It is also (COMPANY NAME)'s policy to require that any person submitting an idea to it must first indicate his/her understanding and agreement to the conditions as outlined above by signing and returning this paper to (COMPANY NAME).

Name (Print): _____

Signature: _____

Date: _____

As can be seen from the preceding agreement, the company is really under no obligation to provide any particular compensation to the inventor for using the disclosed invention, and could theoretically pay nothing. Thus, one way to significantly improve your chances of selling or licensing your invention rights is to obtain a patent, or at least file an application. Concurrently, you should build a prototype that looks as close to an actual manufactured product as possible. Many major metropolitan areas have professional model-makers and designers that can make a working model that looks very close to a high-volume manufactured item. Take some slick photos of the model, perhaps demonstrating its use. If you are a decent actor, make a homemade professional video. Write a one-page product advertisement that tells what the product is, what it will do, and an estimated cost of manufacture and an estimated price. As a rule of thumb, you need to be able to manufacture the item for one-fifth of its projected retail price if it is a consumer item expected to be distributed and sold through normal wholesale and retail channels. Conduct your own informal survey to see what people would be willing to pay as a retail price for your new product.

Marketing to Small Companies

Find out which small companies manufacture and sell products like yours and mail your pitch to their presidents, with a copy of your patent or a notation indicating that you have already applied for a patent. Hand address the envelope with the president's name and mark it with the notation "Personal and Confidential." This will ensure that the president's secretary doesn't open the envelope and discard its contents or send it along to the VP of engineering who will certainly kill it due to the NIH syndrome. The president is only interested in making more profits, and if you get his or her attention, you may find yourself in a meeting discussing a possible sale or license of the patent rights. Remember, 2 or 3 percent of future sales is better than 100 percent of nothing, especially where the company will make all the investment in tooling, inventory, and marketing. You might be able to get an advance against future royalties, which will cover your patent legal expenses and model-maker fees. The company may wish to own the patent rights. You can sell them by transferring full title immediately, with a flexible purchase price based on installment payments representing a percentage of sales, just like a royalty. If the company asks for a copy of the patent application, by all means, provide one, as failure to do so may kill the deal.

However, it is generally not advisable to disclose the serial number, as this could provide an opportunity to challenge your application by way of an opposition or public use proceeding. Also, don't give the claims to the company, because this could give it advance guidance on how to potentially design around any patent you might later be granted.

Marketing at Trade Shows

Trade shows for products and technology related to your invention represent a good opportunity to visit with representatives of other companies that might be interested in commercializing your invention. The people in the booths may give valuable input as to changes that might make your invention more marketable. They might also give you leads to other prospective licensees. They not only know the names of the companies that you should contact, but also the names of the prime contact people within those companies. Don't be bashful about asking for their opinion of your invention, its potential market, and your planned pricing.

Rejection

In attempting to market your invention, you must learn to live with rejection. The plain truth is that most companies will not be interested in your invention. This does not necessarily mean that it does not have commercial potential. As explained, some companies don't accept outside invention proposals, and others that do purposefully kill them off. Simply blanketing companies of all sorts with your unsolicited invention proposal through the mail is not cost-effective. Consider performing your own market survey by asking prospective customers, upon seeing a slick prototype demonstration, whether they would buy the item, and if so, at what retail price. If you have filed a patent application, you can attempt to publicize your invention and its availability via the Internet. For a nominal fee, the USPTO will also publish a notice in its *Official Gazette for Patents* stating that your patent is available for licensing.

You may look into getting free publicity by contacting your local newspaper or television station. They are always looking for quirky inventor stories and someone may learn of your invention this way and contact you about commercializing it. The specialty gift retailer Hammacher Schlemmer & Company in New York runs an annual contest for patented inventions in various categories. Winners gain valuable publicity and sometimes licenses. Many large metropolitan areas have inventor clubs or conventions where inventors can share ideas, war stories, leads, etc.

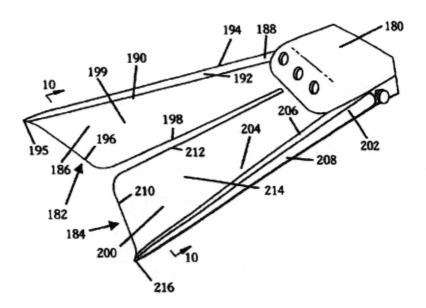

U.S. Patent No. 6,050,868
"High Efficiency Hydrofoil and Swim Fin Designs"
Granted April 18, 2000
(popular Scubapro twin-blade fin for divers)

CHAPTER 10

Patent Licensing

A U.S. patent is fundamentally a right to exclude, so it follows that the patent owner may give permission to a third party to practice the claimed invention. Without such permission, the same activity would be patent infringement. When a patent owner grants permission to another party to practice the claimed invention, a license has been granted.

A license can be implied or express. An *implied license* is one that is not formally set forth in an agreement, but arises from special circumstances, such as when a patent is owned by the president of a closely held corporation, and the corporation makes and sells products embodying the invention with the tacit approval of the president. An *express patent license* is typically a formal contract. It can be an oral agreement, but such agreements may be unenforceable in many states under the so-called "statute of frauds" if they are not to be completely performed within a year of the agreement. Most patent license agreements span the entire term of the patent, and, therefore, they must be formalized into a written contract signed by both parties. The patent owner is normally referred to as the *licensor* and the entity being granted a license is normally referred to as the *licensee*.

Royalties

There are many standard provisions in patent license agreements, and I will summarize the main ones later in this chapter. But first let's talk about the money part. Most patent license agreements call for the licensee to pay a royalty for use of the licensed patent rights. In some cases, patents are cross-licensed royalty free, but this type of arrangement usually is negotiated between large sophisticated competitors that wish to avoid the time and expense of patent litigation. Both realize that as a practical matter, they cannot sell products in a particular technical field and avoid all of the patents owned by their competitor. Usually, a royalty is set forth as a percentage of the net selling price of the goods. This is a pay-as-you-go type of an arrangement that benefits both parties. The licensee only pays based on the extent of use, but the licensor collects more money as sales increase. I have often seen declining scale royalties. They may start at, say, 4 percent, and decline to 3 percent, and then 2 percent as cumulative sales targets are reached. This encourages the licensee to sell more patented goods, and typically results in more royalties being collected by the patent owner than if the royalty rate were flat. This is akin to supply-side economics as applied to patents. This practice was around long before the Reagan income tax cut of the early 1980s.

By far, the single biggest mistake I have observed in patent licenses is the failure to correctly define the royalty base. Agreeing to pay a royalty, for example, "on all improved propane burner heads of the type shown in Exhibit A attached to this agreement" is a prescription for disaster. The product made by the licensee may evolve over the years to incorporate many new improvements developed by the licensee. At some point, the licensee will feel that the product being sold is so fundamentally different than the licensed product that the licensee will stop paying royalties. The inevitable result is a lawsuit between the licensor and the licensee. A much better practice, and indeed the only correct way to define the royalty base, is to provide that the specified royalty shall be paid for all products manufactured and/or sold by the licensee that embody the invention of one or more of the claims of the licensed patent, so long as the patent has not lapsed or expired and the claims have not been held invalid and/or unenforceable in a final court judgment.

License agreements can be reached while the application is pending, and before any patent has been granted. They typically contain all of the same terms and provisions, and in addition, provide that the obligation to pay royalties shall terminate if a patent is not ultimately granted with at least one claim that covers the product manufactured and/or sold by the licensee.

So how much royalty should I get for licensing my patent? It depends on the area of technology. In general, the higher the profit margins in a particular industry, the higher the royalties. As a rule of thumb, patented pharmaceutical inventions normally earn the highest royalty rates. Clearly, an FDA-approved patented drug with a significant market for a widespread ailment can generate tremendous royalty income. The drug company that invented it has to try to recoup hundreds of millions of dollars in developmental costs. I have heard of royalties charged for pharmaceuticals as high as 20 to 60 percent. In general, it is rare for a patent on a mechanical or electrical invention to be licensed for more than 5 percent of the manufacturer's net selling price, excluding trade discounts. Often, the royalties paid for licenses under such patents range between 1 and 3 percent. This makes perfect sense when you consider that it is difficult for a manufacturer of mechanical or electrical goods to consistently operate at higher than a 20-percent gross profit margin.

If the patent license is exclusive, the royalty charged should normally be higher than if the license is nonexclusive. Under an exclusive license, only the licensee can make and sell products embodying the patented invention. Not even the patent owner can do it. Nor can the patent owner grant any other licenses. So if the invention is a good one, and the product has considerable demand associated with it, the patent owner should theoretically be able to charge a higher price because there is no competition for the same goods. This scenario presumes that the market is willing to pay a premium for the advantages that the patented product has over its nonpatented competition. An exclusive license should normally have a guaranteed minimum annual royalty or a provision that allows the patent owner to either terminate the exclusive license or grant other licenses if cumulative sales by the licensee don't reach a given level after a certain amount of time. Otherwise, the licensee may have no incentive to market the patented products, and your patent will be tied up. I don't like "best efforts" clauses because they are often too vague to be effective and difficult to enforce. A nonexclusive license allows the patent owner to grant multiple licenses. They usually contain a so-called "most favored nations clause" that permits earlier licensees the right to a lower royalty rate charged in any subsequently granted license.

The licensee should be required to keep regular accounts showing the sales of its products that embody the licensed invention. Royalties should be paid at least annually, and preferably, within 30 days of the end of each calendar quarter, along with a written report detailing quantity and price information. It's a good idea to have an audit clause in the patent license agreement that permits the patent owner to annually inspect the books of the licensee to ensure that all royalties due have been paid. If the licensee has underpaid by more than 5 percent, the license agreement should require it to pay for the cost of the audit and make up the deficiency.

Standard Provisions for a Patent License

A patent license should contain a number of other standard provisions that address: the territory covered, the term of the license, sublicensing, assignment, field of use restrictions, improvements by the licensor and the licensee, and rights of termination in the event of an uncured breach. The license agreement should also specifically require the licensee to mark all products manufactured and/or sold under the license with the notation "Patent Pending" while the patent application is pending and with "U.S. Pat. No. X,XXX,XXX (the actual patent number)" after the patent is granted. Patent number marking ensures that maximum damages will be recoverable in any patent infringement litigation.

This brings up the very sticky issue of who is responsible for suing infringers. The bottom line is that the licensee will often refuse to take on this responsibility. In the end, if the patent owner won't foot the bill, the whole licensing arrangement may collapse. After all, if the patent owner allows third parties to infringe with impunity, the licensee can hardly afford to keep paying royalties and suffer competition from third-party competitors having lower cost margins.

What about litigation between the licensor and the licensee? Yes, if either party fails to perform under the license contract, they can sue for breach of contract. Surprisingly, the suit must be in state court, unless there is some basis for federal jurisdiction such as diversity of citizenship (plaintiff and defendant residing in different states) or if the breach of contract case is met with a counterclaim for invalidity. In 1969, the U.S. Supreme Court held that a patent licensee normally cannot be barred from challenging the validity of the licensed patent. Furthermore, the licensee usually cannot be enjoined from making and selling the patented goods while pressing a court challenge to the validity of the licensed patent. The court would view unpaid royalties as an adequate remedy for the patent owner should it prevail in the litigation.

I have included on the following pages a checklist for negotiating the key terms of a patent license agreement.

Checklist for Negotiating Patent Licenses

Parties:

1.   Name of Licensor_____
     Address_____
     Principal Office_____
     Incorporated in _____ Short Name _____
2.   Name of Licensee_____
     Address_____
     Principal Office_____
     Incorporated in _____ Short Name _____

Whereas Clause:

1.   Licensor owns inventions _____, patents _____, applications _____, know-how _____, relating to _____.
2.   Licensor represents that it has the right to grant a license relating to _____.
3.   Licensee owns inventions _____, patents _____, applications _____, know-how _____, relating to _____.
4.   Licensee represents _____.
5.   Licensee desires license relating to _____.

Definitions:

(Here define products covered by a limited license and refer to them as "said products." If only certain types of inventions are covered, define the inventions here, reference all licensed patent applications and patents, and refer to them as "said inventions." Sales should also be defined here.)

_____

_____

_____

_____

I.   Patent Rights Granted:

"All substantial rights" to practice said inventions _____ and to make, use, sell, and offer for sale said products _____, and with the right to sue infringers _____. U.S. and/or foreign patents and pending applications and know-how listed in attached exhibits.

Exclusive for ___ years and nonexclusive thereafter.

___Nonexclusive	___to make (manufacture)
___Exclusive	___to have made for own use
___Exclusive except as to Licensor	___to use
___Irrevocable	___to sell ___to offer for sale
___With right to grant sublicenses	___to lease
	___rent

II.   License Restrictions:

Limited to specified field (indicate) ————————————

Limited to specified territory ——————————————

Subject to prior Licensee (identify) ——————————

Subject to Licensor's right to make __, have made __, use __, sell __, offer for sale __.

III.   Sub-Licenses:

To any other party _____

To nominees of Licensor _____

At specified consideration (indicate)_____

Consideration to be shared with Licensor_____

Copies to be furnished to Licensor_____

IV.   Territory:

All countries _____; All countries except ——————

Following countries ——————————————————

United States of America, its territories and possessions ——

Only United States of America ___ and ——————————

That portion of the United States, comprising ——————

V.   Term of Agreement:

For _____ years.

Until (specify date) ——————————————————

Until some future event (specify)_____

For the life of any patent _____

VI.   Date of Agreement:

From date hereof _____

From specific date _____

Effective date_____

When approved by_____

VII.   Improvements of Licensor:

Included _____

Not included _____

Who will file _____

Who will pay costs _____

Assigned to _____

VIII.   Improvements of Licensee:

Included _____

Not included _____

Who will file _____

Who will pay costs _____

Assigned to _____

IX.   Consideration for License:

Royalty free_____

Royalty, percent of _____ profits _____; gross sales _____;
net sales, specific amount (specify) _____; per unit (specify)
_____.

Payment is to be made in U.S. dollars _____; at the then current rate of
exchange _____.

Royalty obligation limited to products embodying or made with one or
more claims of pending patent applications or unexpired valid patents.

X.   Annual Payment for License:

Amount _____ per calendar year _____; per 12-month period
_____.

Payable in advance _____.
Payable at end of calendar year _____; of 12-month period _____.
Credited against earned royalties, yes _____; no _____.
Right to audit Licensee's books annually.

XI.   Assignment of Agreement and License:

Not assignable by either party _____.
Assignable by Licensor, without consent of Licensee _____; with consent
_____.
By either party upon:
Merger _____
To successor of entire business _____
To any company of which a majority of stock is owned _____
To any company of which a controlling interest is owned _____
Binding upon heirs, successors, and assigns_____

XII.   Marking With Patent Pending and/or Patent Numbers:

Licensee's duty.
Form of Notice.

XIII.   Maintenance Fees and Annuities:

Licensor's duty to timely pay.
Timely notice of payment to Licensee.

XIV.   Specific Warranties and Representations:

Licensor has title to inventions and patent rights.
Licensor has maintained confidentiality of know-how.
Licensor is unaware of any claims for infringement or any basis for same.
Licensee will use best efforts.

XV.   Infringement:

Licensor will sue infringers at its expense.
Licensee will sue infringers at its expense and Licensor will join as plaintiff.
Licensor and Licensee will share costs of enforcement and will split
recovery.

XVI.   Arbitration of Disputes:

Licensor and Licensee will submit breach of license disputes to binding arbitration.

AAA arbitration selected.

Three arbitrators to make decision and process for selecting same.

U.S. Patent No. 5,103,459
"System and Method for Generating Signal
Waveforms in a CDMA Cellular Telephone System"
Granted April 7, 1992
(an early Qualcomm patent)

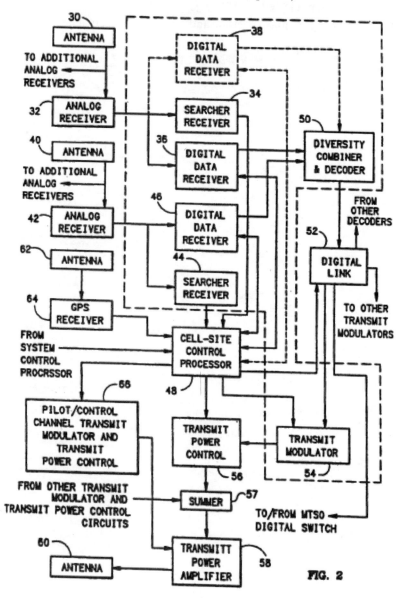

FIG. 2

CHAPTER 11

Patent Litigation

A patent gives its owner the right to exclude others from using the patented invention. However, much to the chagrin of many individual inventors and small businesses, U.S. patents are not self-enforcing. There are no "patent police" as one of my colleagues once told his client whose newly issued patent was being infringed. A civil action must be filed in federal district court against the infringer. Where the defendant is a corporation, it can be sued anywhere it is doing business. Where the defendant is not a corporation, it must be sued where it resides or where the defendant has committed acts of infringement *and* has a regular and established place of business. A U.S. patent is enforceable in all 50 states and its territories. It is an act of infringement to sell, offer for sale, make, use, or import products in the United States covered by the claims of a patent without permission of the patent owner, even if the goods are manufactured in a foreign country.

Infringement

Infringement of one's patent is both good news and bad news. The good news is that the invention must have commercial value or else nobody would bother to copy it. The bad news is that it may take considerable time, money, and effort to resolve the matter. At the outset, the patent owner must decide if he or she (or the company that owns the patent) is willing to license the patent. Licensing was discussed in the previous chapter. In general, it is far easier to get an infringer to take a license than it is to get the infringer to stop infringing. This chapter assumes that the patent owner is either unwilling to license or has been unsuccessful in attempts to do so. In such cases, the patent owner has to decide whether to resort to litigation. Sometimes it takes a lawsuit to force an infringer to take a license and pay royalties.

Patent litigation, like all civil litigation, is fraught with uncertainties. Indeed, the only certainty is that it will take more time and will cost more than you ever thought at the beginning. Patent infringement lawsuits are easy to start and hard to finish. They are often contests of attrition. Great time and expense are usually expended by both sides until one says "uncle." Patent infringement lawsuits are like any other civil lawsuit in that most settle before trial. However, patent litigation is often a "you bet your company" proposition for small businesses. Very large companies are relatively infrequently involved in patent litigation. They usually have in-house patent departments that help them stay clear of competitors' patented designs or obtain licenses where necessary. In the event they run into an unanticipated patent infringement claim with a company of significant size, they can often negotiate a cross-license and avoid the time and expense of going to court.

A patent infringement lawsuit is often preceded by a letter from the patent owner's attorney notifying the accused infringer of the patent owner's patent—and in some cases, formally charging infringement. Caution is advised before such a letter is sent because the prospective defendant may file a declaratory judgment suit in a remote federal district court very inconvenient to the patent owner. Thus, the patent owner may become involved in a lawsuit that he or she cannot financially afford. A declaratory judgment lawsuit typically asks the court to declare that the patent has not been infringed and/or is invalid. Federal jurisdiction arises when the patent owner does something (such as issue a charge of infringement) that creates a reasonable apprehension of suit.

One strategy for the patent owner is to perform the necessary due diligence ahead of time and to then secretly file the lawsuit in a local federal district court convenient to the patent owner and/or its attorneys where jurisdiction and venue are proper. The due diligence would normally include obtaining a sample of the prospective defendant's product and confirming that at least one of the patent claims literally reads on the same, and perhaps a validity study of that claim, along with a potential damage recovery analysis. A cease and desist letter can then be sent to the prospective defendant without mentioning the filing of the suit. If the matter is resolved immediately, the patent owner can dismiss the suit without prejudice. If the prospective defendant files a declaratory judgment action in an inconvenient forum, the later-filed suit must normally give way to the earlier suit filed by the patent owner that is closer to home.

I once represented a large exporter of hay. It had patented a unique method of wrapping a stack of hay bales with stretchable plastic film to produce self-supporting units that could easily be lifted by forklifts from docks on the West Coast, and loaded onto ships bound for Japan. At the client's request, as part of a program to license the whole hay exporting industry under the patent, I sent a letter to a major competitor in Ellensburg, in Eastern Washington, offering a license. The competitor immediately responded with a declaratory judgment lawsuit in Yakima, Washington. I was shocked to learn that there was even a federal district court in such a small town.

Continuing with the hay bale wrapping case, my client filed a motion with the court in Eastern Washington to dismiss the declaratory judgment lawsuit on the basis that there was no case or controversy because the letter merely offered a license, and didn't charge infringement. My client also moved to dismiss the lawsuit for improper venue because its only contacts with Eastern Washington were the letter offering the patent license, a company newsletter mailed into that district, and a trip through the area in a rental car made by a sales representative for my client. Alternatively, my client moved for a transfer of the case to federal district court in California. All motions were denied. But the net result was that my client ended up in a major lawsuit in a very inconvenient forum. The judge granted a motion for summary judgment of invalidity for obviousness. My client didn't appeal, the patent licensing program never came to fruition, and the whole industry adopted the patented method, free of charge.

There are two lessons to be learned from the hay bale wrapping patent litigation. First, under some circumstances, it is better to sue first in your own federal court and then negotiate the license. Second, don't litigate a patent infringement lawsuit at the district court level unless you have the fortitude to last through an appeal to the CAFC located in Washington, D.C. The CAFC spends most of its time reviewing patent cases and reverses approximately 50 percent of the district court decisions. It has exclusive jurisdiction over any appeal involving an issue of patent validity or infringement.

Before you file suit for patent infringement you had better do a search to find out what patents your potential adversary owns. I remember recommending this approach to a client in the telecommunications industry that was hot to sue its competitor for infringement of one it its patents. Much to my client's surprise, the search located no fewer than 12 U.S. patents owned by its competitor. Each of them had to be reviewed for potential applicability to my client's current products. To its great surprise, I found that the competitor could rely upon two of its patents in a counterclaim for infringement. So the lawsuit wasn't started in a situation that was likely to produce a formal cross-license, at best.

By law, a patent owner is entitled to recover its lost profits and not less than a reasonable royalty. If the patent owner can prove that the infringement was willful, the judge may increase the damage award up to three times the actual amount found and award attorneys fees. Normally, such awards are subject to post-judgment interest. Thus, the financial impact of a full-blown patent infringement lawsuit can be devastating. Willfulness is a question of fact normally decided by a jury in a patent case. Willfulness is often found where the defendant was aware of the patent and did not get a formal written noninfringement opinion from an experienced registered patent attorney based upon a thorough review of the patent, its prosecution history, the prior art, and the defendant's product.

Most frightening, and little known by nonpatent attorneys, is the fact that officers and directors of corporations can be named as individual defendants along with their companies and held personally liable for the entire patent infringement verdict. The corporation's limited liability protection will not shield them from personal liability where they knew of the patent and personally made the decision to manufacture the infringing product anyway. It is not necessary for the plaintiff's attorney to "pierce the corporate veil" as it is in other tort litigation. This aspect can ruin the personal finances of officers of closely held companies who are also the principal shareholders. Corporate bankruptcy is not a viable tactical response to a large patent infringement verdict against a company and its president because the president's home and other assets will still be subject to creditors' claims. Furthermore, if willful infringement is found, bankruptcy may not be available to wipe out the judgment. You may recall that O.J. Simpson could not wipe out the $33 million wrongful death tort judgment against him via bankruptcy.

Issues in a Patent Infringement Lawsuit

So what do litigants fight over in a patent infringement lawsuit? The issues are usually *validity*, *infringement*, and *damages*. The patent owner may move the court early on for a preliminary injunction. This is an extraordinary remedy rarely granted by a federal district court and only after extensive legal briefing, hearings, and in some cases, the taking of evidence. Suffice it to say that where the patent has not been offered for license and a particularly strong case of validity and infringement is made out in motion papers, the judge can order the accused infringer to stop selling the accused device even before a trial court verdict has been rendered. The plaintiff may be required to post a large bond to cover the defendant's losses if the patent owner ultimately loses the case. Most patent cases in which preliminary injunctions are granted, however, settle long before trial.

A federal district court judge can theoretically grant a temporary restraining order (TRO) on short notice pending a preliminary injunction hearing. A TRO is an extreme remedy for emergency situations, such as stopping a water district from letting 10 million gallons of water out of a reservoir at noon. I know of only one patent case where a TRO was granted. It involved the ongoing sale and installation of a patented pipe-mounting strap used by plumbers in new home construction.

Validity

By statute, the claims of an issued U.S. patent are entitled to a presumption of validity. The accused infringer in a patent lawsuit (usually the defendant) bears the burden of proving, by clear and convincing evidence, that the claims asserted against it are invalid. This is a very difficult burden indeed, especially when the patent owner (usually the plaintiff) has requested a jury. The burden of clear and convincing evidence is less than the burden in criminal cases, which is beyond a reasonable doubt. However, it is more than a mere preponderance of the evidence that can be visualized as a slight tipping of the scales in favor of a finding. The patent owner is entitled, under the U.S. Constitution, to a trial by jury where money damages are at issue. Patent owners almost universally demand a jury trial, believing that most juries are pro-patent. It should come as no surprise that it takes a lot of evidence and good argument to convince a jury that the beautiful patent document with a red ribbon and gold seal, issued by the U.S. Government after several years of study by an expert examiner, is worthless.

The validity of a patent claim may be challenged on the basis that it fails to meet one or more of the statutory criteria for patentability discussed in Chapter 2. The most commonly asserted grounds for alleged invalidity are that the patent application was filed after the one-year grace period or that the claimed invention would have been obvious over certain prior art references that were not considered by the USPTO examiner. The chances of success for such defenses are highly fact dependent. In general, "on sale" or "public use" defenses are more likely to succeed than an obviousness defense.

Bowing to political pressure, as part of the AIPA of 1999, Congress amended the patent laws to provide a prior use defense primarily benefiting Internet companies, Web hosting companies, and software companies in general. The defense is limited to a charge of infringement of a *business method patent* and requires proof by an accused infringer that, in good faith, it actually reduced to practice the claimed method at least one year before the effective filing date of the patent and commercially used the claimed invention before the effective filing date of the patent. The defense applies even if the method was used secretly. The e-business community successfully lobbied Congress for this special defense to patent infringement. However, after the crash of the Internet sector of the economy, it may only rarely be asserted during the next few years.

The validity of a patent claim can be challenged on the basis that the specification is insufficient or nonenabling; which means it didn't teach enough to enable one of ordinary skill in the art to practice the invention without an unreasonable amount of experimentation. In my experience, this defense is rarely successful. At trial, the dueling technical experts give opposite opinions on the adequacy issue, and the jury readily finds that the defendant did not satisfy its clear and convincing evidentiary burden of proof required to invalidate the claim(s) in dispute.

In the late 1970s and early 1980s, I worked on a patent infringement lawsuit involving a patent on an expensive piece of electronic equipment called a digital shaker table. Simply stated, the device vibrated pieces of electronic hardware in order to gauge whether they would fail in a harsh environment, such as a combat aircraft or spacecraft. The vibration had to simulate the randomness of nature and couldn't be simple oscillatory movement, such as that achieved by a paint-can shaker. The system described in the patent referred to some of the most complex math I had ever seen, including Laplace transforms relating the "time domain" to the "digital domain," and so forth. The Ph.D. technical experts hired by each side had a hard time articulating in plain English what the invention was, and I could just imagine a jury being totally befuddled by the whole case. I was retained by the defendant, who raised an invalidity defense. The patent attorney who had written the original patent application had made a critical mistake. He had referenced various technical articles in lieu of giving detailed descriptions of certain key components of the patented system.

The patent law is very clear that only the disclosure of issued U.S. patents (and pending U.S. patent applications) may be incorporated by reference. Consequently, the defendant asserted that the patent claims were invalid for failure of the patent specification to provide an adequate disclosure. When, as expected, the patent owner's counsel argued that any person of ordinary skill in the art could practice the invention without the details set forth in the referenced articles, we countered that if this were true, then it would have been obvious at the time it was made to that same person of ordinary skill in the art. The patent owner was caught between a rock and a hard place. Either it had an inadequate disclosure or an obvious invention. The case was later settled on terms favorable to my client.

In a patent infringement lawsuit, the patent owner bears the burden of proving infringement of at least one claim by a preponderance of the evidence. In order for a patent claim to be infringed, each and every element and limitation recited in the claim must be satisfied literally or equivalently. An element is satisfied equivalently if there are insubstantial differences between the recited element and the substituted element. In patent lawsuits, it is the exclusive role of the judge to interpret the scope of a patent claim and instruct the jury as to its proper scope. The judge tells the jury what different words and phrases mean so that the jury members can determine if they read on the accused product or process.

I often hear laypeople state very confidently that it is easy to design around a patent. This is a naïve statement. Why would individuals and companies bother to get nearly 200,000 patents in the year 2000 alone if this were true? A better statement would be that an experienced patent attorney can interpret and explain the scope of the claims and suggest design changes that may avoid infringement of some or all of the claims of a U.S. patent. However, such design changes might make the product inferior or downright inoperable. For example, say I owned the first U.S. patent on a heavier-than-air flying vehicle. The claimed invention comprises a fuselage, fixed wings, and means for propelling the craft through the air. A competitor might be able to build a helicopter and avoid infringement because it lacks the claimed fixed wings. However, a helicopter has little range, is relatively slow, and requires tremendous maintenance. I would be happy to own the patent on the fixed wing aircraft because 99 percent of all aircraft sales revenue will fall into that category. Moreover, if there are enough patents in a particular product area, it may be impossible to design around all of them. I doubt it would be possible to make and sell a microprocessor in the United States without infringing at least a half dozen Intel patents.

In 1995, I was "second chair" in a patent infringement trial in Los Angeles, California, involving automated side-loaders for garbage trucks. The entire infringement case boiled down to how the judge was going to interpret the meaning of the claim element "boom assembly secured for pivotal movement." If the judge interpreted that phrase in accordance with the jury instruction submitted by the defendant, the defendant company would win the infringement issue. If the judge interpreted the phrase in accordance with the plaintiff's proposed jury instruction, the defendant company would lose the infringement issue. Each side argued that the specification, prosecution history, and prior art legally dictated its claim construction. The judge came up with his own instruction between the two that had been proposed by the parties, and the plaintiff won the infringement issue. However, my client won a reprieve when the trial judge ruled that the defendant had intervening rights. The patent was a reissue patent and it was admitted that the original claims were not broad enough to read on the defendant's side-loader. The judge found that my client had made substantial investments in reliance on the scope of the original claims before they were broadened via the reissue process discussed in Chapter 8. Therefore, my client was permitted to complete a large supply contract with the city of Los Angeles using its current design subject to the payment of a specified royalty. My client then used this extra time to implement design changes that clearly took it outside even the judge's claim interpretation. Claim interpretation is determined a matter of law and is reviewed on appeal without deference to the trial judge's ruling. However, the case later settled and there was no appellate review.

Anything can and does happen in litigation. You may think you have a "slam dunk" patent case, but in reality, you can be blown out of the water at any time and should, if possible, try to negotiate a settlement. This is especially true if the case will be tried before a jury. A division of one of my clients was, and still is, the leading manufacturer of automatic fare collection equipment for mass transit systems, such as the Bay Area Rapid Transit (BART) subway system in the San Francisco Bay Area. Early in my career, an individual sued BART for infringement of a patent covering an automatic fare collection system. This patent lawsuit presented a real problem for my client, who had indemnified BART as part of its contracts to install its automatic fare collection equipment.

The automatic fare collection patent was a "submarine patent." It didn't actually cover a diving vessel, but was based on an application originally filed in 1957 and kept pending in the USPTO (in secret) for many decades before it surfaced (issued) as a granted U.S. patent. This allowed the inventor to defer his exclusive rights until technology caught up and made his invention practical. If the inventor had issued his patent in the normal course, it would have expired long before it was feasible to commercialize the invention. U.S. patent applications are now published usually within 18 months of filing, and the patent term is measured from the earliest filing date, so this trick can no longer be played.

The automatic fare collection patent had broad claims to a method of issuing a fare card with an initial fare value electronically stored on the card in a stripe of material similar to magnetic recording tape. When the passenger passes through an entry gate at a first station, he or she passes the card through a device that encodes the first station location. Later, upon completion of the subway journey to a second station, the passenger leaves through an exit gate and passes the card through another device that reads the first station location. The applicable fare is calculated and electronically deducted from the initial fare stored on the fare card before the fare card is returned to the passenger for further use. Sound familiar? The original application showed rudimentary vacuum tube and relay circuitry, and the system was not practical until decades later when integrated circuits were widely available. Nevertheless, the claims were broadly worded and allegedly supported by the disclosure. Because the patent had an original 1957 filing date, it was difficult to find prior art predating the filing date that showed or suggested the concept. Prior to 1957, most fare collecting in subways was done by selling tokens that covered a single fare for a specific ride. No one, except, allegedly, the inventor, was thinking about electronically storing a cumulative fare, say $10, on a card, and then sequentially deducting discrete variable fares over a series of different subway trips by passing the card through entrance and exit turnstiles until the cumulative fare was exhausted.

The automatic fare collection patent litigation ground on. Things were looking bleak for my client, and the plaintiff was already counting his millions in damages. Any settlement of the BART case would set a precedent for all other subway systems in the United States that used my client's equipment. Then the lawyers I was working under came up with a promising defense. My client won a summary judgment of invalidity based on the inventor's intervening foreign patent publication. However, the Federal Circuit reversed that decision, holding that if the claim of the CIP was not enabled by the parent application, the published foreign counterpart of the parent could not anticipate that claim, and, therefore, the correct legal test was obviousness. The case was remanded for further trial court proceedings; that is, a trial on obviousness. Although I left the defendant's law firm prior to the issuance of a final judgment, I suspect that the case was settled because, to my knowledge, the fare collection system was never enjoined.

Many people feel that patent litigation today is characterized by excessive pretrial discovery. This involves many depositions of lay and technical witnesses, interrogatories, and burdensome document requests. Depositions involve asking witnesses questions orally under oath before a court reporter. Interrogatories involve written questions that must be answered in writing under oath. Document requests are written lists of various categories of business records and other papers that must be delivered to the other party for review and copying. In patent litigation, protective orders are required to shield various levels of confidential information exchanged between the attorneys for each party, culminating in the ubiquitous "attorneys-eyes-only" designation. In addition, there are numerous motions of all varieties. Many involve attorney squabbles over discovery. A motion for a preliminary injunction is sometimes brought at the outset, requiring Herculean efforts over a couple of months. There is frequently a motion by the accused infringer to separate the liability portion of the trial from the damages portion of the trial. And then there may be a series of summary judgment motions brought by each side on validity and infringement and various defenses. In many cases, the summary judgment motions have little chance of success, but are filed in order to force the other side to show its strongest evidence. Sometimes the patent owner will move to stay (suspend) the lawsuit to complete a preemptive reissue or reexamination. Federal judges almost universally grant such stays if the USPTO has agreed to reopen the prosecution of the patent in suit.

Cost of an Infringement Lawsuit

The minimum cost of taking a relatively simple patent infringement lawsuit through trial would be a half million dollars. This cuts both ways. Certainly, the patent owner has to believe that it has a meritorious case and that the potential damage recovery, and/or an injunction against a competitor, makes pursuing such a case a sound business decision. The defendant, on the other hand, has to believe seriously in its case, and has to view licensing, design changes, or product discontinuance as unsound or impractical options, in order to justify fighting a patent infringement lawsuit. Sometimes, the defendant knows it has a poor defense but hopes to outlast (outspend) the plaintiff. Other times the plaintiff knows it has a weak case but wants to proceed aggressively against a competitor that lacks staying power. Both sides could lose. Not only are huge legal fees expended, but also an enormous amount of executive time gets eaten up, which could be spent more productively elsewhere. A negotiated settlement that both parties can live with is always a better option than rolling the dice on a patent infringement trial. Furthermore, our federal courts are very crowded. Criminal cases always take priority over civil cases. You may not get to trial for three or more years after the complaint for patent infringement is filed. An appeal to the CAFC will take one to two additional years. Can you and/or your business really endure five years of litigation with your patent litigation firm churning out countless hours of high-cost billing?

A couple of years ago, I was involved in a patent lawsuit involving two medical device patents I had written. The later patent was the result of a continuation of the application that resulted in the first patent. The accused infringer's trial attorney called me to the witness stand as a hostile witness, which turned out to be a major mistake. I was able to explain to the jury the prosecution history of the two patents that I had written, and how I had drafted claims in the continuation application to read on the defendant's products. This is a perfectly legal strategy. In effect, I was able to give an expert opinion that the patent claims in suit read on the defendant's products. The jury trial lasted about four weeks. Each side had about six attorneys and six paralegals. I felt that the lead trial attorney representing the patent owner did a marvelous job trying the case even though he was not a patent attorney. He was a brilliant man who had boned up on all the facts and law involved in the case. He used his many years of jury trial experience and exceptional persuasiveness to make a very strong pitch to the jury.

The jurors unanimously agreed that the claims to the medical device were not invalid. However, the infringement issue was a very close call, and the jury hung six to two in favor of infringement. A unanimous verdict is required in federal civil jury trials. I had never before heard of a hung jury in a patent case. The patent owner moved to have the federal judge enter a partial verdict on validity so that only the infringement issue would have to be retried. The damages phase of the case had been delayed pending the outcome of the liability phase. The judge refused to enter a partial verdict on validity, buying into the defendant's argument that validity and infringement were inextricably intertwined and could only be decided together. A new trial date was set, but the case settled. Neither party could stomach the prospect of another marathon trial, and the defendant realized its predicament because the patent owner had only narrowly missed victory in the first trial.

Contingent Fees

There are a few hearty attorneys out there who will actually take patent infringement cases on a contingent fee; that is, a percentage of any damage award. They universally represent patent owners. They hope for a big jury verdict of infringement, but they usually have to endure years of fighting with a huge law firm representing a large "deep pockets" corporate defendant. The most spectacular example of contingent fee patent litigation involved an inventor by the name of Jerome H. Lemelson. Mr. Lemelson obtained many submarine patents on such things as bar code readers and robotic vision systems, keeping his key applications secretly pending for decades. His multimillion-dollar settlements with a number of Japanese automakers gave him a war chest that he used to pursue countless other companies. His patent attorney is reputed to have made more than $200 million in contingent fees in one year alone. The flip side is the story of the unfortunate attorneys who represented Litton Industries on a contingent fee basis in a patent infringement lawsuit against Honeywell relating to the making of highly specialized mirrors used in optical inertial navigation equipment. Initially, they won a jury verdict of more than $1 billion. After a decade of appeals, the award was whittled down to the point where one must question whether the contingent fee would fully compensate the attorneys for their efforts.

Think twice if you are an individual who wants to sue a big company for patent infringement. Many large companies view such lawsuits as shakedowns. If the patent owner isn't selling products embodying the patented invention, the defendant company knows that under the worst-case scenario, it will only have to pay a reasonable royalty if the patent owner prevails. The company will often then embark on a vigorous defense, including a trial and an appeal. The legal departments of large corporations seem to follow the motto "millions for legal fees, but not one penny for tribute!" I wonder if eBay followed this motto before losing a patent jury trial with a $35 million infringement verdict.

Early in my legal career, my mentors warned me not to take a contingent fee patent lawsuit. I didn't listen well enough and had to learn firsthand why these cases are so risky. One of my colleagues obtained a patent on a straightforward but very laborsaving plumbing product that was made of injection molded plastic. The examiner at the USPTO continually rejected the claimed invention for obviousness. Finally, on appeal, the Board of Patent Appeals reversed the examiner by a two to one vote, and the patent issued. My client's product was being knocked off, but he didn't have the money to pay for a patent infringement lawsuit. The competitor had clearly copied my client's commercial product, as the infringing product included nonfunctional features that had been erroneously milled into my client's mold tooling. So I took the case on a contingent fee and filed suit in Houston. The defendant's attorney immediately requested reexamination of my client's patent at the USPTO, and the infringement lawsuit was suspended pending the outcome of the USPTO reexamination proceedings. In reexamination proceedings, unlike a civil lawsuit for patent infringement, the patent is not entitled to a presumption of validity.

The reexamination request regarding my client's plumbing product patent was improper in terms of its form. It presented 18 new patents to the USPTO examiner and, essentially, asked him to take his pick. A reexamination request is supposed to allege that a claim may be invalid over one or two specific prior art patents not previously seen by the examiner. It isn't supposed to present a smorgasbord of prior art patents in the hopes that the examiner may be compelled by one or two of them. By established internal USPTO policy, a reexamination proceeding is conducted before the same patent examiner who handled the original prosecution. It came as no surprise, then, that the same examiner rejected the claims for obviousness over a couple of the new references that were no closer than those considered in the original prosecution. I appealed to the Board of Patent Appeals, which ruled in favor of obviousness. I appealed the Board's adverse decision to the CAFC, which affirmed the obviousness determination. Patent applicants and patent owners usually lose appeals in cases coming out of the USPTO.

My contingent fee patent infringement lawsuit involving the plumbing product was dismissed after I had spent more than 100 hours of time prosecuting the case. Worse yet, my poor client couldn't sell his business for as much as he had planned to, so his retirement was not as comfortable as he had hoped. I learned firsthand that patent infringement lawsuits are dicey from a contingent fee standpoint because liability is so uncertain. Patent cases are not like personal injury auto accident cases where liability is often a foregone conclusion and the only issue is how much in damages the defendant's insurance company will end up paying.

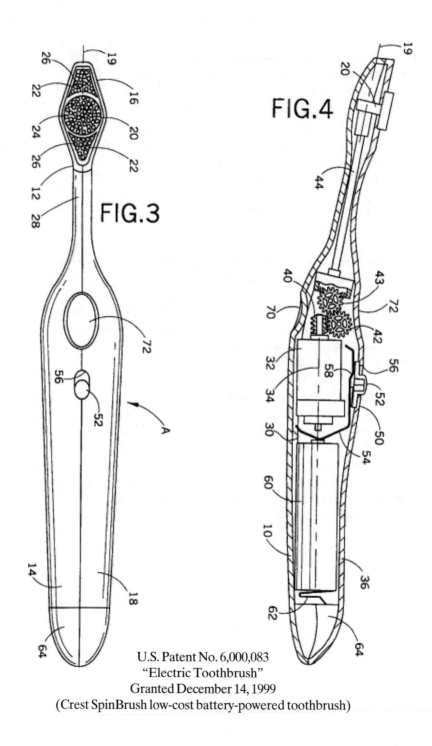

FIG.3

FIG.4

U.S. Patent No. 6,000,083
"Electric Toothbrush"
Granted December 14, 1999
(Crest SpinBrush low-cost battery-powered toothbrush)

CHAPTER 12

Designing Around Patents

I t is frequently very profitable to legally copy a successful product and sell it in competition with the originator. Our free enterprise system permits, and indeed encourages, such competition, because this produces the most products at the cheapest price. However, in order to spur innovation and the development of improved products that enhance the overall well-being of society, the U.S. Constitution provides that Congress can pass laws to grant patents to inventors. Long ago, Congress decided that inventions that are useful, novel, and nonobvious can be patented, and this is still the foundation of U.S. patent law. Trivial differences or modifications to existing devices and methods are not entitled to monopoly-like protection.

Reverse Engineering

Under the U.S. legal system, most of the time, anyone can legally copy another product or method that is not patented. Usually, copying is done by so-called reverse engineering. This involves buying the competitor's product and taking it apart or chemically analyzing it in order to determine exactly how it is made. So long as no trade secrets are misappropriated, there is no legal liability in conducting such activity. Reverse engineering is not misappropriation of trade secrets, as the latter normally requires the stealing of confidential blueprints or formulas, or some other nefarious activity. Companies sometimes sue copycats under a theory of trade dress protection, claiming that "me-too" look-alike products confuse the public as to their source and origin. This special variety of a trademark infringement claim is difficult to win because the copier can easily prevail by showing that the design of the copied features is functional as opposed to merely ornamental. Also, the party asserting trade dress rights is required to prove that the appearance of its product has acquired so-called secondary meaning or distinctiveness, which means that the public automatically associates its configuration with a particular manufacturer. This is usually a very tough burden. Just imagine all the companies that make portable ice chests. Can you name the particular manufacturer of any one of them based solely on its configuration or appearance?

There is nothing sinister, unethical, or illegal about designing around a patent. The U.S. patent system rewards such activity because it often leads to valuable improvements that are beneficial to society. Many design-around products are patentable in there own right. The U.S. Court of Appeals for the Federal Circuit has emphatically stated that designing around patents is a commendable, beneficial activity.

Determining Whether a Device or Method Is Patented

It can be difficult to determine whether a competitor's device or method is patented. The first thing to do is to look at the device and its packaging to see if it has any patent numbers "marked" (printed) on it. If so, you can order the patents, and begin to analyze them using the techniques discussed in this chapter. If not, you might perform a search under the company name to see if you can find any applicable patents. Sometimes you might have the inventor's name and you can locate the patents this way. Don't forget to search published U.S. patent applications, which may signal the future grant of a problematic patent.

If you cannot find any patents or published patent applications, you may proceed to copy any product on the market. However, searches are not 100 percent accurate. As a last resort, you could even ask the manufacturer directly if it owns any patents on the product in your sights, but, surprisingly, such inquiries are rarely answered. Remember, however, that if you write the manufacturer, you are raising a red flag, and the manufacturer is likely to scrutinize your competitive product when it hits the market. A patent may later turn up that covers your copycat design. However, under the so-called marking statute, there is no monetary liability for patent infringement unless and until the patent owner either begins to mark the patent number on its patented product, or sends a formal charge of infringement. Products sold before the earlier date of occurrence of these two events will be free from any monetary damages, even if the patent is later successfully enforced against you. So you can stop manufacturing and selling if you later determine on your own that there is a patent that covers your product, marking commences, or you receive a letter charging infringement. This may force you to eat some inventory and idle valuable tooling and equipment, but you have no other viable option unless you can either buy the patent, obtain a license, or design around the patent.

There are a couple of important exceptions to the patent-marking statute. First, if the patent owner is not commercializing the patented invention, there is no marking requirement. Second, method patents are exempt from the marking obligation because a method is not a tangible item. It is odd that there does not seem to be a requirement to mark a product made by the patented method with the method patent number.

It is prudent to engage an experienced patent attorney to help investigate the scope and extent of patent coverage that a competitor might own on its valuable products. It is common to attempt to design around those patents, again, following the advice of an experienced patent attorney. A word of caution must be stated regarding the reliance on such advice. In close cases, the patent owner may disagree with the conclusions of the patent attorney and litigation may ensue. As explained in Chapter 11, patent litigation is expensive, time consuming, and potentially disastrous from a financial standpoint. Be sure that you get a written noninfringement opinion letter in advance from your patent attorney to protect you and your company from a charge of willful infringement, treble damages, and an award of attorney's fees.

Before turning to the actual design-around process, it should first be made clear that there cannot be any liability for infringement of an invalid patent claim. Consequently, if you can collect and preserve documents and/or testimony that would allow you to prove invalidity before a jury by clear and convincing evidence, you are free to make and sell a product that is covered by the wording of the invalid claim. If you can prove that the claim does not satisfy any of the utility, novelty, and nonobviousness requirements discussed in Chapter 2, you may be able to make out a case for invalidity. Furthermore, the claim may not satisfy the enablement, best mode, and/or definiteness requirements of the U.S. patent law. In theory, the patent claim could be invalid for incorrect inventorship or unenforceable as a result of fraudulent concealment from the patent examiner of material prior art (for example, highly pertinent prior publications). Also, you are generally free to make and sell any product exactly as taught in an expired U.S. patent, save for the possible existence of extremely rare "submarine patents" discussed in Chapter 11.

Infringing a Patent

In order to successfully design around a U.S. patent, you must first understand what is required to infringe a patent. There is an old wives tale that you can avoid infringing a U.S. patent if you change at least 10 percent of the patented device. I have no idea how this rumor got started, but I have heard it repeated as gospel many times by individual inventors and small business owners. This 10-percent rule of thumb has no basis whatsoever in U.S. patent law and may cost you dearly if you rely on it. Infringement of a utility patent is determined by comparing the words of the claims of the patent to the accused method or device. Under the "all elements rule," every element and limitation from at least one claim must be found in the accused device or method in order to find infringement. The elimination of even a single element or limitation will normally avoid infringement of a claim so long as no equivalent element is substituted. If a claim calls for elements A, B, C, D, and E, you cannot avoid infringement by adding element F to the combination of elements A through E. You need to eliminate at least one of the A through E elements without substituting an equivalent element.

When analyzing the claims of a utility patent for possible infringement, one normally looks at each independent claim first. Independent claims stand by themselves and do not refer to, and thereby incorporate, the limitations of any other claims. If a proposed design can be worked out that does not infringe any of the independent claims, it is not necessary to analyze the dependent claims of the patent. This is because there can be no infringement of a dependent claim without infringement of its parent independent claim.

Infringement of a design patent (Chapter 8) is determined in a completely different manner. Under the test for design patent infringement, you compare the drawings of the design patent to the ornamental appearance of the accused article to determine whether the two designs would be indistinguishable in the eye of the ordinary observer. The design-around techniques discussed in this chapter focus on utility patents. Your patent attorney can readily advise you with regard to the extent you must vary the appearance of a product in order to safely avoid infringing a design patent.

The degree of alteration required to avoid any particular utility patent is totally dependent on the scope of its claims, which is the meaning of the words recited therein. This could require a significant modification that would render any noninfringing device less efficient, less reliable, less marketable, and so forth. On the other hand, infringement might be avoided by a trivial modification that has little adverse impact on the noninfringing design from a commercial standpoint.

Let me expand on a hypothetical first discussed in Chapter 11. Assume, for example, that the lone claim of a patent on the first heavier-than-air flying machine calls for a fuselage, fixed wings extending from the fuselage, and engine means mounted to the fixed wings for propelling the flying machine through the air. One could avoid infringing the patent by not having fixed wings, and instead using rotating wings (the blades of a helicopter). But helicopters are slow, can't carry many passengers, have short range, and require frequent maintenance. The patent owner would be very content to have the exclusive rights to the market for 99 percent of the aircraft sold in the United States. One might also be able to avoid infringement by mounting the engines inside the fuselage or to the exterior of the fuselage because the claim literally requires that engines be mounted to the fixed wings. There is some danger here in making this assumption. If the claim was never amended during prosecution before the USPTO, the patent owner may contend that moving the engines to the fuselage still results in infringement under the so-called "doctrine of equivalents." This is an alternative test for infringement besides the test for literal infringement. It was developed by the courts in order to prevent minor inconsequential changes that avoid the literal wording of the claim from escaping liability for infringement.

There cannot be any infringement under the doctrine of equivalents based on overall equivalence. Instead, infringement under the doctrine of equivalents must still be determined on an element-by-element basis. That is to say, each element in the claim must be present literally, or equivalently, in the accused device or method. Your patent attorney will need to review the publicly available file history of a patent to determine whether its claims were amended during prosecution before the examiner in order to overcome a prior art rejection. If so, such claims cannot be expanded beyond their literal terms in determining infringement. Relatively few patents are allowed without some amendments to the claims.

Where the claims of a utility patent were never amended during prosecution, assessing the extent of their scope beyond their literal terms can be very problematic. Usually, a competitive product needs to have nearly all the elements in a claim in order to be viable. Therefore, a competitor normally focuses on a single limitation of the claim and proposes or adopts a lone substituted element. Under the doctrine of equivalents, the test for infringement boils down to whether the claimed element and the substituted element are insubstantially different. Various legal standards have been developed for this test, including interchangeability and whether the two elements perform substantially the same function, in substantially the same way, to achieve substantially the same result. In patent litigation, the issue of infringement under the doctrine of equivalents is usually decided by the jury based on conflicting testimony of technical experts. Under the doctrine of equivalents, the literal scope of a claim cannot be expanded so far that it encompasses the prior art.

Let us return to the hypothetical claim to a heavier-than-air flying machine, and assume that the claim was allowed by the USPTO without requiring any amendment. In infringement litigation, it would be entitled to consideration under the equitable doctrine of equivalents. Assume that the patent owner sued a manufacturer of a flying winged aircraft such as the B2 stealth bomber. The accused infringer would argue that its aircraft has no fuselage and no equivalent of a fuselage. The patent owner could argue that there is literal infringement because the fuselage is the center section of the wing, but this argument would probably fail due to the court's interpretation of "fuselage" based on the drawings and description in the patent. The patent owner could, in the alternative, argue that the center section of the wing is equivalent to a fuselage under the doctrine of equivalents.

It is difficult to predict the outcome of any jury case, but here I believe that the accused B2 bomber manufacturer could successfully argue that:

(1) the same structure, namely, the single large wing, cannot serve to satisfy two different elements of the claim, namely, the fuselage and the "wings"; and (2) under the tripartite function-way-result test, there is no infringement under the doctrine of equivalents because the *way* is so different. The fuselage of the claim is an enclosed, totally aerodynamically streamlined elongated tubular structure that provides no lift. The center section of the wing is a transversely extending hollow body with a lower lifting surface and two vertical flat side sections that join the outer wing sections. The B2 bomber manufacturer could also argue that the *result* of the two elements (fuselage versus center wing section) is so vastly different. Namely, in the flying wing, all of the outer surface of the aircraft is devoted to lifting, with the result of significantly increased payload and extended range capabilities compared to the conventional aircraft of the patent claim that has an elongated fuselage.

An interesting side note of the hypothetical illustrates the relationship of patents to U.S. national defense. Legally, the patent owner would not be able to sue the manufacturer of the B2 bomber, Northrop Grumman, for infringement. The patent owner's sole recourse would be to sue the U.S. Government for infringement in the Court of Claims, and that lawsuit would be defended by the United States Department of Justice. The patent owner's lone remedy would be monetary damages, and no injunctive relief would be available to the patent owner; that is, a federal court could not legally order the government or Northrop Grumman to stop making the B2 bomber, even if infringement were found. For practical reasons—as a matter of public policy—national defense trumps patents.

Having described the basic techniques for designing around a patent, it would be helpful to give an actual example. I was very intrigued that the inventors of an inexpensive battery-powered electric toothbrush were recently able to sell their toothbrush business to Procter & Gamble for a reported $485 million! I was also a little jealous because one of the coinventors, who apparently received a share of this princely sum, was their patent attorney! You may have seen the SpinBrush product in supermarkets. Procter & Gamble is apparently selling millions of units per year under its Crest brand at $4.95 apiece, much to the chagrin of Colgate-Palmolive, which had earlier introduced its battery-powered electric toothbrush at a price of $19.95. I did a quick search on the free USPTO patent database at *www.uspto.gov* and located five U.S. patents using the name of one of the inventors in the article reporting the sale of the patents to Procter & Gamble. If you buy the toothbrush, the applicable U.S. patent numbers are listed on the packaging. Figures from one of the SpinBrush patents are reproduced on page 128.

Electric toothbrushes have been around for decades. Most units on the market are expensive rechargeable devices that sell for $50 and up. There are probably hundreds of issued U.S. patents on various electric toothbrush designs, including battery-powered units, that would constitute prior art against the SpinBrush design. Therefore, my instincts told me that the SpinBrush patents likely had narrow claims, making it relatively easy for Colgate-Palmolive or any other competitor to design around the same and also produce a competitive low-cost battery-powered electric toothbrush. A quick perusal of the patents confirmed my suspicions. One of these patents (U.S. Patent No. 6,189,693) has claims to the combination of an electric toothbrush inside a package that allows prospective buyers to momentarily actuate the ON button to observe the moving bristles. While this is a nice marketing gimmick, it isn't essential, in my view, to successful competitive sales. Claim 1 from U.S. Patent No. 6,189,693 reads:

1. An electric toothbrush comprising;
packaging for containing the toothbrush;
an elongated body portion having opposed first and second ends, a hollow portion and a longitudinal axis;
a head attached to said first end, wherein said head includes a moving portion;
a motor located within said hollow portion of said elongated body portion, said motor being configured to produce a moving motion for the moving portion;
a shaft operatively connected to said motor at a first end and to the moving portion at a second end;
a handle attached to said second end of said elongated body portion; and
a *switch* which is operably connected to said motor, wherein said switch is actuated in a first manner to provide *momentary operation* of said toothbrush when the toothbrush is within the packaging, and is actuated in a second manner to provide *continuous operation* of said toothbrush when the toothbrush is out of the packaging. (Emphasis added.)

I reviewed the prosecution history of the '693 patent, and Claim 1 was allowed only after extensive amendment that overcame an obviousness rejection. You could avoid this claim simply by making a battery-powered toothbrush having a switch without the capability for "momentary" and "continuous" operation. In the actual SpinBrush product, the ON button can be depressed for momentary operation or slid for continuous operation.

Battery-powered toys have been sold in clear plastic packaging that can be temporarily turned ON long before the filing date of U.S. Patent No. 6,189,693. So you could sell your battery-operated toothbrush in the same packaging without a switch that doesn't have both slide ON and push-button ON capabilities. Because Claim 1 of the '693 patent was amended during prosecution to overcome an obviousness rejection, those elements or limitations that were added or argued will not be eligible for expansion in scope beyond their literal terms under the equitable doctrine of equivalents. The patent attorney stated in remarks to the examiner that the amendments were intended to emphasize the "Try Me" feature of the invention.

Another SpinBrush patent (U.S. Patent No. 6,178,579) has claims directed to a particular linkage between the motor and the bristles that includes a plurality of "swivel arms." Undoubtedly there are many noninfringing linkages that could be designed without "swivel arms" or their equivalent that would be equally durable and have comparable performance and low cost. Again, Claim 1 of the '579 patent was extensively amended to overcome a prior art rejection, so the patent owner would not be able to resort to the doctrine of equivalents as to the added or argued elements and limitations.

Another SpinBrush patent (U.S. Patent No. 6,000,083) has a very broad claim to an electric toothbrush with the only significant limitation apparently being the requirement for both moving and stationary bristles. Claim 1 from U.S. Patent No. 6,000,083 reads:

> 1.   An electric toothbrush comprising:
> an elongated body having a handle portion, a head portion, and an elongated body shaft portion intermediate the handle portion and the head portion and wherein the elongated body shaft portion has a smaller cross-sectional dimension than the handle portion, *the head portion including static and moving bristles*, the head portion and body shaft portions being dimensioned for disposition in a human user's mouth for brushing of teeth; and
> a motor disposed in the handle portion and operatively connected to the moving bristles with a gearing and shaft assembly including an elongated shaft closely received in and extending along at least a portion of the length of the body shaft portion for driving the moving bristles. (Emphasis added.)

The prosecution history of the '083 patent shows, once again, that Claim 1 was rejected over prior art and was amended to specify both "static and moving bristles." So this claim is also limited in scope to its literal terms in regard to the requirement for both static and moving bristles. Again, it would seem that comparable performance and consumer appeal could be achieved if the stationary bristles were eliminated in a competitively designed battery-powered toothbrush. A search could locate a prior art patent showing an electric toothbrush with both moving and stationary bristles. If so, the claims of this patent might be invalid, and Colgate-Palmolive could use both moving and stationary bristles.

I was unable to locate any issued U.S. patent or published U.S. patent application on the replaceable brush head for the SpinBrush product. The releasable coupling could easily have been designed to be serviceable and patentable, thus ensuring exclusivity to the substantial follow-on market for SpinBrush replaceable brush heads sold retail at $1.99 each. A court would probably rule that sale of replaceable brush heads by a Procter & Gamble competitor is permissible repair, and, therefore, not contributory infringement of the other SpinBrush patents.

I was able to locate U.S. Design Patent No. Des. 432,312 on the bristle pattern of the SpinBrush toothbrush. This was easy because the number is marked on the packaging for the replaceable SpinBrush brush heads sold by Procter & Gamble. But this design patent could be readily avoided by using a different bristle pattern "distinguishable in the eye of the ordinary observer," yet still functionally compatible with the SpinBrush drive mechanism.

My example of how to design around the SpinBrush toothbrush is not meant to criticize or demean the efforts of its inventors. However, it would appear their major achievement was implementing an extremely low-cost design, high-volume production in China, and great marketing skills in getting the toothbrush into major chain stores. Procter & Gamble didn't pay nearly $500 million for five narrow patents; rather, it paid that much for a successful, growing business that it could take to the next level of sales under its well-known Crest brand. You might ask, then, why bother to patent the SpinBrush design at all? I can give you six reasons:

1. You never know in advance the scope of claims that you might be able to obtain.

2. Undoubtedly, the SpinBrush patents have provided some degree of deterrence. They probably have been valuable in preventing pirate companies from copying the same design and flooding the U.S. market.

3. The SpinBrush patents probably gave some solace to the inventors' financial backers.

4. The SpinBrush patents may have increased the buyout price ultimately paid by Procter & Gamble to the inventors.

5. The product could be touted in marketing as being "patented," and, therefore, presumably newer and better than existing electric toothbrushes.

6. The SpinBrush patents become prior art, which prevents someone from later independently inventing the same thing, patenting it, and suing Procter & Gamble. Not all product areas are as heavily developed and mature as the electric toothbrush art, and, therefore, offer the prospect of obtaining broader, more valuable U.S. patent protection than that obtained on the Crest SpinBrush product.

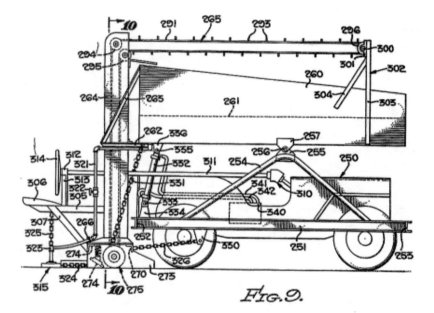

FIG. 9.

U.S. Patent No. 2,642,679
"Ice Rink Resurfacing Machine"
Granted June 23, 1953
(the famous Zamboni machine seen at every hockey game)

CHAPTER 13

Arbitration and Mediation of Patent Disputes

I nstead of fighting it out in court, you may wish to consider the advantages and disadvantages of arbitration. If there is a genuine dispute between two parties that involves an issue of validity or infringement of a U.S. patent, the federal courts will normally decide the case if one of the parties files suit. Except in rare circumstances, state courts cannot decide these issues because their jurisdiction is preempted in these areas. A dispute over breach of a patent license agreement can be decided in state court. Where the parties agree, they may have their patent infringement and patent license disputes decided in arbitration. Arbitration is an out-of-court procedure where one or more experts agreed upon by the parties decide the case instead of a judge or jury. If one of the parties does not agree to arbitration, it cannot be compelled unless there is a valid contract between the parties providing that if one party so elects, any disputes between the parties will be decided through arbitration. If you are about to enter into a patent license agreement and you think you might want arbitration, you had better include a mandatory arbitration provision. Patent infringement disputes usually require the agreement of both sides after the dispute erupts in order for arbitration to take the place of regular federal court litigation.

Arbitration

Arbitration is similar to litigating in court, but the amount of discovery (for example, production of documents and depositions) is usually far less, there are few motions, and there is no judge or jury. Arbitration takes a matter of months, whereas litigation in court takes years if there is a trial and appeal. In a typical situation, arbitration is binding, which means that the decision by the arbitrators is final and cannot be appealed. In some cases, the arbitration decision will be made part of an official judgment that will be filed with a court having jurisdiction over the parties. This allows the decision to be enforced by a federal or state judge if there are problems down the road.

The American Arbitration Association, or AAA as it is known in legal circles, provides a structured set of rules and procedures for arbitration of patent disputes. For a reasonable fee, it will provide lists of qualified arbitrators, a strict set of procedural guidelines, and a physical location for the arbitration hearing. Patent arbitrators are typically experienced patent attorneys who have taken training classes in arbitration techniques. While a single arbitrator can decide a case, usually the parties opt for three arbitrators in order to ensure against a wild-card decision by a single arbitrator. The arbitrators must not have any relationship with the parties or their attorneys that would raise an appearance of impropriety, or bias. You should still employ your own attorneys to prepare and present your side of the case, just as you would if the case were being litigated in federal court. However, arbitration is a much more condensed proceeding. If the parties cannot agree on three arbitrators, they will normally each pick one arbitrator and allow the two arbitrators who have been chosen to pick the third arbitrator.

The arbitration hearing takes place after limited discovery and briefing. At the hearing, the attorneys for both sides present opening statements, followed by their cases in chief, which consist of documents and testimony, and are concluded with closing arguments. The rules of evidence are somewhat relaxed, and the hearing takes a matter of a few days, as opposed to several weeks for a typical patent infringement trial. At the end of the arbitration hearing, the arbitrators meet, review the evidence, and decide the case. In a typical situation, a written decision is rendered within a month or two of the conclusion of the arbitration hearing. There is no appeal, and if you are dissatisfied with the decision, it can only be overturned under extremely unusual circumstances, such as proof that the arbitrators were mentally incapacitated, bribed, or colluded with third parties.

Positives of Arbitration

So what is so good about arbitration? Well, it is generally less expensive than litigating a case in court all the way through a trial and appeal. How much cheaper? It is difficult to generalize, but it might cost one-third or less to arbitrate a patent infringement dispute in terms of your legal fees, the hourly fees paid to the arbitrators, and the AAA administrative fees. If the matter being arbitrated is a patent license dispute, the arbitration provision may provide that the loser pays the winner's legal fees, the arbitrators' fees, and the AAA administrative fees.

Arbitration takes much less time than litigating a case in court through a trial and an appeal. Most arbitrations can be concluded within a year, depending upon the availability of the arbitrators. By way of contrast, it would normally take at least two or three years for a patent infringement case to be tried in federal district court and then decided on appeal by the CAFC. A shorter proceeding means less legal fees, less executive time, and sooner certainty. It also means that you may find out sooner that you lost.

Negatives of Arbitration

With these seemingly major advantages of less cost and time, why wouldn't you always want to choose arbitration over court litigation? Well, for starters, most arbitration is binding and this means you give up the right to appeal or relitigate in court. If the arbitrators misconstrue the scope of the patent claims or misapply the claims to the accused product, there is nothing you can do to fix the error. This could cost you millions, or even your whole company. The finality of binding arbitration decisions alone deters many companies from arbitrating patent infringement cases, because they prefer to have the option of having a trial court judgment reviewed by a panel of three patent law judges at the CAFC. It is possible to have nonbinding arbitration, but most parties won't bother with this because it just adds another layer of cost and delay to the dispute resolution process.

Many companies don't like binding arbitration for a variety of additional reasons. There is a feeling that the arbitrators tend to "split the baby," which means they give each party a little of what they think is just, and thereby satisfy the business objectives of neither party. Patent cases are so complex that many companies want the thorough discovery and motion proceedings that are involved in federal court patent infringement litigation. Many patent owners are convinced that they will only get a fair shake if the case is decided by a jury, and arbitration does not provide any way to have trial by jury. In some cases, a party may have superior resources and will not want its opponent to benefit from the reduced cost of arbitration proceedings. A defendant in a patent infringement case may want to drag out the case as long as possible, hoping to wear down the patent owner until they will agree to a cheap settlement. Such a strategy can really only be effectively pursued via court litigation.

I remember that there used to be a very large patent law firm in which one of the named partners made a nationwide reputation, and a fine income, during a 40-year career of litigating patent cases in federal court. Thereafter, he went on the "chicken lunch circuit" preaching the supposed benefits of arbitrating patent cases. Of course, by this time he was in the twilight of his career and was making a handsome living in what is called "alternative dispute resolution." This basically means that he was available for hire as an arbitrator or a mediator in patent cases.

Mediation

A mediator tries to get the parties to agree to resolve their dispute without resorting to arbitration or litigation in court. In mediation, the two sides come together and explain their positions and demands, and the mediator shuffles back and forth between the parties in a series of group meetings and one-on-one closed-door sessions in the hopes of getting each party to see the other party's case and come to a joint solution. Mediation techniques were first developed and perfected to resolve labor disputes, and, later, family law disputes. The problem with mediating patent disputes is that the mediation process tends to ignore the merits of each side's arguments about validity and infringement and focuses instead upon fashioning some sort of resolution that both parties can agree upon. However, the patent owner wants the defendant to stop making what it is selling and to pay money damages for infringement. The defendant doesn't want to stop selling its product, change its design, or pay any money whatsoever. It is hard to mediate a resolution of such issues. You can mediate what pay raise you give to the teachers' union, but it is not so simple when it comes to patent infringement cases.

During my career as a patent attorney, I have been counsel of record in approximately 20 patent infringement lawsuits, but I have never represented a client in an arbitration. My experience has been that it is very uncommon for parties to agree to arbitrate a patent infringement case. In contrast, arbitration of patent license disputes is very common because many patent license agreements have mandatory arbitration clauses that one party chooses to invoke. Such cases usually involve an issue of whether royalties are due for a particular modified design, or an issue of determining the royalty base—whether the royalty percentage should be based on (multiplied against) the price of the entire product or merely the cost of a component. I do not know of a single case in which a patent infringement dispute was resolved by mediation, although I am sure this has occurred from time to time.

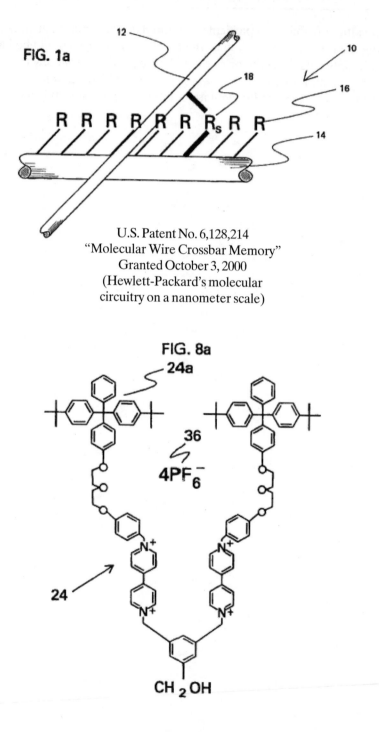

FIG. 1a

R R R R R R R_s R R

U.S. Patent No. 6,128,214
"Molecular Wire Crossbar Memory"
Granted October 3, 2000
(Hewlett-Packard's molecular
circuitry on a nanometer scale)

FIG. 8a

24a

36

$4PF_6^-$

24

CH_2OH

CHAPTER 14

Inventors and the IRS

D eath and taxes—inventors can't avoid them, the same as everyone else. This chapter will give an overview of federal income tax treatment of invention-related development expenses and patent-related income. Many financial advisors will tell you that it is not how much money you make, it is how much money you keep after taxes that is critical in determining your standard of living and your ability to save. I am not a tax lawyer or a CPA, so make sure you run any specific situations by your tax professional. Keep in mind that the following comments are meant to help you optimize the income tax returns that you and/or your company file with the Internal Revenue Service (IRS). State income tax laws vary across the United States, and you'll need to look into their application as well. You may be lucky enough to reside in a state with no *personal* income tax, such as Nevada, Texas, and Florida, but your corporation may still have to pay some state *corporate* income tax on patent-related income.

Federal Income Taxes

The general rule of thumb when it comes to federal income taxes is that if expenses related to a given activity are deductible in determining taxable income, income produced by that activity will be counted in determining taxable income. In order to increase your odds of surviving an IRS audit without a deficiency or penalty assessment, you should keep detailed written records of invention-related development expenses and patent-related income. In borderline cases, it may be advisable to get a written opinion letter from a tax lawyer supporting your position that certain invention-related expenses are deductible in a particular manner and/or that certain patent-related income is entitled to certain favorable treatment. This could insulate you from any charges of criminal tax evasion, but only if you make a full disclosure to your tax lawyer and get the opinion in advance of taking the action in question.

Usually, expenses incurred in the creation of an asset must be capitalized according to Section 263 of the IRC. This means that you must add up all the expenses paid in connection with developing an asset, and then deduct equal portions of the total amount annually over the life of the asset. For example, if you build a hotel on a piece of land, the cost of the building is recovered by deducting an equal amount of that cost each year over a 39-year period. You cannot deduct the entire cost of the building against your income in a single year.

However, an inventor may, pursuant to Section 174 of the Internal Revenue Code (IRC), deduct "research or experimental expenditures" that are paid or incurred during the year in connection with a trade or business associated with the technology to which his or her invention relates. It is not necessary to add up all these expenditures and then deduct an equal portion each year over the life of a patent. One commentator says that the term "in connection with" was deliberately used in Section 174 in order to alleviate the more stringent requirement that the taxpayer have an actual ongoing business concern, as previously required, in order for such expenditures to be deductible. The IRS Regulations make it relatively clear that the costs of developing patentable inventions fall within the definition of "research or experimental expenditures." The IRS Regulations also state that research or experimental expenditures generally include "...all such costs incident to the development or improvement of a product." The IRS Regulations define a "product" to include any "pilot model, process, formula, invention, technique, *patent*, or similar property, and includes products to be used by the taxpayer in its trade or business as well as products to be held for sale, lease, or *license*" (emphasis added). These deductible expenditures include the cost of obtaining a patent in terms of attorney's fees and USPTO fees. Salaries of research employees, tooling for prototypes, and materials related to the invention would be currently deductible. The applicable IRS Regulations give the following example:

> [A] taxpayer undertakes to develop a new machine for use in his business. He expends $30,000 on the project of which $10,000 represents the actual costs of material, labor, etc., to construct the machine, and $20,000 represents research costs which are not attributable to the machine itself. Under Section 174(a) the taxpayer would be permitted to deduct the $20,000 as expenses not chargeable to capital account, but the $10,000 must be charged to the asset account (the machine).

Under Section 41 of the IRC, 20 percent of the "qualified research expenses" incurred in the development of a patented invention may be credited against the taxpayer's tax liability. The definition of "qualified research expenses" under Section 41 is more narrow than the definition of "research or experimental expenditures" under Section 174. The three-part test for whether expenses are "qualified research expenses" is as follows:

> 1. They must be expenditures deductible under Section 174;
> 2. They must be undertaken for the purpose of discovering information that is technological in nature, the application of which is intended to be useful in the development of a new or improved business component of the taxpayer; and
> 3. Substantially all of the activities supported by the expenditures must constitute elements of a process of experimentation related to the development of a new or improved function, performance, reliability or quality of a business component. (Philip F. Postlewaite et al., *Federal Income Taxation of Intellectual Properties and Intangible Assets*. Warren, Gorham & Lamont: Boston, Mass., 1998.)

Notably, there can be no qualified research expenses tax credit if the research relates to "style, taste, cosmetic, or seasonal design factors."

The Taxpayer Relief Act of 1997 reactivated favorable long-term capital gains treatment of certain patent-related income. Usually, a taxpayer must hold a property for at least a year in order for the income from its sale to be entitled to the capital gains rate of 20 percent, as opposed to the ordinary income rates for individuals that can exceed 39 percent. Under Section 1235 of the IRC, proceeds from the sale of a patent can be entitled to long-term capital gains treatment no matter how short the holding period, and even if the taxpayer is considered to be a professional inventor. In order to receive capital gains treatment on the income, the recipient must be a "holder" as defined in the IRC. In addition to the inventor, a holder of the patent can be someone who bought invention rights from the inventor, but only if the latter obtained his or her interest before the invention was actually reduced to practice; for example, before a prototype was built and successfully tested. This aspect of the federal income tax law was designed to make it more attractive for investors to finance new technology ventures, thereby making it easier for inventors to finance their research and development efforts.

The ability to deduct "research or experimental expenditures" related to an invention from ordinary income can be extremely advantageous due to the fact that these deductions are not recaptured upon the later sale of the rights to the resulting technology. Assume for the sake of illustration that you spent $400,000 over several years developing a new snowmobile, and that you later sell all the rights to the technology, including patent rights, to the manufacturer of Arctic Cat snowmobiles for $1 million. You could deduct $400,000 from your ordinary income, and the entire $1 million in proceeds would only be taxed at 20 percent. Without favorable tax treatment, the first $400,000 would be taxed at a much higher personal tax rate (for example, 39 percent or higher), and only $600,000 would be entitled to the more favorable 20-percent rate.

In order for the proceeds of the sale of a patent to be entitled to favorable capital gains treatment, the sale must convey substantially all of the rights to the invention. Thus, royalties paid under a nonexclusive license would be taxed as ordinary income. What about royalties paid under an exclusive license? They would likely be treated as capital gains income, but you should ask your tax professional about this one. I have frequently seen a sale of a patent structured so that full title to the patent is conveyed immediately, but the purchase price is paid in installments over the life of the patent based on the annual sales volume of products embodying the patented invention. This looks a great deal like a license, but it apparently offers capital gains advantages to the seller in the opinion of some tax professionals.

Let's look at several hypothetical examples to further illustrate how inventors and investors can take advantage of the special federal income tax treatment of invention-related development expenses and patent-related income.

Tax Example 1: *The Solo Medical Inventor*

Dr. Nightingale conceives a new way to measure red blood cell count by illuminating a sample with different colors of light and comparing the amounts of each color reflected. She builds and successfully demonstrates a prototype and promptly files a U.S. patent application within one year of her conception of the invention. Still within the same year, Dr. Nightingale enters into an exclusive license agreement with a company covering her patent pending invention. Her uncle is the majority owner of the company that licenses her invention. Her tax lawyer tells her that she can deduct all the development expenses and legal fees from her ordinary income and claim capital gains treatment on the royalties. Because Dr. Nightingale is a medical doctor, she has a high personal income, but the favorable tax treatment gives her plenty of deductions against her relatively high ordinary income and a tax rate of 20 percent on her royalty income, instead of a rate of more than 39 percent. She now has more money to pursue other important potentially life-saving inventions, in part because the tax on her royalty income is only slightly more than half what she would otherwise pay the IRS. As an aside, before he signs the exclusive license agreement, Dr. Nightingale's uncle had better confirm that she has not previously signed an employee invention agreement obligating her to assign all rights to her blood cell measuring invention to her employer. Employer and employee invention rights are discussed in Chapter 16.

Tax Example 2: *The Wealthy Investor*

Mr. Rich is a wealthy venture capitalist. Through his networking contacts he meets a bright young scientist with an idea for sending large amounts of computer data between adjacent high-rise buildings using a modulated point-to-point laser that beams energy from a transmitter on one rooftop to a receiver on another rooftop. The scientist only has a theoretical concept of his invention in mind, and has never built or tested any hardware to prove that it will work. Mr. Rich decides to invest (through a suitable legal entity that is formed by a corporate attorney) in the production of a prototype. This makes him a participant in the "reduction to practice" of the invention from a federal income tax standpoint. Nine months later, before building a prototype, the inventor files a U.S. patent application on his laser invention and all the patent rights are sold to a large company for $2 million. Mr. Rich's share of the $2 million proceeds are subject to only a 20-percent federal income tax rate, instead of an ordinary income tax rate of more than 39 percent.

Tax Example 3: *The Marketing Executive*

Mr. Bell, a marketing executive, learns of a patented rotisserie that has never been commercialized but has been demonstrated in the form of a finished prototype. He is confident he can sell the rights to the invention to one of his contacts in the food equipment industry. Mr. Bell wants to avoid investing any cash, so he convinces the patent owner to agree to give him a percentage of the proceeds of any sale or exclusive license of the patent rights. Mr. Bell is not an inventor or an investor prior to an actual reduction to practice of the rotisserie invention. However, he can still qualify for capital gains treatment on his share of the proceeds of the sale by holding his interest in the invention for more than the long-term capital gains holding period. During this period, Mr. Bell adds value to the product by suggesting changes to make it cheaper to manufacture, arranging contacts with a Chinese manufacturer, and producing a marketing video. After plenty of effort over two years, Mr. Bell consummates an exclusive license of the patent rights to one of his contacts. Mr. Bell then receives a share of the royalties on a quarterly basis over the 10-year remaining life of the patent. He pays only the 20-percent capital gains rate on this income, allowing him to retire comfortably in Hawaii where he regularly sees the patented rotisserie for sale on the Home Shopping Network.

Under Section 162 or Section 212 of the IRC, legal expenses incurred in prosecuting an action for patent infringement will be deductible if the claim arose in connection with the taxpayer's trade or business or an activity engaged in for profit. Patents acquired from another party as part of the taxpayer's trade or business may, under normal circumstances, be amortizable under the straight line method using a useful life of 15 years, rather than the actual statutory term of the patent. Finally, if a patent owner recovers damages from an infringer in the form of lost profits, the damages received will be treated as ordinary income.

The foregoing general overview and the three examples should open your eyes to some of the special federal income tax advantages enjoyed by inventors, their financial backers, and patent owners. Again, let me stress that I am not a tax lawyer or a CPA. You should consult with your tax professional about your particular situation to ensure that you are entitled to deduct certain patent related expenses, take a tax credit, or claim favorable tax treatment on patent-related income. Federal income tax law is extremely complex, and even more so when it collides with inventions and patents! Furthermore, Congress changes the income tax laws on a frequent basis, and in addition, there are constantly new regulations and Tax Court rulings that affect the interpretation and application of these laws.

PCT

WORLD INTELLECTUAL PROPERTY ORGANIZATION
International Bureau

INTERNATIONAL APPLICATION PUBLISHED UNDER THE PATENT COOPERATION TREATY (PCT)

(51) International Patent Classification 7 :		(11) International Publication Number:	WO 00/47398
B30B 9/32, B26F 1/20, 1/24	A1	(43) International Publication Date:	17 August 2000 (17.08.00)

(21) International Application Number: PCT/US00/01357

(22) International Filing Date: 20 January 2000 (20.01.00)

(30) Priority Data:
09/248,394 12 February 1999 (12.02.99) US

(63) Related by Continuation (CON) or Continuation-in-Part
(CIP) to Earlier Application
US 09/248,394 (CON)
Filed on 12 February 1999 (12.02.99)

(71) Applicant (for all designated States except US): CP MANU-
FACTURING [US/US]; 1428 McKinley Avenue, National
City, CA 92050 (US).

(72) Inventor; and
(75) Inventor/Applicant (for US only): DAVIS, Robert, M.
[US/US]; 1775 Navajo Road, El Cajon, CA 92020 (US).

(74) Agent: MEADOR, Terrance, A.; Gray Cary Ware & Frei-
denrich, LLP, Suite 1700, 401 B Street, San Diego, CA
92101–4297 (US).

(81) Designated States: AE, AL, AM, AT, AU, AZ, BA, BB, BG,
BR, BY, CA, CH, CN, CR, CU, CZ, DE, DK, DM, EE,
ES, FI, GB, GD, GE, GH, GM, HR, HU, ID, IL, IN, IS, JP,
KE, KG, KP, KR, KZ, LC, LK, LR, LS, LT, LU, LV, MA,
MD, MG, MK, MN, MW, MX, NO, NZ, PL, PT, RO, RU,
SD, SE, SG, SI, SK, SL, TJ, TM, TR, TT, TZ, UA, UG,
US, UZ, VN, YU, ZA, ZW. ARIPO patent (GH, GM, KE,
LS, MW, SD, SL, SZ, TZ, UG, ZW), Eurasian patent (AM,
AZ, BY, KG, KZ, MD, RU, TJ, TM), European patent (AT,
BE, CH, CY, DE, DK, ES, FI, FR, GB, GR, IE, IT, LU,
MC, NL, PT, SE), OAPI patent (BF, BJ, CF, CG, CI, CM,
GA, GN, GW, ML, MR, NE, SN, TD, TG).

Published
With international search report.

(54) Title: MACHINE FOR PERFORATING AND CRUSHING CONTAINERS

(57) Abstract

An apparatus and method of use is
disclosed for a machine used for perforating and flattening or crushing containers (30) of varying sizes and materials.
The disclosed machine has a frame (12)
having an input opening (26) and a discharge opening (28). A first plurality of
shafts (18) and second plurality of shafts
(20) are rotatably supported by the frame
(12). The first plurality of shafts (18)
are disposed in a first plane and the second plurality of shafts (20) are disposed
in a second plane. The second plane is
acutely angled with respect to the first
plane. One or more motors rotate the
first and second plurality of shafts, each
shaft having perforating elements (44) po-
sitioned along them. The perforating elements (44) are offset between adjacent
performing shafts such that adjacent perforating elements overlap but do not touch
the adjacent shaft. The perforating elements (44) have a plurality of spikes capable of perforating the container being

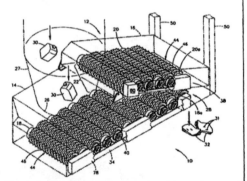

perforated and crushed. In use, containers (30) are introduced into the frame (12) through the input opening (26). The containers enter
and engage the first plurality of shafts (18) and the second plurality of shafts (20) disposed on intersecting planes. As the containers travel
between the first and second plurality of shafts (18, 20), the area between the first and second plurality of shafts becomes progressively
smaller and closes in on the containers, crushing them between shafts of the first and second plurality of shafts with the spikes puncturing
the containers, relieving them of any pressure or contents. After flattening or crushing, the containers are discarded through the discharge
opening (28). In another embodiment, a pair of rotatable crushing members located near the intersecting planes, further crushing the
containers as they exit the first and second plurality of shafts.

U.S. Patent No. PCT/US00/01357
"Machine for Perforating and Crushing Containers"
Published August 17, 2000
Corresponding to U.S. Patent No. 6,131,509
Granted October 17, 2000
(commercial recycling equipment of CP Manufacturing Inc.)

CHAPTER 15

Foreign Patent Protection

C ontrary to popular belief, there is no such thing as an international patent. Several treaties help U.S. inventors and companies obtain patents overseas, but with very limited exceptions, it is still necessary to obtain a patent separately in each foreign country.

Filing a Foreign Patent Application

According to the Paris Convention Treaty, so long as a foreign patent application is filed by a U.S. inventor within one year of the U.S. filing date, the foreign-filed application is entitled to the benefit of the so-called priority filing date of the parent U.S. patent application. However, whereas the U.S. has a one-year grace period to file a patent application, most foreign countries require absolute novelty. As a practical matter, this means that if an inventor wants to preserve his or her right to seek foreign patents, the U.S. patent application must be filed prior to the first disclosure of the invention on a nonconfidential basis.

Of paramount importance is the fact that a U.S. inventor must file his or her patent application in the USPTO first, or else risk criminal penalties for what amounts to unauthorized export of technical data. A U.S. inventor must then either obtain a foreign filing license, or wait until six months has expired before filing corresponding foreign patent applications. The USPTO reviews every newly filed patent application to determine if it relates to national security. Of particular sensitivity are inventions relating to atomic energy, nuclear weapons, electronic warfare, encryption, germ warfare, and so forth. The USPTO will defer to the Department of Defense (DOD) in deciding whether to issue a secrecy order, in which case the application will be prosecuted but will not be published and will not issue until the DOD lifts the secrecy order, which is reviewed annually. I once filed a patent application on a method of remote piloting of a drone aircraft based on a simulated chase plane view. A secrecy order was imposed and the patent did not issue for 13 years.

A U.S. inventor runs a risk of significant legal sanctions if he or she decides unilaterally to file foreign without first filing in the USPTO on the assumption that the invention could not possibly have any effect on national security. For example, an inventor cannot legally file a foreign patent application on a lasagna maker without first obtaining a U.S. foreign filing license or waiting for six months after filing an application in the USPTO.

Another treaty of significance is the Patent Cooperation Treaty (PCT) administered by the World Intellectual Property Organization (WIPO) based in Geneva, Switzerland. There are more than 100 PCT signatories, including the United States and most of the world's industrialized countries. A U.S. patent applicant can effectively refile his or her application in the USPTO as a PCT application within the one-year Paris Convention allotment and preserve the option to seek foreign patents in most of the industrialized world. An initial examination authority is designated, which can be the patent office of any PCT member country that will accept applications for examination. The application is automatically published by WIPO on or about the 18-month anniversary of the U.S. filing date. The application is examined for form, a search is done, and initial positions are taken as to novelty and inventive step. The latter is the international equivalent of the nonobviousness requirement in the United States. Responses may be filed with amendments to the specification and claims, along with argument. The initial examining authority will make a final determination on patentability, which is forwarded to each of the designated foreign patent offices. These patent offices are not obligated to follow the determinations on patentability in the final PCT office action, which are merely advisory. If a Chapter II Demand is filed by the 19-month anniversary, the applicant can postpone completion of the national phase filings until the 30-month anniversary of the filing date, and in some cases, up to the 31-month anniversary. A Chapter II Demand is simply a document that formally asks the PCT authority to give an 11-month extension of time to file corresponding patent applications in individual foreign countries. Many countries have waived the requirement to file a Chapter II Demand by the 19-month deadline.

Foreign Patent Systems

Europe has a common patent office in Munich, Germany, called the European Patent Office (EPO). Patent applications filed in the EPO go through an examination similar to that in the USPTO, and if claims are deemed to meet the conditions for patentability, a Notice of Intention to grant a patent is published. If no opposition is filed, or if one is filed and the applicant prevails, a European patent is granted. However, it is not a patent in the usual sense, because it must be nationalized in each of the 16 European countries previously designated where exclusive rights are desired. The result is that you end up with individual patents in the United Kingdom, Germany, France, Italy, Spain, etc., or a subset of these countries. The EPO can be designated when a PCT application is filed, and an EPO application can be filed out of the PCT prior to the national phase deadline.

There are several other regional patent systems besides the EPO system. These include the African Regional Industrial Property Organization (ARIPO) and the Organisation Africaine de la Propriete Intellectualle (OAPI), which are based on groupings of African countries. The Eurasian patent covers the Russian Federation and many of its former Asian republics. Not surprisingly, few U.S. inventors or companies file patent applications with these regional systems. Do you really need a patent in Burkina Faso, Benin, Côte d'Ivoire, Mauritania, Chad, or Togo?

In virtually all foreign patent offices, your application will have to be examined as to form and for patentability. Just as in the United States, this will involve Office Actions from the foreign patent examiner and the responses filed. It is often necessary to redraft the background portion of the specification and to substantially change the format of the claims into the so-called "characterizing" form in which the first part of the claim recites prior art and the inventive portion follows the words "characterized by" (for example, "A pencil characterized by an eraser at one end thereof"). The EPO has a strict unity of invention rule that effectively dictates that your EPO application can have only one independent claim.

Nearly all foreign patent systems have counterparts to the novelty and nonobviousness requirements of the U.S. patent law. However, there are so many complexities and subtleties to each foreign patent system, it is necessary to engage a patent agent in each country to act as your advocate. It is clear that this adds considerably to the cost of obtaining a foreign patent. Also, the level of uniqueness required for patentability varies widely from country to country. You may not get a patent in a particular country, or if you do, it will have claims narrower than those in its U.S. counterpart. The EPO examiners are notorious sticklers. They perform thorough prior art searches and generally require substantial detail in the claims to meet the "inventive step" requirement. Any prior art cited by a foreign patent examiner must be made of record in the parent U.S. application if it is still pending in order to satisfy the duty of disclosure. This adds to the cost of U.S. prosecution and can prevent you from getting broader claims allowed.

Cost of Foreign Patent Protection

The cost of seeking foreign patent protection in most industrialized countries is very steep, with the exceptions of Canada and Australia. Many U.S. companies file in Canada as a matter of course. Despite the proximity of Mexico and the advent of the North American Free Trade Act (NAFTA), patent application filing in Mexico by U.S. inventors and companies is only a small fraction of that which takes place with respect to Canada. In general, with the exception of pharmaceuticals, there is relatively little filing of patent applications by U.S. inventors and companies in Africa, the Middle East, South America, and Eastern Europe. By far, most foreign filing by U.S. inventors and companies is concentrated in the EPO and Asia. Outside of the EPO, the most common choices for nationalization are the United Kingdom, Germany, France, and Italy. With regard to Asia, the most frequent choices are Japan, Taiwan, South Korea, and the People's Republic of China. Nearly all foreign patent systems require annuities to be paid each year to prevent the pending applications and issued patents in their countries from lapsing. These annuities can amount to a significant financial burden for an individual or a small company.

An inventor may receive a substantial up-front royalty payment from a manufacturer. The inventor may be tempted to spend most of that up-front payment pursuing foreign patents. The subsequent royalty stream may not be enough to offset the cost of seeking foreign patents, and as a consequence, the inventor may not make any real money from his or her invention even if it is successfully commercialized. This is because the cost of pursuing foreign patents may exceed the cumulative royalty payments. An inventor may try to negotiate a deal that requires the manufacturer to bear the cost of seeking and maintaining foreign patent protection if it believes that such protection will be cost-effective in foreign markets.

Deciding Whether to Seek Foreign Patent Protection

This leads me into a discussion of the factors to take into account in deciding whether it is worth the cost to seek foreign patents on your invention. It really depends upon the nature of your invention, its place of manufacture, and its markets. As a general rule of thumb, in most instances, the cost of seeking and maintaining foreign patent protection, with the exceptions of Canada and Australia, is prohibitive for an individual inventor or small business. It can easily cost $50,000 to $100,000 to obtain patents in a handful of European and Asian countries. The annuities can easily run $500 and more per country per year just to maintain these patents. Remember, a U.S. patent can be used to stop the importation and sale in the U.S. of infringing products made overseas. Furthermore, you don't need a German patent to sell in Germany, only to stop a competitor from manufacturing or selling your invention there. You do need a German patent to obtain royalties for products made or sold in Germany that embody your invention. Ask yourself if you are really prepared to file suit in a German court to stop an infringer in Germany and you begin to realize that the practice of acquiring foreign patents, in most cases, is best left for medium to large multinational companies.

Many times in my career I have seen companies with annual sales of between $10 and $50 million spend money needlessly on foreign patents to the detriment of building their portfolio of U.S. patents. In most cases, these smaller U.S. companies would have been better off getting 10 U.S. patents on various improvements to their product line rather than patenting a single invention in four European countries and Japan. Too often, small businesses believe that one invention is the most important to the company, and patent it overseas. Later on, they find out that another invention turned out to be more important in the long run, and in some cases, it wasn't even patented in the United States because the foreign filing costs busted the patent budget.

This is not to say that foreign patents cannot be extremely valuable. From a strategic standpoint, they can preserve high profit margins in overseas markets. Canada is a natural extension of the U.S. market. The currency exchange rate between the U.S. and Canada makes the legal fees and government fees in Canada very inexpensive for U.S. inventors and companies. Furthermore, the Canadian Patent Office seems to give a great deal of deference to the fact that a U.S. patent has been granted. This translates into an extremely expedient and inexpensive Canadian prosecution. The same factors play out in Australia. It often costs less than half of the U.S. prosecution costs to obtain Canadian and Australian counterpart patents, adding markets with roughly 40 million people to your area of exclusive rights.

Whether to file foreign patent applications and where to file them, besides Canada and Australia, involves weighing a number of factors. In general, foreign patent filings should be limited to principal markets and/ or places of manufacture for the product in question. For example, all of the components of Rokenbok radio-controlled building sets are made in China, like most toys. So if the company obtains Chinese patents, it controls the biggest and cheapest source of manufacture, and, therefore, needs not seek patents in Latin American countries, for example. Inkjet printers are not manufactured in Turkey, and not many people have personal computers in that country. Therefore, the cost of seeking and maintaining lots of Turkish patents on inkjet printers is probably not justifiable from a cost standpoint. In some cases, a very large company need only obtain one or two key patents in such a country in order to lock it up, so to speak. I have seen small- to medium-sized companies file patent applications in the home countries of their principal foreign competitors. If, for example, your Italian competitor cannot make a similar product at its factory in Milan, it is unlikely that it will set up another plant in a different country to manufacture that article just to avoid your Italian patent.

One needs to bear in mind the concept of so-called "working" that is inherent in the patent law of many foreign countries. Under this concept, the foreign patent law allows a competitor to obtain a compulsory license under your foreign patent after a certain number of years, say five years, if you or your licensee are not exploiting the foreign patent by manufacturing or selling the patented article in that country.

In the end analysis, the prudent approach for many individuals and small business owners who strongly believe that their invention has significant overseas potential is to file a PCT application near the end of the 12-month Paris Convention period. This usually costs less than the cost of the U.S. filing. Upon the timely filing of a Chapter II Demand, an extra 18 months is effectively purchased for optional national foreign filing by the 30-month deadline. If you plan to sell or license your invention rights to a multinational company, in many cases it will be seriously interested in foreign patent coverage. You need to strike a deal with such a company before the 30-month PCT deadline passes in order to shift the substantial cost of national phase filings over to your assignee or licensee.

If an inventor does not timely file a PCT application, then all national phase filings (for example, filing a Brazilian counterpart to a U.S. application) must be completed by the 12-month anniversary of the U.S. filing date. If the inventor files a PCT application and then files a Chapter II Demand by the 19-month deadline, the inventor can postpone filing the national phase application in particular foreign countries to the 30-month anniversary of the U.S. filing date—the difference being 18 months. As noted earlier in this chapter, many countries have done away with the requirement of filing a Chapter II Demand by the 19-month anniversary of the U.S. filing date in order to postpone filing in those countries until the 30-month deadline, but this presumes the inventor has timely filed a PCT application within 12 months of the U.S. filing date. Also, some systems, such as the EPO, extend the filing deadline to 31 months.

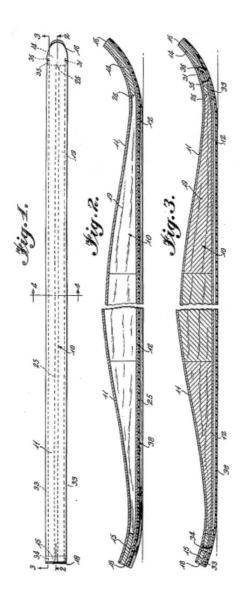

U.S. Patent No. 2,694,580
"Composite Wood and Metal Ski
Having Plastic Running Surface"
Granted November 16, 1954
(Head snow ski that replaced
all-wood snow skis)

CHAPTER 16

Employer and Employee Invention Rights

I nventions, patent applications, and patents are so-called intangible property, as opposed to real property. The latter term generally refers to land and buildings. The ownership of intangible property in the United States is covered by the laws of each individual state, but the laws are similar across the country when it comes to their applicability to inventions and patents. Under the U.S. patent laws, patents are granted in the names of the inventors. In the absence of any overriding contractual obligations, an individual owns the full title to a patent that lists the person as the sole inventor. Unless there is an overriding contractual arrangement, joint inventors each own an undivided equal interest in a U.S. patent. Absent any agreement to the contrary, each joint inventor of a patented invention may make, use, offer to sell, or sell the patented invention without the consent of the other owners and without accounting to them for any share of royalties or other income. Inventors can, pursuant to state law, agree to assign their patent rights to each other, to their employer, or to some other third party. Usually this is done in a written contract.

Employees and Invention Agreements

Where the contract to convey all the rights to an invention is specific to a certain invention or patent, it is usually referred to as an assignment. However, most companies that have anything to do with developing and selling new products and services have their employees sign employment invention agreements. By their terms, these prospective agreements obligate employees to assign all the rights to any inventions made by the employee in the course of his or her employment that are related to the employer's business or its research, or is made with its time, facilities, or equipment. In a typical situation, such agreements are signed at a time in advance of making the invention, which is normally the first day of employment. Usually, an employee invention agreement requires the assignment of both U.S. and foreign patent rights. Nearly all states allow employee invention agreements of this type to be enforced. The consideration for the agreement is the salary and other benefits provided to the employee. Some experts have opined that an employee invention agreement executed sometime after the commencement of the employment relationship is unenforceable unless the execution is in conjunction with either a raise or some other additional consideration.

You may ask, *What happens if my employee made a valuable invention related to my business using my equipment, but he never signed an employee invention agreement in advance? Can I demand that he assign the rights to my company?* In California, and in many other states, the employer has no legal right to demand the full rights to the invention or any resulting patent absent a binding express agreement with the employee obligating him or her to assign. Whether you could fire such an employee for refusing to assign his invention rights and escape liability for unlawful termination is a question of employment law, which is outside the scope of this book. Most states have a statute of frauds that requires any contract that is not to be performed within a year of its making to be in writing. Because many inventions are made by employees after their one-year anniversary of employment, the employer better make sure that it does not rely upon oral contracts with its employees to assign inventions made in the course of their employment.

"Shop Right" Doctrine

Some states have a safety net for companies that didn't have the foresight to have their employees execute an employment invention agreement. Under the so-called "shop right" doctrine, an employer gets a paid up, royalty-free license to use an invention made by an employee using its time, facilities, and equipment. However, the employee retains title to the invention and any resulting patent. The "shop right" generally limits the employer's right to use the invention to the employer's own facilities. The mere fact that an employer pays for the legal fees to obtain a patent on an invention does not give rise to any contractual obligation on the part of an employee to assign the underlying invention rights to the employer.

Hired-to-Invent

In California, and perhaps some other states, a few court cases have held that, even in the absence of any agreement, a company can insist on the assignment of invention rights from an employee or consultant where that person was hired to solve a specific problem and the invention does, in fact, solve that problem. This hired-to-invent exception is very narrow. The general rule is that the invention rights belong to the inventor if there is no express agreement to assign. California has gone further in protecting employees by enacting a statute that prohibits an employer from requiring, in a written employee invention agreement, that inventions be assigned to the employer if they are not related to the employer's business or research, and not made with its time, equipment, and facilities. For example, any employee invention agreement in California so broad as to require an employee of Microsoft to assign the inventor's rights to a fishing rod invention would be unenforceable to that extent.

Fiduciary Duty

There is one other important exception to the general rule that an employee owns all rights to an invention absent an express agreement to assign. Where the employee is also a corporate officer or director, the employee has what is known as a "fiduciary duty." This means that the employee cannot make an invention potentially valuable to the corporation and then exploit it outside the corporation for gain, even if the employee has not agreed to assign invention rights to the corporation.

Invention Disclosure

Most employee invention agreements also require the employee to keep company inventions and other trade secrets confidential. They may require the employee to fill out and submit to company management a written invention disclosure on any company-related inventions made during the course of employment. Large companies usually have a patent policy document given to engineers and other technical employees that explain the strong interest of the company in obtaining patents on its new products and the results of its research and development in order to maintain competitiveness. They typically spell out the process of filling out a preprinted invention disclosure form for review by a patent committee. Such patent policy documents explain that company patents help prevent copying, provide a basis for collecting royalties, and permit infringement disputes to be settled by cross-licensing.

In the early 1980s, the in-house general counsel for one of my clients received a letter from an outside patent attorney offering to license the rights to a patented invention for adding electronic warfare training capability to its very successful system for training Top Gun fighter pilots in actual air-to-air combat. Upon investigating the matter, the in-house counsel determined that the inventor was one of the company's current employees who had signed the company's standard employee invention agreement upon the commencement of his employment. The employee was notified of this fact and was requested to assign the patent rights to the company. Upon his refusal, his employment was terminated, and the company sued for breach of contract. The ex-employee's defense was that the invention was not related to his employer's business because its current air combat training system in service with the U.S. military had no electronic warfare training capability. However, the evidence showed that the inventor had used manuals on the company's system to develop a compatible add-on electronic warfare training feature. Internal company documents showed that it had planned to add this feature. The employee had also consulted with other company engineers on ways to implement his invention into the company's air combat training system. The result of the trial was, not surprisingly, a verdict in favor of the company, and pursuant to a court order, the ex-employee was required to execute an assignment of all his invention rights to his ex-employer. This was the first trial that I ever conducted in my legal career, and while I was proud of the favorable verdict, I realized that the trial had been the legal equivalent of shooting fish in a barrel.

From an employer's standpoint, it is important for the employee invention agreement to require the employee to list any inventions previously made by the employee that are, therefore, exempt from its terms. This will shift the burden to the employee to prove, later on, that an invention was made before he or she started working for your company.

Employee Financial Incentives

Many employee invention agreements will include financial incentives to the employee to disclose the invention to his or her employer.

These should be limited to flat bonuses, such as $500, on the filing of a U.S. patent application, and $500 on the issuance of a patent. Without such encouragement, many company engineers don't want to be bothered with filling out an invention disclosure form, talking to the company patent lawyer, and reviewing various draft patent applications. It's a good idea to provide a maximum bonus of $1,000 or some other figure that will be divided amongst two or more coinventors. Otherwise, employees tend to list lots of fellow employees as coinventors so they can all get a sizeable bonus.

From the employer's perspective, no employee invention agreement should ever promise the employee inventor a percentage of sales or profits derived from the invention. This is a ticket to a lawsuit. Not only does it create an accounting nightmare, but it inevitably will lead to a dispute over how profitable the invention turned out to be in the long run. At one time, a major U.S. aerospace company had such an employee agreement. That company got into a dispute over the amount of payments due several employee inventors for an invention that had to do with protecting the space shuttle during transport. The employees claimed that the aerospace company had grossly underaccounted for the amount of savings attributable to the use of their invention. At trial, the jury agreed, awarding the employees something in the neighborhood of $18 million. After the dust settled, no doubt a bunch of lawyers were fired or demoted, and the ill-fated incentive-laced employee invention agreement was replaced for new employees and amended for existing employees.

Procedure for When an Employee Leaves the Company

When an employee quits, retires, or is terminated, it is a good idea to have an exit interview with that person. During the exit interview, the person should be reminded of the terms of the employee invention agreement that he or she executed at the commencement of employment. The person should be asked if they have disclosed all such inventions to their employer. If not, curative steps can be taken at that time. While you cannot stop an employee from going to work for a competitor, they should not be allowed to give that new employer invention rights that belong to the ex-employer. Therefore, you should monitor U.S. patents obtained by your competitors listing your ex-employees as inventors. You may discover a patent that appears to relate to your product line or research and its filing date may be soon after the ex-employee left your company. If this is the case, an investigation should be conducted to determine if you can prove that the invention was likely made while the ex-employee was still working for your company. If so, you may want to demand an assignment from the ex-employee. It is most helpful if the employee invention agreement requires the assignment of inventions first conceived and/or reduced to practice during the term of employment. It is also good practice that when you hire new employees, to tell them they should not tell you details about inventions they made before coming to work for you. However, your employee invention agreement should require a brief listing of such inventions, in general terms, to avoid disputes later on about whether they belong to the employer, prior employer, or to the individual.

A sample Employee Invention and Nondisclosure Agreement is reproduced here. Also reproduced is a sample Invention Disclosure form and a sample Company Patent Policy.

Acme Advanced Products
Employee Invention and Nondisclosure Agreement

Name: Position:

1.   I am now or will be a paid employee of Acme Advanced Products, Inc., hereinafter referred to as "ACME."

2.   In the course of my job, I may make new contributions and inventions* of value to ACME.

3.   This Agreement concerns all contributions and inventions conceived or made by me alone or with others:
     a.   while I am employed by ACME; and
     b.   that relate to the business or research of ACME or result from tasks performed by me for ACME.

4.   As to these contributions and inventions, I agree:
     a.   to disclose them promptly to ACME;
     b.   they will be the sole property of ACME and I will assign them to ACME; and
     c.   to assist ACME in obtaining patents and other intellectual property protection in all countries, at ACME's expense.

5.   I further agree:
     a.   to not disclose ACME's trade secrets** to outsiders; and
     b.   to keep written records of my work for ACME and to deliver them to ACME's management upon request.

6.   All inventions that I have already conceived or reduced to practice that I claim to be excluded from the scope of this Agreement are listed below.

7.   I understand that copyright in all computer programs that I shall write, prepare, modify, edit, debug, outline, or otherwise work on during the course of my employment with ACME shall belong to ACME under the "work for hire" doctrine [17 USC Section 201(b)].

8.   So long as I am employed by ACME and for two years thereafter, I will not disrupt, damage, impair, or interfere with the business of ACME whether by way of interfering with or raiding its employees, disrupting its relationships with customers, agents, representatives, or vendors, or otherwise. I understand that I am not restricted from being employed by or engaged in a competing business after termination of my employment with ACME.

9.   Upon termination of my employment with ACME, I agree to participate in an exit interview with representatives of ACME to discuss my continuing obligations regarding ACME's trade secrets and otherwise under this Agreement.

10. This Agreement is made under and shall be construed according to the laws of the State of California.

11. This Agreement does not apply to any invention excluded by Section 2870 of the California Labor Code, a copy of which is attached hereto.

By:

(Date)   (Employee's Name)

*   "Contributions and inventions" includes all ideas of products, methods, or services, whether or not patentable.

**   "Trade secrets" include all confidential information and ideas relating to ACME's business, such as computer programs, customer lists, designs, and specifications.

California Labor Code § 2870
(January 1, 1991)

Section 2870.   Employee agreements; assignment of rights

(a)   Any provision in an employment agreement which provides that an employee shall assign, or offer to assign, any of his or her rights in an invention to his or her employer shall not apply to an invention that the employee developed entirely on his or her own time without using the employer's equipment, supplies, facilities, or trade secret information except for those inventions that either:

1) Relate at the time of conception or reduction to practice of the invention to the employer's business, or actual or demonstrably anticipated research or development of the employer; or

2) Result from any work performed by the employee for the employer.

(b)   To the extent a provision in an employment agreement purports to require an employee to assign an invention otherwise excluded from being required to be assigned under subdivision (a), the provision is against the public policy of this state and is unenforceable.

Acme Advanced Products
Invention Disclosure No. XX

The invention herein described was evolved during the course of my employment and is being submitted pursuant to the terms of the Employee Invention and Nondisclosure Agreement. (See instructions for filling out this form on next page.)

1. **Invention Title:**

2. **Inventor(s) Name(s) and Addresses:** (*including middle initial*)

Name: _____ Citizenship: _____
Address: _____
Name: _____ Citizenship: _____
Address: _____
Name: _____ Citizenship: _____
Address: _____

3. **Purpose of the Invention:** _____

4. **Conception:**
   ✎ Date Invention Conceived _____, ____.
   ✎ Date Disclosure Written _____, ____.

5. **Reduction to Practice** (if any):

    ✎ Date of Construction of Device_____, _____.
    ✎ Date Device Completed_____, _____.
    ✎ Date Device Tested_____, _____.

6. **Sale, Use, or Publication:**
    ✎ Date Product Incorporating Invention First Offered for Sale

    ___, _____.

    ✎ Date Device Incorporating Invention First Used _____, _____.
    ✎ Date Invention First Published_____, _____.

7. **Brief Description of Invention** (attach previously prepared description, drawings, etc., when available):

_____

8. **Prior Art:** The prior art that is the closest to the subject invention is listed below. (Cite U.S. patents, publications, articles, and/or brochures when available.)

_____

_____

9. **Sign Full Name(s)** (*including middle initial*):

_____ Date: _____
_____ Date: _____
_____ Date: _____

10. **Witness:** The invention was disclosed to me by the above inventor(s) on the date indicated. The description was reviewed by me, and I understand the same:

_____ Date: _____

Instructions for Filling Out Invention Disclosure Form

Title of Invention: The title should describe the novel functions and/or structure of the device, preferably in 10 words or less. Do not use only a proposed trademark or internal code name. These may be given in addition to a descriptive title to help identify the project.

Inventor(s) Name(s): This/these should be the names of all the people, both employees of the company and outside individuals, who creatively contributed to the making of the invention. Note that the mere recognition of the problem does not make a person an inventor. For example, the mere idea of making an illuminated sprinkler is not an invention. The person who designs a sprinkler with built-in LEDs is the inventor.

Purpose of the Invention: In one sentence, describe what the ultimate goal of the invention is in terms of functionality. The purpose of the invention should not be described in terms of simpler, more reliable, more efficient, and other laudatory terms.

Conception: The date of conception is the date on which the inventor(s) first came up with the idea.

Reduction to Practice: This term refers to the actual physical making of a model or prototype that embodies the invention previously conceived.

Sale, Use, or Publication: The offer for sale date is the date that customers, or prospective customers, were first contacted about a potential new product, regardless of whether the product was fully tested or developed. The first use date normally refers to the first date that an actual physical embodiment of the invention was used on a nonexperimental basis. Publication of an invention normally refers to an unrestricted oral or written dissemination of details of the invention under circumstances where no obligation of confidentiality exists.

Brief Description of the Invention: Give a general description of the structure and function of the preferred design for the invention. If blueprints or drawings are available, representative copies should be attached to the Invention Disclosure form. The same is true of photographs.

Prior Art: This refers to any publications, such as existing U.S. and foreign patents, whether owned by ACME or not; trade publications; trade literature; technical books; etc. Copies of the most relevant prior art should be attached to the Invention Disclosure form.

Names: Each inventor should sign and date the Invention Disclosure form.

Witness: A coworker, who is not one of the coinventors, should read the Invention Disclosure form, and then sign and date the same at the end. Notarization is not required.

Acme Advanced Products
Company Patent Policy

Introduction

Acme Advanced Products, Inc. ("ACME") is the world's leading manufacturer of electrical connectors for the automotive industry. The competitive nature of our markets requires that we constantly seek to develop new products in order to effectively compete with Amp, Molex, Berg, and others. Many of the new products that we develop can best be protected through patents, but only if timely action is taken. Neither copyright nor trade secret protection can be used to prevent others from independently developing products similar to ours. The names and/or logos under which we sell our products can be protected as trademarks.

Employee Invention Agreement

All employees of ACME are required to sign an agreement covering their responsibilities to the company with regard to inventions and confidential information. The agreement provides that all inventions conceived during employment that are related to our business belong to ACME. Under this agreement, trade secrets and other information of a proprietary nature are not to be disclosed to outsiders unless pursuant to a previously executed confidential disclosure agreement that has been approved by an officer of ACME.

Why Patents Are Important to Acme

Only by developing new products, and by improving existing products now being marketed, can our company continue to grow and prosper. To develop and maintain a position of leadership, ACME must look to its staff for ideas. Prolonged and expensive development programs are sometimes required before new products can be commercially exploited. If ACME had to seek new ideas outside of the company, substantial royalty payments would usually be involved. These would represent added cost to the products offered by our company, thereby tending to reduce our competitiveness.

Company-owned patents serve many purposes. First and foremost, patents are essential to prevent copying of the products that we develop. Patents are a tangible product of the research and development efforts that are supported by our company. They also add to the professional standing of the technical people involved and, by extension, to ACME's reputation. They also serve as a basis for negotiating where we desire to obtain a license to patent rights held by others. Company-owned patents also enable ACME to license others, and, therefore, provide a basis for royalty income. Patents also protect ACME against a charge of infringement should others develop and patent inventions in areas in which we are also active.

What Is a Patent?

A U.S. patent is a grant to an inventor by the United States Government of the right to exclude others for a limited time from making, using, or selling the patented invention. The period of exclusivity granted by a patent is the reward for providing new ideas to our society. Utility patents are granted for inventions that include new processes, machines, articles of manufacture, and compositions of matter. Design patents only protect the ornamental outer appearance of a product. By way of contrast, infringement of a utility patent is determined by reading the claims at the end of the patent and comparing the words against the structure of an accused device.

Foreign patent laws differ from country to country in the kind of protection they afford. From time to time, ACME may decide to file patent applications in foreign countries.

A utility patent application consists of a specification, drawings, and claims. The specification is a description of at least one preferred embodiment of the invention. It must contain sufficient detail to enable someone skilled in the pertinent art to make the invention without undue experimentation. The drawings are typically prepared by a patent draftsman based on sketches, blueprints, or other materials supplied by the inventors. The claims define the boundaries of the patent grant. They also define what is, and what is not, an infringement.

It is not necessary that an invention be built or tested before a patent application is filed.

Patentable Inventions

To be patentable in the United States, an invention must be useful, novel, and nonobvious compared to the prior art.

Almost all inventions meet the usefulness requirement. Useful does not mean that the invention is practical.

In general, the novelty requirement means that the invention has not been known before. In the United States, a patent application must be filed within one year of the first offer for sale, public use, or publication of an invention, the one year commencing from the earliest of the foregoing events to occur. Where ACME desires to obtain foreign patent protection, a U.S. patent application must be filed before the first nonconfidential disclosure of the invention, and there is no one-year grace period as is the case where only U.S. patent rights are desired.

The nonobviousness requirement for patentability is based upon the subjective determination of a patent examiner. He or she compares the differences between what is being claimed and what the prior art shows or suggests. Many engineers and scientists erroneously come to the conclusion that a new method or device is obvious on the basis of hindsight reconstruction. Often, an employee's reaction to seeing another's invention is that he or she just as easily could have made the invention, or perhaps one even better. In the end analysis, it is preferable to have patent attorneys employed by ACME express an opinion as to patentability.

Determining Who Inventors Are

In the United States, a patent application must be filed in the name of the true inventor or inventors. An inventor is one who makes a positive contribution to at least one claim of the patent application. If two people work on the same project and one merely carries out the ideas and suggestions of the other, a joint invention usually does not result. Each person must add something creative to the claimed invention if he or she is to be considered a true coinventor under the U.S. patent laws.

It is not necessary that any particular feature or aspect of an invention that is claimed in a U.S. patent application be solely attributable to a particular person in order for that person to be a coinventor. Frequently, inventions are conceived in a brainstorming session where the precise contribution of each participant is not discernible.

In difficult cases, it may be necessary for ACME to have its patent attorneys explore the inventorship issue.

What You Can Do to Protect Your Invention

It is essential for employees to make regular notations of ideas, concepts, and improvements, preferably in notebooks. Each page, or at least a group of pages relating to a single idea, in an employee's notebook should be signed and dated by the person keeping it, and signed and dated by a coworker after reviewing the same. Notarization is not necessary.

If any of ACME's staff believes that he or she has come up with an idea, concept, or design of possible significant interest to the company, an Acme Invention Disclosure form should be properly filled out and turned into ACME's engineering manager. The invention disclosure will be promptly evaluated and the employee advised of its disposition.

In addition to providing a vehicle for permitting ACME's patent attorneys to consider an invention, an invention disclosure that is signed and dated by both the inventor and a witness provides evidence of the date of the invention. This evidence may be valuable in disputes with third parties over priority of inventorship.

Consideration of Invention
Disclosures and Filing of Patent Applications

When an employee of ACME submits a completed Invention Disclosure form to our engineering manager, it will be docketed and duly considered. ACME may engage outside patent attorneys to evaluate the invention. In some cases, a patentability search may be conducted. The inventor should also submit and/or note the closest prior art of which he or she is aware. This information will be passed on to our outside patent attorneys for consideration.

When a patent application is to be filed, the patent attorneys engaged by ACME will prepare a draft of the application. In some cases, the patent attorneys may make inquires to the inventors directly to obtain additional technical disclosure as well as the inventors' comments about the prior art. After review of the patent application by the ACME inventors, the patent application will be revised, if necessary, and filed at the earliest possible opportunity.

Once the application is filed in the U.S. Patent and Trademark Office, it is assigned to one of approximately 1,600 patent examiners. The examiner will have particular expertise in the area to which the invention pertains. The U.S. Patent and Trademark Office will perform its own patentability search regardless of whether ACME performed its own search. It is typical that there is a series of Office Actions from the U.S. Patent and Trademark Office setting forth rejections over prior art and, on occasion, objecting to certain formal matters. In order to overcome prior art rejections, the patent attorneys prepare and file amendments, distinguishing the claimed invention from the prior art patents and/or narrowing the scope of the claims to articulate features that distinguish over the cited prior art patents.

If the prosecution is successful, then the government will issue a formal notice of allowance. Upon payment of the necessary government fees, the application issues as a patent. As a result of the GATT treaty, U.S. utility patents based on applications filed on or after June 1, 1995, will have a term of 20 years from the application filing date, instead of the traditional 17 years from the date of grant. The term of a design patent is 14 years from the date of grant.

Conclusion

This policy document is not meant to be exhaustive, but to provide relatively general and useful information on the subject of inventions and patents. Further inquires are encouraged and may be directed to ACME's engineering manager.

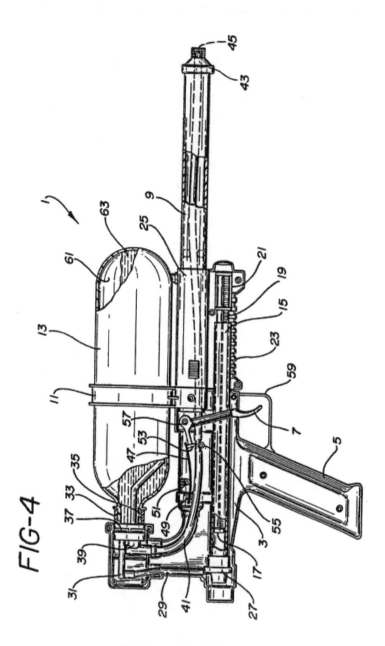

FIG-4

U.S. Patent No. 5,074,437
"Pinch Trigger Pump Water Gun"
Granted December 24, 1991
(Super Soaker squirt gun manufactured by Laramie Corp.)

CHAPTER 17

How to Select
a Patent Attorney

A fter reading the preceding chapters, I think you will agree that it is indispensable to employ an experienced patent attorney if you are interested in obtaining a worthwhile U.S. patent. In order to be a patent attorney, an individual must have at least an undergraduate degree in engineering, physics, chemistry, or some other technical field, or equivalent technical experience. The USPTO tries to ensure that patent attorneys have the scientific knowledge required to communicate with inventors regarding their fields of endeavor. Some patent attorneys who practice in the pharmaceutical and biotech fields even have Ph.D. or M.D. degrees, along with undergraduate and law degrees.

Patent Attorney Credentials

In addition to a technical degree, to be a patent attorney, one must graduate from law school and must take and pass the bar of one of the 50 states or the District of Columbia. In addition, the candidate must take and pass a very tough federal patent bar exam. The USPTO will not allow a candidate to sit for the patent bar exam unless he or she has at least a technical undergraduate degree or equivalent technical experience. USPTO examiners with at least four years of experience at the USPTO are eligible to have the requirement of passing the patent bar examination waived. An attorney in good standing duly admitted to a state bar and/or the District of Columbia bar who has taken and passed the patent bar exam is officially called a "registered patent lawyer" or "registered patent attorney." Individuals who have the requisite technical degree or equivalent technical experience but are not regular attorneys may also take the federal patent bar exam. If they pass that exam, they are called "registered patent agents." Usually, patent agents only work for large corporations or large patent law firms. This is because their handling of matters outside patent prosecution would be considered the unauthorized practice of law in all states. Matters outside of patent prosecution would include drafting assignments, licenses, or other contracts, and appearing in court.

While there are close to 1 million attorneys in the United States, there are probably only 20,000 or 30,000 patent attorneys in active practice. Each patent attorney or agent is given a unique registration number that must be listed next to his or her signature on all correspondence with the USPTO. Registration numbers are sequentially granted to those passing the patent bar examination. While newly awarded patent attorney registration numbers are currently in the high 40,000s, most patent attorneys with registration numbers under 20,000 are deceased or retired.

Patent attorneys are typically located in the major metropolitan areas of the United States near centers of industry and technology. Many of them work for corporations or the federal government and are not available to handle matters in private practice. Considering the ongoing worldwide technology revolution, it should come as no surprise that patent attorneys are usually in demand, particularly experienced patent attorneys. At the same time that demand for patent law services has increased, many young engineers and scientists have opted against becoming patent attorneys. They dislike the grueling years of law school and the prospect of taking and passing two bar exams. For example, California has a state bar exam pass rate of between 50 and 60 percent, and the federal patent bar exam has a pass rate of anywhere from 20 to 60 percent. Young engineers and scientists also disdain the lost income from three additional years of schooling, not to mention law school tuition. By the time they do the math, they see that it would take many years to make up for the lost income and law school expenses, even if they passed both bar exams, which is no sure thing. Thereafter, they get to apprentice in a law firm for five more years where, heaven forbid, they won't receive any stock options! You get the picture.

Applying Pro Se

Before talking about how to select a patent attorney, let me first talk about the "do it yourself" alternative. As in all legal matters, an inventor is legally entitled to represent himself or herself pro se before the USPTO in seeking a patent. But the old adage "he who acts as his own attorney has a fool for a client" is nowhere more true than in the field of patents. In nearly 30 years of practicing patent law, I have never seen a patent that was written and prosecuted by someone not registered to practice before the USPTO that was worth the paper it was written on. The drafting of the claims, the drafting of the specification to support those claims, and the responses to examiner's actions are critical not only in determining whether a patent will be granted in the first place, but also in determining whether the claims provide the broadest scope of coverage and have the highest chance of surviving a validity challenge.

It is true that the USPTO examiner will try to give extra assistance to a pro se applicant. After recommending that the inventor retain a registered patent attorney or agent, the patent examiner may draft a suggested claim. However, the examiner cannot suggest adding new description or drawings, even though the inventor-drafted specification may be woefully inadequate. Such additions cannot be made, as this would violate the prohibition against the introduction of new matter. New disclosure cannot be added to an already pending application because priority is measured by what was disclosed and claimed at the time of filing. Furthermore, any claim drafted by the examiner is likely to be overly narrow and will not give the inventor the full breadth of protection to which he or she is entitled considering the relevant prior art. The examiner is not an advocate for the inventor, but rather a government employee charged with the responsibility of lawfully moving applications through the examination process.

For many years, I was a principal in a patent law firm. Like other patent law firms, we tried to hire the best and brightest candidates. Roughly, half of the new patent attorneys we hired and extensively trained actually panned out; that is, they had the aptitude to eventually do a good job on patent prosecution in a reasonable amount of time. Even then, we had to invest three to five years of intensive training just to find out if each new patent law trainee could hack it. My patent attorney colleagues from around the country have told me they have had the same experience. Our new hires were very bright people who had engineering and law degrees and passed two tough bar exams. Is it any wonder that a layperson cannot possibly hope to do a competent job obtaining a U.S. patent on his or her own?

Employing a Patent Attorney

Let us go back to the only practical alternative, which is employing a registered patent attorney (or patent agent) to handle your patent matters. Only these individuals are legally permitted to represent inventors before the USPTO. Regular attorneys are not legally allowed to represent clients before the USPTO, although they may handle patent litigation in federal court. The U.S. Government has preempted the area of patents, and, therefore, none of the 50 states may pass laws purporting to protect inventions or that in any away abridge or interfere with a U.S. patent. The U.S. Supreme Court has ruled that a state may not prohibit a registered patent attorney from performing legal services in connection with representing an inventor before the USPTO even if that patent attorney is not a member of the bar of the state in which the services are being performed. This is a great advantage for older patent attorneys because it allows them to semi-retire in any state and keep prosecuting patents for long-time clients, without having to take a new state bar examination.

While many registered patent agents are well qualified to prosecute patent applications, in some cases, an individual inventor or small business owner would be better served to retain a registered patent attorney. As already mentioned, a patent agent is not legally permitted to draft assignments, licenses, confidential disclosure agreements, and other contracts, or give advice regarding the same, and you are likely to need such advice. Furthermore, you may need advice about other forms of intellectual property, such as trademarks, copyrights, and trade secrets. Patent agents generally have minimal knowledge of these subjects, and they are not legally permitted to advise clients about them. In addition, patent agents cannot represent clients in patent infringement litigation, so they cannot help you if you need to enforce your patent or defend yourself or your business against a charge of patent infringement.

Now then, exactly how do you select a good patent attorney? The same way you select any other professional, such as a doctor, dentist, or accountant. Most people cannot rate law schools. So ask for recommendations from other business owners and general attorneys. If the same name keeps turning up, chances are that this patent attorney has a good reputation that is well deserved. Don't just pick a patent attorney out of the yellow pages because you like the sound of his or her name or because the bragging in their ads sounds impressive. The patent attorney you retain should have a minimum of at least five years of patent law experience, and, more preferably, at least 10 years of experience. Ask your prospective patent attorney how many patent applications he or she has prosecuted. It should be at least 50. You can search the free USPTO patent database on the Internet by attorney or firm name and get a list of all the patents handled by that firm or patent attorney since 1976. This will give you some idea of the technologies that they have handled. If the firm or patent attorney represents Fortune 500 companies, chances are they are well qualified. These companies typically have in-house patent attorneys who know the best outside patent attorneys and are able to hire whomever they want. However, don't necessarily dismiss a patent attorney even if he or she has no such clients. The patent attorney may prefer not to work for large entities and may instead prefer to work with start-ups.

You will find good patent attorneys in the intellectual property departments of large general practice law firms, in patent law firms (also known as "patent boutiques"), and in solo practice. If you decide to use an experienced patent attorney in a law firm, get that patent attorney to agree in advance to carefully scrutinize any patent application prepared on your invention by a junior patent attorney or patent agent in his or her firm. Also, try to get a written fixed-fee quote for the cost of preparing and filing the application. Insist on a written fee agreement that spells out what you will be charged for, as well as indicates the patent attorney's hourly rate. Also, remember that once the patent preparation process starts, if you keep giving your patent attorney new invention disclosure and/or additional alternate embodiments, this may increase the cost beyond the fixed-fee quote.

Read the draft patent application carefully before executing it, and be sure that it meets the best mode requirement discussed in Chapter 5. Try to include as many alternative embodiments as you can. Review the patent drawings carefully and be sure to list as an inventor anyone involved in the conception of the subject matter of any of the claims. Advise your patent attorney about any facts raising any potential U.S. statutory bars and make sure you get the application filed in the USPTO before the first potential U.S. statutory bar. File the U.S. application before the first nonconfidential disclosure of your invention if you want to preserve your foreign patent rights. Make sure you give your patent attorney all of the closest prior art so that he or she can take it into consideration in drafting your patent application and comply with the duty of disclosure by filing it in the USPTO with an Information Disclosure Statement (IDS). If you later discover relevant prior art, forward it to your patent attorney as soon as possible.

A word about legal fees is in order at this point. In one of the do-it-yourself books on patents that I reviewed, the author said that there are more patent attorneys than there is patent work. There are generally not enough good patent attorneys to handle all of the available patent work. He also said that if you decide that you need to hire a patent attorney, don't talk to one unless you are given an initial free conference. I don't know a single experienced patent attorney who will consult with an inventor for free. They have plenty of paying work and don't have to give away their time and expertise. If you find a patent attorney who will give away his or her time, he or she may not be very experienced or very good. There are probably some good patent attorneys who give free initial conferences, but not many. By and large, legal services are like any other product or service when it comes to pricing; namely, you get what you pay for.

Forget about writing the patent application yourself and asking a patent attorney merely to edit the same in the hopes of saving on legal fees. Most experienced patent attorneys will decline to be involved in such projects. In almost all cases, I have not been able to incorporate any patent application text that inventors have written on their own. It would usually cost just as much to have an experienced patent attorney rewrite an amateur patent application than it would cost the patent attorney to write it from scratch. The latter product would almost always be the superior legal instrument. The best way to proceed is to gather any existing documentation and drawings, and the most relevant prior art patents and publications, and discuss them in person with your patent attorney. He or she will help you identify the potentially patentable invention and will ask for any additional invention disclosure that is needed to prepare a suitable patent application directed to that specific invention.

It will undoubtedly cost you many thousands of dollars to seek and obtain a well-drafted patent on your invention. However, patent legal costs are a small fraction of what it will cost to develop the invention for commercialization, to make the tooling necessary to manufacture the product, and to market the product. Anything worth doing is worth doing correctly. Take advantage of the one-year grace period under the U.S. patent law to find out if your invention justifies the cost of seeking a patent in the first place.

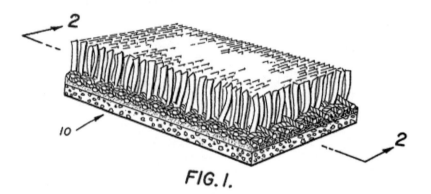

2

10

2

FIG. I.

U.S. Patent No. 3,332,828
"Monofilament Ribbon Pile Product"
Granted July 25, 1967
(Astroturf carpet material made by
Monsanto Co.)

CHAPTER 18

Preserving Evidence to Prove Priority of Invention

I t is very important to remember that in the United States, generally the first person to make an invention is entitled to a U.S. patent, provided that the person files within the one-year grace period measured from the first to occur of an offer for sale, public use, or publication of the invention. Most foreign countries adhere to a first-to-file patent rule. In the United States, a person can file a U.S. application on his or her invention and obtain a valid patent even though he or she filed after another person filed on the same invention. In order to establish priority, a person should be in a position to prove that he or she *made* the invention first.

The United States is under continual international pressure to abandon the first-to-invent aspect of its patent system in favor of the nearly universal first-to-file rule, but so far, sufficient inducements from other countries have not been offered. The United States has considered going to a first-to-file patent system, while retaining its long tradition of giving the inventor a one-year grace period within which to file, the one year commencing from the earliest offer for sale, public use, or publication. However, some experts feel that this would lead to many complex litigations to determine if one patent applicant derived his or her invention from another inventor.

As discussed in Chapter 1, an invention is *made* in the United States when both conception and reduction to practice have occurred. Conception is the mental part of thinking up the solution to the problem to the point that it would be operable for its intended purpose if physically put into practice. Reduction to practice can be either constructive or actual. Constructive reduction to practice is achieved once a U.S. patent application has been filed on the invention. Actual reduction to practice occurs when the invention has been physically demonstrated to operate as intended. The U.S. patent law gives equal weight to both types of reduction to practice. The U.S. patent application can be filed before the invention has ever been demonstrated to work as conceived.

Determining Priority

In determining priority between competing U.S. patent applications claiming the same invention, or a U.S. patent application and an issued patent claiming the invention, in general, the first person to conceive and reduce to practice will prevail. Of course, it is a fundamental rule that each person who files a patent application must be a true inventor, and must not have derived the claimed invention from another person's efforts. The USPTO has a special proceeding called an interference whose function is to determine priority of invention in such circumstances. Three administrative law judges make the decision with a right of appeal to the U.S. Court of Appeals for the Federal Circuit. In rare cases, a defendant in a patent infringement lawsuit may claim that the patent asserted against it is invalid because the defendant or some third party was the first inventor. In such cases, the judge or jury will decide the priority of invention issue.

An inventor who is second in time to conceive but first to reduce to practice can win an interference if the inventor who was first to conceive fails to establish diligence in reducing the invention to practice from a time just prior to the date of conception by the second to conceive. If the first to conceive reduces the invention to practice before the reduction to practice date of the second to conceive, the diligence or lack thereof by the first to conceive is irrelevant. Diligence is regular work toward building a prototype of the claimed apparatus or making the claimed composition. It should not be surprising that many times people are independently working on the same problem at the same time. This is because problems tend to materialize chronologically, and persons skilled in the art begin to devote their efforts toward solving them when they become apparent. For example, when the EPA made low volume (1.6 gallon) gravity-operated flush toilets mandatory, many inventions were made over the next few years on new flapper valve and flush valve mechanisms that would ensure proper flushing of such toilets.

Because ownership of valuable patent rights may ultimately depend upon proving priority of invention, it is important to preserve evidence of both your conception and your reduction to practice. If there is a time lag between your date of conception and your date of reduction to practice, then it is also important to preserve evidence of your diligent efforts to reduce your conception to practice. The U.S. Court of Appeals for the Federal Circuit has established strict rules that prescribe the type of evidence necessary to establish priority of invention. In general, *corroborating evidence* is needed to prove an inventor's dates of conception and actual reduction to practice, along with the inventor's diligence. Constructive reduction to practice is easily proven by showing the filing date of your U.S. patent application.

Corroborating Evidence

Corroborating evidence is testimony besides the inventor's own testimony or physical evidence, such as documents or models that can be authenticated and validated date-wise by others, that support or confirm what the inventor has sworn to in terms of his activities and the dates thereof. For example, an inventor might testify that he built and successfully tested his first laser-guided chain saw on New Year's Day, 1990. However, the inventor's testimony, standing alone, would not prove this activity on that date. The inventor might be able to produce a photograph of his prototype being used to cut down a tree. If the photograph was taken by a neighbor on that day, and the neighbor could authenticate the photograph and date as the same in sworn testimony, the inventor would have proof of an actual reduction to practice on January 1, 1990, provided the photograph and the neighbor's testimony indicated that the claimed laser guide was in the chain saw and successfully operated for its intended purpose. The law requires corroborating evidence to prove dates of conception, reduction to practice, and diligence because of a concern that a party claiming inventorship rights might be tempted to describe his or her actions in an unjustifiably self-serving manner. Simply stated, the purpose of requiring corroboration is to prevent fraud by insisting upon independent confirmation of the inventor's testimony.

I recall a case in which I was involved where a party had obtained a U.S. patent on goggles with overlapping, transparent, tear-away strips worn by motocross riders so that they could pull them away each time mud splashed on the goggles. Priority of inventorship became an issue when the patent was asserted against a major manufacturer. An issue arose as to whether the entries in an engineering notebook were genuine in terms of the dates indicated thereon. The notebook was the well-known bound type with a black-and-white speckled color. It turns out that these have serial numbers printed in them, so if the purported handwritten dates in the entries predated the date of manufacture of the notebook, it could be proven that the entries had been backdated. The manufacturer of the notebook could readily supply the date of manufacture based on the serial number. I think the case settled.

Courts apply a "rule of reason" analysis to determine whether an inventor's testimony has been sufficiently corroborated. All pertinent evidence is examined to determine if the inventor's story is credible. Documentary or physical evidence that is made contemporaneously with the inventive process provides the most reliable and convincing proof that what the inventor is saying is true. This kind of evidence avoids the risk of litigation-inspired fabrication or exaggeration. Post-invention oral testimony is suspect, as there may be a motive inspired by litigation to corroborate the inventor's testimony.

Invention Disclosure Document

Fortunately, the USPTO has made it easy to preserve evidence of your date of conception by establishing the Invention Disclosure Document program. For a fee of $10, the USPTO will accept and preserve for a period of two years a simple description of an invention written by the inventor. The Invention Disclosure Document, including drawings and sketches, must be on white letter-size paper or European size (A4) paper, written on only one side, with each page numbered. No particular form of description is required. An Invention Disclosure Document is typically prepared by the inventor and is rather informal. It need not include patent claims, although its description may include a minimal number of reference numerals that appear in the drawings. Attachments such as videotapes and models are not permitted. The Invention Disclosure Document must be accompanied by a separate letter signed by the inventor stating that he or she is the inventor and requesting that the papers be received under the Invention Disclosure Document program. The following statement is recommended:

> The undersigned, being the inventor of the disclosed invention, requests that the enclosed papers be accepted under the Invention Disclosure Document program, and that they be preserved for a period of two years.

A Disclosure Document request form (PTO/SB/95) can be used as a cover letter and can be printed off the USPTO Website at *www.uspto.gov*.

Within a few weeks, the USPTO will acknowledge receipt of an Invention Disclosure Document. The USPTO prefers that two copies be filed so that one can be returned with a date stamp and a unique number. The inventor should supply a self-addressed, stamped return envelope to facilitate receipt of the acknowledgment copy. The USPTO will also send a warning telling you that the Invention Disclosure Document is not a patent application and that the inventor must still file a patent application within the one-year statutory grace period. The two-year period of retention of the Invention Disclosure Document is not a "grace period," but merely the period within which the USPTO will keep a copy of that document in confidence. If a U.S. patent application is filed within this period, it may reference the Invention Disclosure Document, which will then be saved in the patent application file. The Invention Disclosure Document will be destroyed unless it is referred to by its title, filing date, and number in a separate letter in a related U.S. patent application filed within the two-year period.

An Invention Disclosure Document may be mailed to the USPTO at the following address:

Commissioner for Patents
PO Box 1450
Alexandria, Virginia 22313-1450

The Great Lakes Patent and Trademark Center at the Detroit Public Library (GLPTC) is the USPTO's authorized agent for accepting documents filed under the Disclosure Document program. This eliminates much of the delay in USPTO processing. The address of the GLPTC is:

Great Lakes Patent and Trademark Center
Detroit Public Library
5201 Woodward Avenue (second level)
Detroit, Michigan 48202

A numbered and dated Invention Disclosure Document acknowledged by the USPTO can be submitted in any proceeding and will be accepted as corroborating evidence of the matters set forth in it. As such, it can be extremely valuable in winning a priority battle in the USPTO or in court litigation. It avoids the necessity of showing your invention to someone that you may not trust in order to establish a future corroborating witness. I have also heard of inventors filing an Invention Disclosure Document themselves, and then stating to others, including potential investors, that they have "filed on their invention in the USPTO." While technically a true statement, such a representation could be held to be misleading by a court if an investor should later decide that he was wrongfully induced into backing a venture to commercialize the invention based on the misimpression that a regular utility patent application was already pending. Nevertheless, such a statement in other contexts may not be illegal or unethical and may help an inventor gain credibility and access at a time when his finances do not permit him to bear the cost of preparing and filing a regular utility patent application.

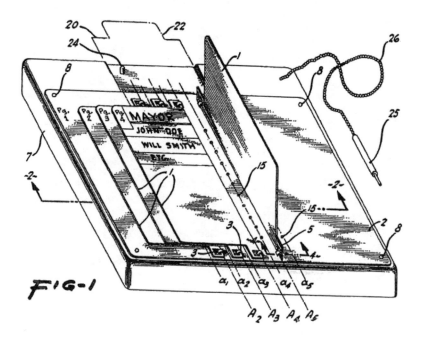

FIG-1

U.S. Patent No. 3,201,038
"Data Registering Device"
Granted August 17, 1965
(punch ballot machine used in Florida
in Bush v. Gore presidential election)

CHAPTER 19

Patents and Politics

T he USPTO is a federal agency within the Department of Commerce, which itself is part of the executive branch of the U.S. Government. The USPTO is subject to the policy direction of the Secretary of Commerce, but otherwise retains responsibility for decisions regarding the management and administration of its operations. Supposedly, the USPTO exercises independent control of its budget allocations and expenditures, personnel decisions and processes, and procurement. By statute, the USPTO is responsible for the granting of patents, the registering of trademarks, and the dissemination of information to the public concerning these forms of legal protection. So far, so good. However, just as you might expect, like any federal agency with thousands of civil service employees and an annual budget of approximately $1 billion, the USPTO gets caught up in its share of political battles.

USPTO Hierarchy

The head of the USPTO was formerly called the commissioner of patents, and then later, the commissioner of patents and trademarks. For some reason, in recent years, the head of the USPTO got the official title of "Under Secretary of Commerce for Intellectual Property and Director

195

of the United States Patent and Trademark Office." The director of the USPTO is nominated by the president and must be confirmed by the United States Senate. Each time there is a change of administration in the White House, a new director of the USPTO comes on board, along with a new secretary of state, secretary of commerce, and so forth. In the latter half of the 20th century, the commissioner of patents was typically a former chief patent counsel of a big industrial company, such as General Electric. His nomination and confirmation were never controversial. Towards the tail end of the 20th century there was a shift, and the head of the USPTO began to come out of the political ranks. At the time of the writing of this book, the current director of the USPTO is a former Republican congressman from California. Political tensions have affected the USPTO on both the domestic and international fronts.

Patent Law and Foreign Countries

Internationally, the United States has been under pressure to harmonize its patent laws with those of other foreign countries. Foreign governments and companies have long complained about peculiar aspects of our system, which they feel put them at a competitive disadvantage. The United States altered its patent laws in the mid-1990s as part of the process of ratifying the GATT treaty in order to change its patent term from 17 years measured from the date of grant to 20 years measured from the earliest filing date. Also, U.S. patent applications are now automatically published 18 months from filing, regardless of whether a patent is ever granted, unless a nonpublication request is timely filed under very limited circumstances. These changes were implemented to reduce the likelihood of so-called "submarine patents" being granted. These were U.S. patents based on applications filed decades ago, but kept secret and pending for many years in order for technology to catch up, so that they would be issued at a time when great royalties could be extracted. (See page 122 for more on "submarine patents.") Jerome Lemmelson was infamous for filing applications on bar code reading and vision robotics, which he kept pending for as long as four decades by filing a seemingly endless stream of continuation applications. Finally, when the patents issued, he asserted them against several Japanese automakers, and gained hundreds of millions in royalties, which he then used as a war chest to fund many lawsuits against companies that wouldn't sign a blanket license agreement.

Foreign governments and companies have long detested the system in the United States that awards the patent to the first inventor instead of the first to file a patent application on the invention. This sometimes leads to complex and lengthy legal proceedings called *interferences*. Foreigners used to be at a distinct disadvantage in such proceedings. Their inventive actions outside the United States were given little, if any, evidentiary weight in determining who was first to mentally think up the invention, how much activity was engaged in to make the invention work, and when the invention was successfully turned into a functioning prototype, process, or composition. Recent amendments to the U.S. patent law have leveled the playing field in terms of the ability of foreigners to rely on their activities outside the United States in seeking to win a priority battle. Nevertheless, the United States has steadfastly refused to abandon its "first-to-invent" patent system.

In return for modifying its patent laws, the United States has won some concessions from foreign governments. Usually, these have been pledges to more strictly enforce their own domestic patent laws against pirates. At the time of writing this book, one major controversy is the alleged unlawful production in China of mass numbers of DVD players by local manufacturers that allegedly do not have the required licenses under the Chinese patents owned by U.S. and European companies.

Patent Law in the United States

Domestically, beginning around 1990, the USPTO became a pawn in various federal budget battles, and the outcome has been a diversion of substantial fees collected by the USPTO from inventors and patent owners to pay for federal programs wholly unrelated to the day-to-day operations of examining patent and trademark applications and educating the public about this process. During my career as a patent attorney, the cost of obtaining and holding a patent for its full term has increased more than 4,000 percent! It used to cost less than $200 in U.S. Government fees. As of the writing of this book, it now costs $750 just for the base filing fee, $1,300 for the issue fee, and $6,090 for the maintenance fees. Add all that up and you get $8,140, not counting the minimum annual CPI increase to all these fees. If you can establish that you are a small entity, such as an individual inventor or a small business, you are entitled to a 50-percent discount, but you lose that discount if you sell or license your U.S. patent rights to any non-small entity.

USPTO Fees

In the summer of 2002, President Bush attempted to have Congress pass a stealth tax on inventors and companies performing research and development. He introduced legislation that sought to dramatically increase USPTO fees so much that it was estimated that U.S. patent filings would drop 30 to 50 percent. His proposed fee increase included such things as a $10,000 surcharge for filing a continuation or divisional application. President Bush's proposed USPTO fees amounted to approximately a 500-percent increase. Had it passed, the president's fee bill would have meant that during my career as a patent attorney, the cost of getting and holding a U.S. patent full term would have increased approximately 20,000 percent! Fortunately, the proposed legislation was held up in the U.S. Senate long enough for it to get on people's radar screens. Whether President Bush will still be successful in the future in implementing such massive USPTO fee increases remains to be seen. If individuals and companies cannot afford to obtain U.S. patents, or as many patents, they certainly cannot afford to carry on as much research and development. Then innovation declines, business formation stalls, and the United States becomes less competitive worldwide. President Bush's primary motive for the huge proposed fee increase was to fund "homeland security." While few would deny the need for increased defense expenditures in the wake of the September 11, 2001, tragedy, they should be paid by the public and business at large, and should not be borne disproportionately by inventors and technology companies. After all, at its core, a nation must be strong economically in order to be able to best protect its citizens.

The ongoing USPTO fee diversion, which has taken place every year for the past 10 years, still represents a serious threat to the U.S. economy. Congress only gives the USPTO the authority to collect fees from patent applicants and owners. The money goes into the general treasury and must be annually appropriated by the House and Senate to fund the operations of the USPTO. Each year for the past 10 years the U.S. Congress has appropriated for USPTO operations between $1 and $200 million less than the USPTO has collected. The remainder of the funds has been diverted and spent on various social programs and so-called "national debt reduction." Each fall during the federal budget wrangling, certain pet projects need funding and it is easy to use the USPTO as a "honey pot" to pay for them. For years, the USPTO has not had enough money to modernize its computer systems. Worse, it cannot afford to increase the pay of examiners sufficiently to lower their turnover rate. This means that well-trained, experienced patent examiners regularly leave for the private sector. *So what?* you might say. Sometimes patents that should be granted are not, and individuals and companies suffer losses from a lack of patent protection. Worse, in some cases, patents that should never be granted are issued and eventually lead to lengthy and expensive court battles, and damage to some sectors of the economy.

A class action lawsuit has been filed claiming that the annual diversion of fees collected by the USPTO for non-USPTO uses is unconstitutional. The lawsuit alleges that Article I, Section 8, Clause 8 of the U.S. Constitution only gives Congress the power to collect such fees as are necessary and incident to the function of examining patent and trademark applications, and that anything more that is collected for non-USPTO purposes amounts to an unlawful tax. I read a summary of the defense asserted by the U.S. Justice Department that alleges that the money has not been diverted, but is still somewhere in a mythical account available for the USPTO to use. This is a classic example of "Neverland" federal budget gimmickry. The Department of Justice's argument makes Worldcom's alleged accounting irregularities look tame by comparison. As this book nears publication, a federal judge has just ruled against many of the U.S. Government's defense motions.

The Press and the Misrepresentation of Patents

There is another political threat faced by the USPTO. Lately, the popular press has formed a bad habit of misrepresenting the scope of newly granted U.S. patents. For example, a few years ago, the national press published an inflammatory story that Amazon.com had just been granted a U.S. patent that would give it the right to collect a fee or percentage of every financial transaction on the Internet. When I looked at the patent, it turned out that its claims were so narrow that Internet competitors could easily design around them. But after repeated stories of this type that predicted dire consequences for the U.S. economy, various members of Congress put pressure on the director of the USPTO. He set up special review bodies and quality control checks and extra scrutiny on patent applications in given technical areas, such as methods of doing business. As a result, patent applicants in certain technical fields face extra costs and delays, and, in effect, a higher standard of nonobviousness not authorized by the U.S. patent law. The software industry is famous for complaining about the issuance of certain U.S. patents on the basis that the claimed system or method is old. If that is truly the case, and the claimed system or method is commercially valuable, the patent will be invalidated in either reexamination or infringement litigation. If it is not the case, the inventor should have his reward of exclusive rights for teaching the public about an important software advancement.

Patents and Politics Summary

In summary, the patent laws and the operations of the USPTO and its funding are subject to constant changes due to ongoing political pressures. There are relatively few patent attorneys, and their lobbying strength is negligible. Therefore, individual inventors and small business owners doing product development should inform their members of Congress that the USPTO needs adequate funding and that user fees should not be diverted to non-USPTO uses. The founding fathers who drafted the U.S. Constitution had a vision that inventors should be rewarded with exclusive rights, not so that they would profit, but so that their discoveries would be published in order "[t]o promote the progress of science and useful arts." There is no industrialized country in the world that does not have a viable patent system. We should not allow the U.S. patent system to be destroyed by excessive taxation.

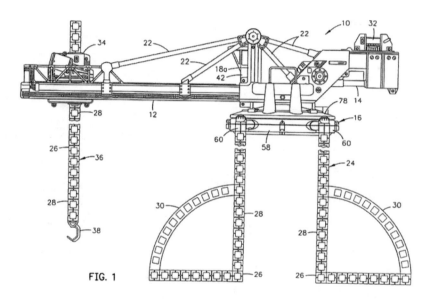

FIG. 1

U.S. Patent No. 6,475,058
"Rotary Tower Crane With Vertically
Extendable and Retractable
Lifting Boom"
Granted November 5, 2002
(Rokenbok radio-controlled toy crane)

CHAPTER 20

Myths About Patents

I n nearly 30 years of private practice as a patent attorney, I have heard many myths about patents from inventors and company executives. It is amazing how these myths are treated as gospel. Frequently, I hear that a certain course of action was taken in complete reliance on the myth, usually to the detriment of the person or business that followed it. Surprisingly, these people never bothered to seek qualified legal advice in advance. In this chapter I will dispel 25 of the most common myths about patents to help protect you against the loss of valuable patent rights or financial liability for patent infringement. These 25 myths are not discussed in any particular order. I have heard many more, but these particular myths seem to come up most often.

25 Most Common Patent Myths

Patent Myth No. 1:

I can protect my invention by writing up a description of it and mailing it to myself.

The so-called "poor man's patent" is absolutely worthless. It is clear that no unofficial description of an invention could ever afford exclusive rights. They can only be obtained by timely filing a U.S. patent application. Anyone can mail an empty envelope to themselves, and then years later, steam it open and stuff in a backdated description of an invention. Inventors are actually trying to preserve evidence of their date of conception by mailing an invention description to themselves, relying on the U.S. Postal Service postmark as an official date. A long line of Federal Circuit court decisions requires written or oral corroboration for a description of an invention to be admissible evidence on the issue of conception of the invention. In other words, at least one individual must sign and date the description and indicate that they understood it at the time, or must later testify that they were told of the invention on the date alleged by the inventor or observed evidence of its conception at that time. Witnessed engineering or scientific research notebooks are usually the best evidence of a date of conception.

Patent Myth No. 2:

I can write my own patent and it will be good enough.

I have never seen a U.S. patent that was written and prosecuted by a person who was not a patent attorney or patent agent that was worth the paper it was written on. Yes, like all areas of the law, a person need not be a patent attorney in order to represent himself. However, the old adage that says "he who represents himself has a fool for a client" is nowhere more true than in the field of patent law. Whether you get a patent in the first place, and if so, whether the scope of its claims gives you the maximum amount of protection to which you are legally entitled is largely dependent upon the skill and experience of the patent attorney or patent agent who handles the matter. It takes years of training to make a competent patent attorney, and the process is very complex.

Patent Myth No. 3:

Infringement can be avoided if I change
10 percent of a patented invention.

Patent infringement is determined by comparing the claims of the patent to the accused device, composition, or method. Each and every element and limitation of at least one claim must be found in the competitor's product. The presence or absence of infringement cannot be quantified numerically. Even if someone could explain how you measure a 10-percent change of a patented design, it certainly would be no guarantee against infringement liability. Chapter 12 discusses in detail the entire process of attempting to safely design around a patent.

Patent Myth No. 4:

I will make a lot of money if I patent my invention.

A patent derives its value from the potential commercial value of the underlying invention that it covers. Simply stated, unless someone wants the product, nobody will ever want to copy it. You will not make any money from your patent unless you, your assignee, or licensee can successfully commercialize the invention. The patent prevents copying, and therefore allows you to charge higher prices and make more profit. Of course, if you can sell or license your patent, that will represent income. But patenting the invention is only part of the process of building a business around the invention. Chapter 9 discusses invention marketing and Chapter 10 discusses patent licensing.

Patent Myth No. 5:

I can get an international patent that covers all foreign countries.

There is no such thing as an "international patent." As explained in detail in Chapter 15, each country has its own patent laws and grants its own patents. Therefore, it is necessary to file a patent application in each country where patent protection is desired. There are certain treaties such as the Patent Cooperation Treaty (PCT) and European Patent Convention (EPC) that perform some initial receiving, publication, searching, and examination functions, and allow you to delay filing and prosecuting the so-called "national phase" patent applications.

Patent Myth No. 6:

Methods of doing business are not patentable.

This was true in the United States for a couple hundred years, but the U.S. Court of Appeals decided a case in 1998 that effectively overturned the long-standing prohibition against patenting methods of doing business. The floodgates opened, and a tidal wave of patent applications were filed on all sorts of Internet-related business methods.

Patent Myth No. 7:

Patents last for 17 years.

Again, this was true for a couple hundred years. However, in the last decade, Congress changed the U.S. patent law as part of the process by which the United States ratified the international treaty known as the General Agreement on Tariffs and Trade (GATT). The term of a U.S. utility patent is now 20 years from the filing date of the application on which it is based. If the patent is based on a string of applications, the 20-year term is measured from the earliest filing date in the string. For U.S. patents based solely upon one or more applications filed before June 8, 1995, the term is automatically the longer of 17 years from the grant date or 20 years from the earliest filing date. The terms of many U.S. patents were extended when the U.S. patent law was changed in the mid-1990s, and some companies were later liable for infringement when they incorrectly assumed that certain patents owned by their competitors had expired 17 years from their grant date.

Patent Myth No. 8:

Big companies will steal your invention.

I have never seen a big company "steal" an invention. In general, they will not even consider unsolicited invention proposals from outside the company. If they do, they normally insist that the inventor first file a U.S. patent application on the invention. If a big company wants to make a product that is patented, it will either buy the patent, license the patent, or attempt to design around the patent. In rare situations, the big company might seek to invalidate the patent if it can find prior art that establishes a clear case of lack of novelty of the claimed invention. There is just too much potential financial liability for a large company to disregard the valid patent rights of others. A jury could find willful infringement, and a judge could then award triple the damages found by the jury and the patent owner's attorney's fees incurred in bringing the lawsuit to a successful conclusion. Little companies are far more likely to thumb their nose at a patent because they have never experienced the financial devastation of a patent lawsuit. Only the true inventor can file a U.S. patent application, so a big company couldn't steal an invention by filing its own patent application by listing as inventors its employees who did not make the invention. The oath would be invalid, and there could be criminal penalties for submitting a false oath.

Patent Myth No. 9:

Your patent attorney will steal your invention.

Again, I have never heard of this actually happening. Patent attorneys are bound by strict codes of conduct imposed by state bars and the USPTO. They would never risk their licenses to practice patent law in the hopes of somehow illicitly profiting from a client's invention.

Patent Myth No. 10:

If I invent something on my own time,
I own the patent rights, not my employer.

This whole subject is discussed in detail in Chapter 16, which covers employer and employee invention rights. Where an employee signs a standard employee invention agreement, and the invention is related to the employer's business, the employer normally owns all the patent rights, regardless of whether the invention was conceived or made by the employee during off hours or while on vacation.

Patent Myth No. 11:

I have to physically demonstrate my invention by
building a working model before I can get a patent.

There is no requirement under U.S. patent law that an inventor actually build or even test the invention in order to be entitled to a patent. Indeed, many valuable patents are based on applications filed on inventions that, at the time, had only been conceived, and not actually reduced to practice.

Patent Myth No. 12:

If I get a patent, I am free to manufacture and sell my invention.

Wrong! A patent is only a right to *exclude* others from making, using, offering for sale, or selling the invention defined by its claims. It is not an affirmative right to make anything. The reason is simple: there may be earlier unexpired patents with broader claims that "dominate" your patent. See my example of the patent on the pencil and the subsequent patent on the pencil with an eraser, on page 14.

Patent Myth No. 13:

Once a patent has expired, I can't be sued for infringing the patent.

There is a six-year statute of limitations on the recovery of patent infringement damages. So you could, for example, be sued five years after a patent expired, but you would only potentially be liable for one year's worth of damages.

Patent Myth No. 14:

You cannot patent minor variations of conventional products.

If an invention as claimed is new and nonobvious over the prior art, you are legally entitled to a U.S. patent, regardless of how "minor" the variations are. Shortly after Thomas Edison perfected the electric lightbulb, an extremely valuable patent was obtained by a different inventor on a lightbulb with frosted glass. It diffused the otherwise bright glare emitted by Edison's lightbulb that used perfectly clear glass.

Patent Myth No. 15:

You cannot patent a new combination of old parts.

Wrong again! Almost every patented invention is a rearrangement of old parts, or a new combination of old parts, or the same combination with a slightly modified part. Again, the basic three-part test for patentability requires usefulness, novelty, and nonobviousness.

Patent Myth No. 16:

You cannot get a patent on a new use for an old product.

It is surprising, but you can get a patent on a new use for an old product. So long as the claimed method would have been nonobvious to a
person of ordinary skill in the art, you are legally entitled to receive a U.S.
patent for the same. For example, if I claimed a method of improving the
yield of tomato plants by applying an aqueous (water) solution of 1/1,000
percent aspirin by weight to the soil in which the tomato plants are being
grown, I could get a patent, assuming the examiner found the method to
be nonobvious.

Patent Myth No. 17:

You can patent a computer program.

If the claim says, "A computer program, comprising: (list of steps in
Microsoft Visual Basic)," the USPTO will almost surely reject it. When patent
attorneys say that computer software is patentable, it is, but you have to
present it as a recitation of functional steps that are in English (or partly
mathematical) and not in a recognized programming language.

Patent Myth No. 18:

The notation "patent pending" appearing on a product
or its packaging indicates that the product is patented.

This notation merely indicates that a patent application has been filed,
but not that it has turned into a patent. If the product is patented, it should
bear the proper statutory notice that includes the seven-digit patent number (for example, "U.S. Patent No. 6,357,639").

Patent Myth No. 19:

You have to have knowledge that a patent exists
before you can be liable for infringing the patent.

In order to prove patent infringement, there is no need to show intent
on the part of the infringer. Therefore, there is no need to prove that the
accused infringer was even aware of the patent. If the patent owner is making, selling, or offering for sale the patented invention in the United States,

it cannot recover any damages occurring before the patent owner either marked its products with the patent number or charged the accused infringer with infringement. There is no such requirement, however, and no limitation on the recovery of damages if the patent owner is not making, selling, or offering for sale the patented invention in the United States. However, if the patent owner wants to recover increased damages and/or attorney's fees, it must prove willful infringement, in which case the accused infringer's knowledge of the patent and subsequent conduct will be highly relevant.

Patent Myth No. 20:

It is easy to invalidate a patent.

A patent is presumed valid, and this can only be overcome by clear and convincing evidence. This is a very substantial burden of proof. You have to pay for a very expensive lawsuit and hope you have extremely strong evidence of lack of novelty, obviousness, or some other technical defect. Reexaminations rarely succeed in knocking out all the claims.

Patent Myth No. 21:

The U.S. Patent and Trademark Office is located in Washington, D.C.

It has actually been located in Arlington, Virginia, for about 40 years. Recently, the USPTO moved to a massive new office complex in Alexandria, Virginia.

Patent Myth No. 22:

I can get the term of my patent extended.

You cannot get the term of your patent extended without a special law passed by Congress and signed by the president, unless you fall into one of the narrow statutory exceptions. For example, patent term extension is available where there are unreasonable administrative delays during prosecution, or in the case of drug patents, based on delays attributable to obtaining FDA approval,which is required to sell the drug.

Patent Myth No. 23:

I am free to manufacture and sell a product shown in an expired patent without risking any infringement liability.

This is a dangerous assumption. There could be other unexpired "submarine" patents that cover different aspects of the design shown in the issued patent. These are U.S. patents that are based on a string of continuation applications all filed before June 8, 1995, which still get a 17-year term when issued.

Patent Myth No. 24:

You can get a patent on anything.

Not every invention as claimed meets the utility, novelty, and nonobviousness requirements of U.S. patent laws.

Patent Myth No. 25:

Patents are worthless.

The USPTO collects more than $1 billion in fees annually. More than 200,000 U.S. patents are granted annually at great expense to the companies that obtain them in order to achieve the many significant advantages discussed at the end of the Introduction, and again in Chapter 21. True, some patents are worthless, but it is because the underlying inventions have no commercial value, the patents are invalid for failure to comply with the patent laws, or the patents have been poorly drafted.

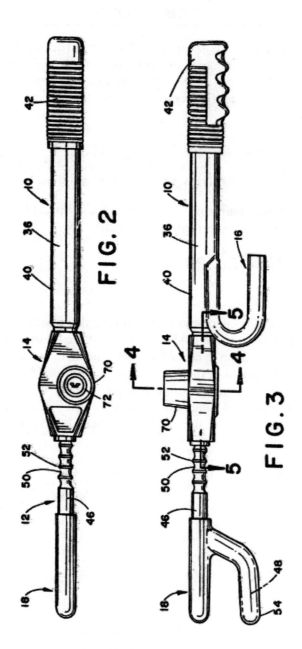

FIG. 2

FIG. 3

U.S. Patent No. 4,738,127
"Automobile Steering Lock"
Granted April 19, 1988
(popular Club antitheft car steering wheel lock)

CHAPTER 21

Deciding Whether to Seek Patent Protection

(H) opefully, the preceding chapters have given you new insight about the patent process, the exclusive rights afforded by a patent, and what happens after you get a patent. At some time in your career there will undoubtedly come a time when you ask yourself whether you should seek patent protection on your own invention, or on the invention of an employee. Perhaps that time is now, because you are reading this book. It is helpful to review the reasons for seeking a patent, as previously discussed in the Introduction:

1. Stop competitors from copying your invention and selling products embodying it without your permission.
2. Provide a basis for financial reward by either selling the patent or licensing it in return for royalties.
3. Prevent someone from patenting the invention and impairing your ability to commercialize it.
4. Allow patent infringement disputes to be settled via cross-licensing instead of paying money.
5. Add asset value to your business.
6. Increase the prestige of your company, its scientists, and its engineers.

It is certain that the first three reasons listed are of paramount importance. But the latter three reasons should not be underestimated. Let me illustrate an example of adding asset value to a small business. I represented a small manufacturer of portable lift conveyors for carrying roof tiles, tar paper, and other building materials from a pickup truck to the roof of a one- or two-story building. The conveyors had twin parallel endless conveyor belts supported on pulleys carried by an extensible boom. The conveyer belts had upstanding cleats that would prevent a load sitting on the belts from sliding backwards. Expensive and failure-prone electromechanical mechanisms were normally required to keep the cleats side-by-side by varying the drive speed of separate pulleys to account for minute differences in the lengths of the conveyor belts. My client invented a way of using a single endless conveyor belt that was wrapped into two parallel upward load-carrying segments and two crisscross lower return segments. The single belt is supported on pulleys carried by towers mounted on the boom that allow the boom to be leaned against the edge of a roof, while ensuring that the parallel cleats stay even with each other and don't become entangled on their return run. This eliminated the complex electromechanical mechanisms previously required to keep the cleats side-by-side. See U.S. Patent No. 6,053,305 granted April 25, 2000. Customers love the new arrangement, and my client's warranty claims and repairs have been greatly reduced. The patent will prevent copying by his competitors until April 12, 2018. Perhaps equally as important, the patent will allow my client to sell his small lift conveyor business for a much greater price when he gets ready to retire.

Commercial Value of the Invention

Fundamentally, a patent application and any resulting patent reflect the commercial value, or *potential* commercial value, of the underlying invention. This should be intuitive because there is no intrinsic value in the right to exclude someone from making, using, or selling something that nobody wants. The more the demand there is for an article, the greater the worth of a patent controlling its manufacture and sale.

It is normally a poor investment of time and money to file a patent application on your great idea if it did not arise in the context of your regular ongoing business or come forth from observing a crying need in the marketplace. Try to be objective. Most inventors fall in love with their inventions, yet they need the well-reasoned, unemotional evaluation of marketing experts in the appropriate field regarding sales potential and pricing levels. If your product is a consumer item that will be sold through normal retail channels, can you make it for approximately one-fifth of its selling price? Inventors also need input from manufacturing experts to determine the feasibility of producing the desired volumes at reasonable cost. The inventor of the 3rd Grip fishing pole holster discussed in Chapter 1 paid for a booth at the well-known Fred Hall Fishing Expo in Long Beach, California, and sold his product himself, allowing him to directly gauge the reactions of sports fishermen. He sold approximately 500 units in four days based on a suggested retail price of $19.99. This convinced him to make the arrangements to have the product produced in China in large volume for importation into the United States. The decision to manufacture was only arrived at after a limited production in the United States, and the manufacture of several thousand units in Mexico. Each manufacturer suggested materials and design alterations to lower the cost of production.

Market Evaluation of the Invention

Chapter 9 identifies relatively inexpensive, reliable sources for market evaluations of inventions. *Stay away from invention promoters!* You have probably heard their late-night television advertisements promising market studies and contacts with prospective manufacturers. Nearly all such companies are frauds. For a fee of $5,000 or more, they perform a shallow patent search, and file a design patent application or a very poorly drafted utility patent application. They also give you one or more large three-ring binders full of useless boilerplate information, much of which is readily available via the Internet. Finally, their supposed "contacts" with prospective manufacturers boil down to sending form letters to addressees in their database, which are almost universally rejected or discarded by their recipients.

Meeting With a Patent Attorney

As I have already explained, forget about writing a patent application yourself. Your chances of getting worthwhile protection via this route are almost zero. Consult with an experienced patent attorney or patent agent selected through the process discussed in Chapter 17. He or she will give you a feel for the potential patentability of your invention and, perhaps, suggest a patentability search. The search results will go a long way toward determining whether you might be able to obtain a patent on your invention, and if so, what the scope of its claims might be. Ask yourself whether the claims of such a patent would adequately protect you in the marketplace or would be easy for a competitor to avoid. The claims of the 3rd Grip fishing pole holster patent discussed in Chapter 1 require a rigid tube or its equivalent for slidably receiving and supporting the handle of a fishing pole. As a practical matter, without such structure, any knockoff made by a competitor just won't work very well. So that patent has real value to its owner, assuming that sales of the product take off. Also, don't forget that in the world of consumer products, there is a certain marketing cachet that can be conveyed to prospective customers by indicating that the product is patented or "patent pending" in the United States. To the ordinary person, this tends to indicate the product is new and unique, and not just some garden variety device that has been around for years.

Meeting with a patent attorney or a patent agent and having a reasonably extensive search performed, along with a formal written patentability opinion, costs less than $1,000 in most metropolitan areas for noncomplex inventions. Figure that the process of preparing, filing, and prosecuting the application to issuance will take about two years and cost $6,000 to $10,000 for a noncomplex invention. Expect your attorney to spend about 25 to 35 hours preparing the application, and about five to 15 hours preparing and filing two amendments, one in response to each of two Office Actions from the USPTO examiner. Amendments can easily cost $1,500 and more to prepare and file in the USPTO. Beyond the initial conference with the patent attorney, which may last one to two hours, further conferences will probably not be necessary. The patent attorney may ask for your input on the prior art cited by the USPTO examiner in the Office Actions, but usually the patent attorney is fully capable of distinguishing the prior art references on his or her own.

Remember that many metropolitan areas have talented and experienced industrial designers, mold tooling experts, machinists, model-makers, and consulting engineers. For fees that are typically below those charged by a patent attorney, they can provide valuable advice about the manufacturability of your design. They can often suggest valuable improvements, and for this reason, you need to have them sign consulting agreements in advance in which they agree that anything they coinvent during their engagement will belong to you. Such consulting agreements should also require that your invention be maintained in confidence. You can obtain standard form consulting agreements of this type from your patent attorney, and most reputable consultants will not balk at executing it. Don't ask your patent attorney or patent agent to sign a confidentiality agreement. He or she is already bound by strict ethical rules to maintain all client confidences. In many cases, a prototype of your invention can be constructed using custom-made parts, sometimes produced via stereo lithography, that will make the prototype appear as if it were a manufactured item. Such a prototype can be invaluable in explaining your invention to potential manufacturers, partners, investors, and so on.

Investors

A word about seeking investors is in order. Most states have laws that effectively prohibit you from selling percentages of an invention, or a future stream of income, to the public at large. Before you ask for and receive investment funding for developing and commercializing an invention, talk to a business attorney about whether you need to set up a formal partnership agreement or form a corporation. I remember a slick operator in San Diego, California, who ripped off many investors by selling percentages in his invention that he claimed could magnetically separate pure gold from gold ore. It seems almost inconceivable that investors had so little scientific knowledge that they actually believed that this gold mining scheme was technically feasible. Didn't these investors ever ask for a demonstration or an analysis from a properly credentialed scientist or engineer? This is why states have so-called blue sky laws, namely, to prevent gullible people from buying equity in various harebrained schemes, including inventions. Such blue sky laws heavily regulate the sale of equity interests to inventors and require substantial governmental filings and/or "buyer-beware" disclosures in advance.

Deciding Not to Seek a Patent

If you decide against seeking a patent, there are several ways to prevent others from later patenting the same invention in the United States and asserting the patent against you or your business. You can publish your invention in a newspaper, journal, or over the Internet by setting up a Website or adding a description of the invention to someone else's Website. This will start the one-year statutory bar period under the U.S. patent law, effectively barring any third party from obtaining a patent on the invention based on an application filed more than one year after your publication date. Under the first subsection of the novelty statute, the publication of your invention may immediately prevent others from independently inventing and validly patenting the same invention. If you offer products embodying your invention for sale in this country, such as by displaying them at a trade show or other exhibition, this will also start the one-year statutory bar period. You may want to distribute dated brochures describing and illustrating your product so that these can be cited as publications against applications filed more than one year after their dissemination. You can also file a statutory invention registration with the USPTO by paying a nominal government fee, although this would typically involve a patent attorney and be more costly than the other ways of making sure that your invention goes into the public domain. Remember that the U.S. patent law provides a one-year grace period for filing a U.S. patent application. So keep track of the date you first offered the invention for sale in this country, used it in public in this country, or published it anywhere. You may later change your mind and decide to file a U.S. patent application before the one-year statutory bar date arrives.

CHAPTER 22

What Is a Trademark?

T rademarks are all around us from the time we wake up in the morning and brew Folgers coffee to the time we take Tylenol PM pain reliever at bedtime. In short, trademarks are source identifiers. They allow us to rely on a word and/or symbol to reassure us that the product we are buying is the one we know and trust in terms of quality. Trademarks facilitate a mass production consumer economy. Before the Civil War, most products were made by hand in small numbers by local tradesmen. The cobbler, the baker, the barrel-maker, and so forth, were people individually known to their customers who trusted them to provide acceptable goods at a reasonable price. Beginning with wooden matches and soap, many products in the mid- to late-19th century began to be mass-produced in containers and other packaging marked with familiar words and artwork to build brand identity. The term "brand" is really just a layman's term for a trademark, and has its origins in the branding irons used by cowboys to burn unique identifying ownership symbols into the hides of live cattle.

Law of Trademarks

The law of trademarks arose to protect the public from being mistaken or deceived into buying goods from one producer when, in fact, they were made by another. The theory was simple: Manufacturers should be able to build up goodwill around words or symbols associated with a

219

particular type of product (for example, Colt revolvers) by providing a functional and durable product and standing behind that product. Then customers and prospective customers will be more likely to buy products with that brand, knowing that it indicates a good buy from a respected producer. Consumers are protected by the law of trademarks because other companies are prohibited from using trademarks that are so similar in sound, appearance, or meaning as to cause a likelihood of confusion as to their source and origin when used on the same or similar products.

Trademarks are often the single most valuable assets of a company. They can be worth billions of dollars. I would much rather own the trademarks of Johnson & Johnson than all its other assets combined, including all its property, buildings, bank accounts, and patents.

What Constitutes a Trademark

Most trademarks are words or symbols, or a combination of the two. Sometimes numbers are included. The most well-known trademark, Coca-Cola, is internationally used in a stylized white letter script form for the world's most popular soft drink beverage. Almost everyone is familiar with the Nike "Swoosh," a stylized check-mark symbol used around the world for athletic shoes and apparel. When a trademark is a symbol—a design or other piece of artwork besides words, letters, and numbers—it is typically referred to as a "logo." Trademarks are often a combination of words and a logo, in which case they are referred to as a composite trademark. A good example of a composite trademark comprises the words Old Spice and a stylized sailboat used for deodorant and cologne by Procter & Gamble. The seemingly ever-present Starbucks composite trademark is reproduced at the beginning of this chapter and consists of the words "Starbucks" and "Coffee" superimposed on a green ring surrounding a stylized mermaid.

Federal Registration Symbol

The (®) symbol is the federal registration symbol, which can only be legally used in the United States if the trademark has been registered in the USPTO. In fact, the (®)symbol must be used by the trademark owner on the product in order to collect the maximum amount of monetary damages against an infringer. You may sometimes see the (™) symbol used as a superscript at the end of a trademark. The use of this symbol is not sanctioned or regulated by any trademark statute that I am aware of, and its usage merely reflects an industry custom to place others on notice that the user claims exclusive rights to the words and/or symbol as a trademark for particular goods. Trademark infringement actions are discussed in Chapter 26. The rights and remedies of a trademark owner vary greatly depending upon whether the trademark rights are based on federal registration with the USPTO, registration with one or more of the 50 states, or merely on so-called "common law" rights solely based on use.

Trademarks can also be colors, sounds, and even fragrances, although this is rare. It is very difficult to register a single color as a trademark because, usually, it is deemed merely descriptive or generic, and the law of trademarks disfavors any one party getting a monopoly on one color for a particular type of goods. For example, attempts to register yellow for earth-moving equipment, green for farm machinery, and black for outboard motors by Caterpillar, John Deere, and Mercury (Outboard Marine Corp.), respectively, have failed. On the other hand, Owens Corning owns a federal trademark registration on the color pink for fiberglass building insulation. Harley-Davidson successfully registered the deep rumbling sound of its engines as a trademark for its motorcycles, and a few perfume fragrances have been deemed distinct enough to warrant federal registration.

Trade Dress

A distinctive trade dress can receive trademark protection, such as the blue and yellow color scheme of the aerosol spray can for WD-40 lubricant. From time to time, companies have tried to confuse people into buying other lubricants in similar cans with a canary yellow shield and navy blue background. This can raise a likelihood of confusion with respect to an impulse purchaser even when the competitor doesn't use the actual WD-40 letters and words.

I recently learned of a dishwasher detergent being sold at a Costco store in a box with the same exact bright metallic green color as Procter & Gamble's Cascade brand. However, because the Kirkland brand is prominently displayed on the box, Costco, the company, has no doubt taken the position that there is no likelihood of confusion relative to Procter & Gamble's best-selling dishwasher detergent.

Service Marks

Words or symbols that are used to identify a particular source of a service are called service marks and are subject to the same protection as trademarks. Examples are Southwest for airline services, Roto-Rooter for drain-cleaning services, and the AT&T globe logo for telephone services. You probably would also recognize the red umbrella logo used by Travelers Insurance Company. Where the service mark is not federally registered, companies often use an (^{SM}) symbol as a superscript at the end of the service mark.

In the next few chapters, when references are made to trademarks, it is safe to assume that the same principles apply to service marks. Of course, the identical words and/or symbols can function as both a trademark and a service mark. For example, IBM is a well-known trademark for computer hardware, but it is also a well-known service mark for computer consulting services.

Trade Names

A trade name is the name under which a business operates. It may be a corporate name, or the name of a partnership or sole proprietorship. A trade name may also function as a trademark or service mark where goods and/or services are sold under or provided in connection with the same words. A good example is International Business Machines.

Not every word and/or symbol can serve as a valid trademark. In general, words that are generic—the common, everyday term for a type of product—cannot be the subject of exclusive rights conferred by a federal trademark registration. For example, McDonald's could not register "Hamburger" for a sandwich product with a ground meat patty. Nor could it register "Hot and Juicy" for the same product, because the trademark law will not confer exclusive rights for terms that are merely descriptive of an attribute or characteristic of a product. However, if a mark is only suggestive of the goods, it can be federally registered as a trademark. Thus, the phrase Big N' Tasty is federally registered by McDonald's for "specialty sandwiches."

Trademarks should be used as adjectives, not as nouns, to avoid becoming generic, such as Escalator for moving stairs and Zipper for a slide fastener. These were once valid trademarks, but became the common ordinary term for a type of product. Thus, Kimberly-Clark always refers to Kleenex facial tissue. In addition, as discussed in Chapter 24, one cannot use or register a trademark for goods where its use would create a likelihood of confusion with a trademark already registered or in use. Contrary to popular belief, these rules cannot be avoided simply by misspelling the term or using it in a foreign language. For example, one could not federally register "Pollo" for chicken breasts because it is the Spanish word for chicken. Nor can somebody legally sell "Jillette" shaving cream.

Slogans or tag lines are often protected as trademarks. One example is the slogan "We Love to Fly and It Shows" used for many years by Delta Airlines. Another example is the "We Try Harder" slogan used by Avis. And who can forget the "Only Her Hairdresser Knows for Sure" tag line used so successfully by Clairol for hair color? More recently, Volkswagen of America has had considerable success with its "Drivers Wanted" television advertising campaign.

Product Shapes

Product shapes can, on rare occasions, be registered as trademarks with the USPTO. However, in order to receive trademark protection, the product configuration must be distinctive; that is, the consuming public must associate the shape with a particular manufacturer. Even then, the product configuration must not be utilitarian—it must not be functional—and must be purely aesthetic. The product configuration that has most often qualified for trademark protection is the distinctive shape of a bottle, such as the narrow-waist shape of the traditional Coca-Cola bottle.

Where a novel product configuration is developed, the owner of the design would be wise to file for a U.S. design patent within the one-year grace period, as discussed in Chapter 8. Design patents are easy to obtain and do not require proof of distinctiveness and nonfunctionality—two factors otherwise required for federal registration of a product configuration as a trademark.

In the past few years, the U.S. Supreme Court has sanctioned the concept of giving trademark-like protection to a distinct restaurant decor. The types of designs and artwork that can function as trademarks are almost limitless. Consider the tartan plaid registered by 3M Company as a trademark for adhesive tape, and the three white stripes registered by Adidas as a trademark for athletic shoes and clothing.

Internet Domain Names

This chapter would not be complete without a discussion of Internet domain names. A domain can legally function as both a trademark and a service mark. The trademark is normally the intermediate part of the domain name address, which are the words and letters between "www" and ".com." Virtually everyone is now familiar with Amazon for Internet-based retail services, eBay for Internet-based auction services, and Google for Internet search engine services. However, it is extremely important to understand that when a domain name registration company says that your proposed domain name is available, this does not mean that you are free to use the intermediate part as a trademark or service mark without being sued for trademark infringement. Nor does an indication of domain name availability by a domain name registration company indicate that the intermediate part of the domain name will be registerable with the USPTO and therefore, as a practical matter, protectable. A domain name registration does not create any trademark rights. Trademark rights are based on actual use on goods in commerce or in connection with services in commerce. Trademark selection, registration, and enforcement are discussed in the following chapters.

CHAPTER 23

Choosing a Trademark

T his chapter focuses on the best way to select a word trademark. Selecting a logo is a much easier process and flows naturally from the word mark that you ultimately select. The logo should be compatible with the word mark. You don't need a high-priced agency to select a good trademark. Some of these agencies charge $100,000 and more to select a new trademark for a large corporation. All you need is a little creativity and a basic understanding of the rules that govern your selection. In general, a good trademark is short, memorable, easy to spell, and suggestive of the type of product and its positive attributes. It should not have any negative connotations, and it must not be generic or merely descriptive of the goods themselves or some aspect or characteristic of the goods. Where the goods are to be sold internationally, the mark should not have an undesirable translation. Nova was selected many years ago by General Motors for a compact car, but it was an absolutely terrible trademark in Latin American countries because "no va" loosely translates into "won't go." "Its Finger Licken' Good" was a very poor marketing slogan for Kentucky Fried Chicken in China because it loosely translates into "tastes so good you'll bite your fingers off."

It is best to come up with a long list of possible new trademarks because, as described in the next chapter, many of them may be knocked out when you subsequently perform a search and find conflicting trademarks that are already registered, pending, or in use. It is often a good idea to brainstorm with other people involved in your business, particularly those having responsibility for marketing the company's products.

Trademark Rights

The mere suggestion of a possible trademark that is a word or words is not a property right. You don't need to have a fancy written agreement in order to acquire rights to a suggested word trademark so long as you don't promise any compensation to the party that suggests the mark. Trademark rights are acquired through use in commerce; that is to say, by selling goods with the mark on the goods, packaging or containers, or on attached tags. Service mark rights are acquired by advertising and/or performing services under the mark. The only real exception to these rules is that the filing of a U.S. trademark or service mark application with the USPTO on the basis of an intent-to-use (ITU) constitutes constructive use of the mark, but the mark must actually be used later on, and a statement of use (SOU) timely filed in order for the ITU application to mature into a registration.

If you want to have a contest in which the winner's suggestion will become your new trademark, clearly spell out in writing to the participants that you will provide a nominal award, say $250, to the contest winner and that they give up all their rights in the name, whatever they might be, in return for a $250 prize. Just to be on the safe side, make the winning contestant sign a short written agreement to this effect in order to receive the prize, and if he or she won't sign the agreement, drop the mark like a hot rock and pick another mark. Why set yourself up for a lawsuit even if it has no merit?

If the proposed new trademark has any design component (a symbol, drawing, picture, or some other graphic or artistic component, including the layout of the words, special coloration, etc.) make sure you have the creator (artist) sign a copyright assignment if it was not created by an employee of your company in the normal course of his or her employment. Here's a war story that demonstrates why. There is a major company in Carlsbad, California, that makes Cobra golf clubs. The company sells its clubs with two trademarks, namely, the word "Cobra" and a logo consisting of a stylized venomous cobra snake that was also federally registered as a trademark for golf clubs. A few years ago, the management of Cobra Golf felt that the snake logo should be updated, so they hired an outside artist who quickly drew an updated snake, apparently for a small fee. However, at the time, Cobra Golf failed to get the outside artist to sign a written assignment of his copyright rights in the updated snake illustration. Because he was not an employee of Cobra Golf, his copyright rights were not automatically transferred to Cobra Golf under the work for hire doctrine of U.S. copyright law. Cobra Golf then extensively adopted and used the new snake logo as a trademark for its golf clubs and its associated golf apparel. Eventually, the artist (or his clever lawyer) realized the mistake made by Cobra Golf in not getting a copyright assignment, and his lawyer arranged for him to get regular monthly payments of thousands of dollars for past and continued use of his artwork. For a while, Cobra Golf paid the artist the money, but when the artist got a little greedy and wanted even more money, litigation erupted. When Cobra Golf was later purchased for more than $500 million, the artist got a bonanza, reportedly more than $3 million to settle his copyright infringement claim!

It is not necessary to register a copyright claim to any artwork in your trademark so long as the trademark is federally registered in the USPTO. However, it is absolutely indispensable to have any non-employee sign a written assignment of any artwork he or she created that is used in your trademark.

Techniques for Selecting a Trademark

So now let's turn to useful techniques for selecting a new trademark. Think about how the trademark will look and feel in an advertisement and then work backwards. Will the trademark grab your attention? Is its memorable? Does it impart positive qualities and attributes regarding your product? KC Masterpiece certainly does a good job of informing prospective customers that the barbecue sauce must be good because it is associated with Kansas City, Missouri, which is famous for good barbecue, and further because it is a masterpiece—award-winning and top quality.

Try not to use words right out of the dictionary that are regularly associated with a certain type of product, because they are likely to already be registered, or they are merely descriptive and, therefore, incapable of being registered. For example, "Laser Level" would be a poor choice for a carpenter's tool that uses a laser to provide a visible leveling line.

Your best chance of coming up with a good trademark is to "coin" a new word that isn't found in an English dictionary. Good examples are Sunkist, Citibank, KitchenAid, Waterpik, and Microsoft. Notice that each of these trademarks has a common theme: they are a joinder of two words or portions thereof, sometimes with misspellings. In fact, one of the easiest and best ways to coin a new trademark is to write up a list of descriptive terms for your product and then join parts of them together. Thus Microsoft was formed by joining the front portion of "microcomputer" with the front portion of "software." Another good example is Chironetwork for franchised chiropractic clinics. I like LensCrafters for a chain of retail stores that provide optometric services and glasses.

Stay away from overused terms that do not result in distinctiveness, because you want to differentiate your goods from the competition with a unique and memorable term. Everyone seems to use "Pro" with some other words. It has ceased to have much positive connotation. In addition, "Pro" is usually associated with other equally washed-out terms to form a mark that customers won't remember and that is probably unregisterable. For example, without doing any research, I can tell you that the odds are pretty high that you could not use and/or register "Pro Series" as a trademark for fishing rods. Why would you want to anyway? Wouldn't "Master Angler" be a better choice, assuming it passed a search?

If you want to appeal to customers with lots of disposable income, try thinking up a trademark that sounds foreign but isn't a real word. For example, Häagen Dazs makes consumers think that the ice cream must be Scandinavian, and, therefore, good tasting and deserving of its high price. But it is not a real term in any foreign language. The same goes for Rokenbok for radio-controlled construction toys.

PC software may still be available, such as NamePower from Decathalon Corp. in Cincinnati, Ohio, and Namer from Salinon Corp. in Dallas, Texas, for helping create new trademarks. These programs essentially spew out combinations of words and portions thereof based on words that you input. They don't have brains that take into consideration the meaning of the words, your markets, and your customers, but they are quite creative in coming up with a large number of permutations and combinations that you can readily discard or give further consideration. A lot of these might be missed if you do the process manually. A great deal of the tedium is avoided using such name creation software.

Try to avoid using initials, acronyms, and letter/number combinations. There are studies that have indicated that trademarks made up exclusively of letters that don't form a word, such as TXS, are 40 percent less memorable than trademarks made up of words or portions of those words. They look and sound like stock trading symbols, which almost nobody can remember. While everyone knows about WD-40 lubricant, which was derived from "water displacement formula number 40," it takes many, many years of marketing to build up brand identity around this genre of trademark. Don't count on having a wonderful unique product and stellar marketing similar to what WD-40 Company has enjoyed for decades.

Be careful about using geographic terms. Normally, the USPTO won't register a trademark if it is primarily merely geographically descriptive. So don't use state and city names for a product, unless you want to spend a ton of legal fees trying to register the mark and a ton more legal fees trying to police it. It has been done, but rarely successfully. Here are a couple of contrary examples: Oregon is registered for canned berries, California Pizza Kitchen is registered for restaurant services, and Fig Newton is named after Newton, Massachusetts, a town located near the original cookie-making company.

The USPTO will also not register a surname such as "Johnson" or "Jones." So think twice about using your own name as a trademark. Also, what happens if you want to sell your business? Do you really want to sell the exclusive rights to your own name? Again, one can get around the prohibition against registering surnames, but it takes a lot of time and money. Examples are Bill Blass for clothing and Vidal Sassoon for hair care products.

A trademark should be pleasing to view and to hear. For example, "Alida" is more appealing to hear than "Alidak." The font and any logo associated with the trademark can go a long way in producing a pleasing visual image, or one that immediately conveys the utility of the product. Everyone recognizes the ubiquitous bunny logo of the Playboy company, which conjures up a playful risqué image. Reproduced at the beginning of this chapter (page 224) is the composite trademark for the patented 3rd Grip fishing pole holster illustrated on page 20. The word portion suggests that the product provides another hand that holds your fishing pole. This allows a fisherman to bait his hook or remove fish without having to lean his pole up against a railing. The design part is a fanciful illustration of a shark reminding the potential customer of the excitement of deep-sea fishing. Of course, a pleasing and readily identifiable combination of colors is always a good thing to build into your trademark. Personally, I like the purple and orange color scheme of the FedEx service mark.

Finally, when all else fails, consider purchasing an existing federal trademark registration along with all of the goodwill associated with it. You would be amazed to learn that many federal trademark registrations can be purchased for $10,000 or less. Frequently, a company is no longer using a trademark and would be glad to sell it for a small price, because the federal registration will ultimately be canceled or lapse anyway. You will save time and money searching and registering your own mark, which, by the way, is not always successful. Be very wary of taking a license to use someone else's trademark unless it is a famous mark, such as the Dallas Cowboys, that will automatically bring you lots of sales. Otherwise, trademark license royalties represent unnecessary overhead and will eat into your profits.

Int. Cl.: 35

Prior U.S. Cls.: 100, 101 and 102

United States Patent and Trademark Office

Reg. No. 2,420,512
Registered Jan. 16, 2001

SERVICE MARK
PRINCIPAL REGISTER

EBAY, INC. (DELAWARE CORPORATION)
2125 HAMILTON AVENUE
SAN JOSE, CA 95125

FOR: ON-LINE TRADING SERVICES TO FACILI-
TATE THE SALE OF GOODS BY OTHERS VIA A
COMPUTER NETWORK AND PROVIDING EVALUA-
TIVE FEEDBACK AND RATINGS OF SELLERS'
GOODS AND SERVICES, THE VALUE AND PRICES
OF SELLERS' GOODS, BUYERS' AND SELLERS'

PERFORMANCE, DELIVERY, AND OVERALL
TRADING EXPERIENCE IN CONNECTION THERE-
WITH, IN CLASS 35 (U.S. CLS. 100, 101 AND 102).

FIRST USE 1-15-1998; IN COMMERCE 1-15-1998.

OWNER OF U.S. REG. NO. 2,218,732.

SER. NO. 75-587,191, FILED 11-12-1998.

ANTHONY MERCALDI, EXAMINING ATTORNEY

CHAPTER 24

Searching a Trademark

Y ou are at risk of being sued for trademark infringement if you use a trademark that is so close to someone else's trademark such as to cause a likelihood of confusion when used on the same or related goods. In determining a likelihood of confusion, compare the two trademarks in terms of similarity in sound, appearance, and meaning. Also, consider the similarity of the goods, their respective channels of trade, and the relative sophistication of their customers and prospective customers. The closer the marks are, the more different the goods need to be to avoid a likelihood of confusion. For example, I will have a real problem if I sell leather purses under "Volcano" if that same word is already federally registered for leather belts, because the marks are identical and leather purses and belts are often sold in the same retail outlets. But there would be no infringement problem if I sold "Volcano" water skis. It is unlikely that customers and prospective customers of leather belts would think that the same company sells water skis. Could I sell "Vulcan" leather shoes and not have an infringement problem with the federal registration for "Volcano" for leather belts? This is a close one. I would counsel against adopting "Vulcan" under these circumstances. "Vulcan" and "Volcano" are similar in sound and appearance, and both conger up images of fire. Why spend lots of time and money building up goodwill around "Vulcan" only to face a lawsuit down the road that you either have to defend at considerable cost and risk, or settle by changing your mark and starting over?

Registering an Internet Domain Name

So after you have made a list of proposed trademarks for your product according to the techniques described in the previous chapter, prioritize them from best-liked to least-liked and begin searching to see if there are any potential conflicts. Starting with your favorite mark, the first thing to do is to see if the mark is available as a domain name on the Internet with a ".com" extension. Go to *www.networksolutions.com* and run an availability search in the ".com" extension. Registering the proposed trademark as a ".com" domain name will allow you to set up a Website to publicize your new product under that name. However, understand that just because the domain name registry indicates that your mark can be registered as the intermediate part of an Internet domain name address does not mean that you are free to sell goods under that mark or to register that mark in the USPTO. The domain name registration companies only look for the identical name. They do not check for similar names and they do not consider the type of goods you intend to sell. Simply put, unlike the USPTO, the Internet domain name registry programs do not do any analysis for likelihood of confusion. I could probably quickly register *www.DISNEYDOGS.com* as an Internet domain name. However, it wouldn't be very long after I began selling stuffed animals under the registered name "Disneydogs" that I would get sued for infringement by the Walt Disney Company.

You may wish to search the ".net" extension as well, but I wouldn't bother with searching the ".org," ".edu," or ".gov" extensions. There is little risk that nonprofit, educational, or governmental entities will have separate trademark rights that will conflict with your proposed trademark usage. I also don't think it is necessary to either check or register your mark in the ".biz," ".tv," ".us," and other extensions that have recently been established.

USPTO Trademark Search

Assuming you can get a ".com" domain name registration including your favorite proposed trademark, go to *www.uspto.gov* and perform a trademark search on the mark using its New User Form Search (Basic) engine. You may need to click the "Help" button to get you up to speed on how to do the search, but it can be mastered fairly quickly. The individual "hits" can each be clicked on to evaluate the nature of the goods and the owner.

The Boolean and Advanced Search options on the USPTO trademark Website are fairly complicated in terms of mastering the search command syntax, but this may be necessary in some cases to get a better feel for the availability of your proposed mark for use and registration as a trademark.

If a search on the New User Form Search (Basic) at *www.uspto.gov* does not reveal that the identical mark or something close is already registered (or the subject of a pending application) for the same goods, or closely related goods, you are probably wise to go back and immediately register your mark as a domain name for $35 or whatever the cost, which is nominal. Don't wait; the domain name may be gone tomorrow. This presumes that you have done a basic likelihood of confusion analysis in your mind and that you are satisfied that there is no likelihood of confusion. In close cases, you will need to consult an experienced trademark attorney to make this judgment. Err on the side of caution when determining whether there is a potential for a likelihood of confusion.

In some cases, you may be investing a substantial sum of money to print brochures, develop a TV advertisement, or build a whole ad campaign around a particular trademark before you are absolutely certain that there is no conflict with another prior use, registration, or pending mark. The search on the USPTO database only covers marks that have been registered or which are the subject of pending applications. It does not cover trademarks that are the subject of registrations in various states, listed in phone books, listed in trade directories, etc. Nor does the USPTO database tell you about marks that are in use, but not registered. In addition, the search engines on the USPTO trademark database do not look for marks that have a similar sound, appearance, or meaning. They generally are limited in their search capabilities to looking for similar word marks based strictly on spelling similarity. The established leader in trademark research is Thomson & Thomson of North Quincy, Massachusetts. If you retain an attorney, the attorney may have Thomson & Thomson conduct a thorough search that overcomes the shortcomings of searching on the USPTO trademark database and provide an extensive report for analysis. Expect to pay $1,500 to $2,000 for a full comprehensive trademark search and an opinion letter from your attorney based on a review of the search report. Thomson & Thomson can also search proposed logos. No matter how much searching you do, it is still not possible to know with 100-percent certainty that you will be able to federally register your new trademark or that you will not be sued for infringement for using it. However, with a full comprehensive trademark search from Thomson & Thomson and a clearance opinion from an experienced trademark attorney, you can probably achieve 95-percent reliability.

Int. Cl.: **41**

Prior U.S. Cl.: **107**

United States Patent and Trademark Office

Reg. No. 975,685
Registered Dec. 25, 1973

10 Year Renewal

Renewal Term Begins Dec. 25, 1993

SERVICE MARK
PRINCIPAL REGISTER

LOS ANGELES RAIDERS, THE (CALI-
FORNIA LIMITED PARTNERSHIP)
332 CENTER STREET
EL SEGUNDO, CA 90245, BY CHANGE
OF NAME FROM OAKLAND RAID-
ERS (CALIFORNIA LIMITED PART-
NERSHIP) OAKLAND, CA

OWNER OF U.S. REG. NOS. 731,309
AND 731,310.

FOR: ENTERTAINMENT SERVICES
IN THE FORM OF PROFESSIONAL
FOOTBALL GAMES AND EXHIBI-
TIONS, SOME OF WHICH ARE REN-
DERED THROUGH THE MEDIUM OF
TELEVISION AND RADIO, IN CLASS
107 (INT. CL. 41).

FIRST USE 7-0-1960; IN COMMERCE
8-0-1960.

SER. NO. 72-436,589, FILED 9-25-1972.

*In testimony whereof I have hereunto set my hand
and caused the seal of The Patent and Trademark
Office to be affixed on Apr. 19, 1994.*

COMMISSIONER OF PATENTS AND TRADEMARKS

CHAPTER 25

Registering a Trademark in the United States and Overseas

I n the United States, trademark rights are based on use. However, registration, particularly in the USPTO, gives many substantive and procedural advantages. Many foreign countries allow exclusive rights to be based solely upon registration, which can be very problematic as discussed later in this chapter.

Federal Trademark Registration

There was a time when many companies registered their trademarks with the government of various states. So, for example, you might own a California state trademark registration, a New Jersey state trademark registration, a Texas state registration, and so forth. The USPTO has long permitted trademarks to be registered, which gives you national exclusive rights, but only trademarks that have been used in interstate commerce can be federally registered. For many years, the term "interstate commerce" was narrowly interpreted by the courts. Nowadays, almost all goods or services are sold "in interstate commerce" as that term has been judicially interpreted. Therefore, except in rare cases, applications can be lawfully filed in the USPTO on virtually all trademarks and service marks. This has effectively rendered state trademark registrations obsolete. Why spend all the time and money to register a trademark in every state where you sell when you can cover all 50 states and U.S. territories with a single federal registration?

Here are some benefits of obtaining a federal trademark registration for your trademark from the USPTO:

1. The certificate of registration is prima facie evidence of the validity of the registration, the registrant's ownership of the mark, and the registrant's exclusive rights for the listed goods.

2. A third party, seeing your federal registration during a search, may decide against adopting a mark that would create a likelihood of confusion. Even if they proceed, an examining attorney at the USPTO may refuse registration of the third party's mark citing your prior registration. Even if the third party succeeds in getting its application allowed, you can file an opposition based on your registration, and the Trademark Trial & Appeal Board (TT&AB) of the USPTO may sustain the opposition and prevent the third party's application from maturing into a trademark registration.

3. A federal trademark registrant can bring its infringement actions in federal court where the court can grant a nationwide injunction.

4. After five years of consecutive use subsequent to the obtaining of the federal registration, the owner can file a declaration and have its registration made incontestable, which provides a number of procedural advantages in trademark litigation, such as foreclosing an infringer from seeking to have your registration canceled on the basis that the mark is allegedly merely descriptive of the listed goods.

5. When you obtain a federal registration you are legally entitled to display the registration symbol (®) to inform the public that the mark is federally registered.

6. If a trademark is the subject of a federal trademark registration, the trademark may be registered with U.S. Customs to stop the importation of infringing goods.

7. Finally, some foreign countries require that the trademark owner obtain a U.S. trademark registration as a prerequisite to obtaining a registration in those countries.

These benefits are provided by registration of a trademark on the Principal Register. There is another register called the Supplemental Register, which is used where registration has been refused based on descriptiveness.

Federal Trademark Application

A federal trademark application can be based on actual use of the mark in interstate commerce, or it can be based on an intent-to-use (ITU). The former generally requires that goods be sold in more than one state of the United States with the trademark affixed to it on tags attached to the goods, or on containers for the goods. A mere advertisement of the goods that displays the trademark is not considered trademark usage that will support federal registration. However, an advertisement of services containing a service mark will suffice for purposes of registering a service mark in the USPTO. If you have not yet used the mark, but have a bona fide intent to do so, you can file an ITU application.

Both types of federal trademark applications (use and ITU) are examined at the USPTO for form and for possible conflict with any other mark in use or in another pending application or registration. Office Actions are typically rendered addressing matters of form, and often initially refusing registration on a substantive ground, such as a likelihood of confusion with another mark or mere descriptiveness. These often can be overcome via amendments to the application or legal argument. If the application is allowed, the USPTO will publish the mark for opposition. A third party then has 30 days to file an opposition on various grounds, including likelihood of confusion with its own mark, even if the trademark examining attorney has already ruled on that issue relative to the third party's mark. A trademark opposition proceeding is a mini-lawsuit with discovery and a trial held before three administrative law judges of the TT&AB of the USPTO. If no opposition is timely filed, or if one is filed, and you prevail, your registration will be granted in the case of a use-based application. If the application is an ITU application, you will be given six months to file a statement of use (SOU) indicating the date of first use of the trademark in interstate commerce and providing specimens of use. The filing of the SOU can be delayed up to 30 months from the date of the USPTO Notice of Allowance by timely filing requests for extension of time every six months.

Once a federal trademark registration has been granted, a combined Section 8 and 15 Declaration should be filed between the fifth and sixth anniversaries of its grant date to prevent the registration from being canceled and to make the registration incontestable. The latter status prevents a party from seeking to cancel the registration based on the allegation that the mark is merely descriptive of the goods. It also precludes certain other defenses in trademark infringement litigation. Trademark registrations need to be renewed around the 10th anniversary or else they will be canceled. They can be renewed every 10 years thereafter; however, the mark must be in use at the time of each renewal. Unlike U.S. patents, U.S. trademark registrations can be renewed indefinitely, as long as the mark is still in use. The original Coca-Cola trademark registration is much more than 100 years old.

The USPTO Website allows a non-lawyer to file his or her own trademark application without using a lawyer. You can either file electronically or download the forms, fill them out, and mail them in. The instructions are fairly clear. I don't recommend that inventors prepare and file their own patent applications for reasons previously explained in Chapters 6, 7, and 18. However, a trademark application form is fairly easy to fill out and the consequences of not doing it correctly are far less severe than filing an inadequate patent application. In a worst-case scenario, an ITU application may not be sufficient to provide you with a constructive first-use date and another party may beat you to the punch and get the trademark before you can file a legally correct ITU trademark application. In this case, you may end up having to switch to a new trademark, but if you have not yet used the mark, which is why you filed an ITU application in the first place, you shouldn't be sacrificing any goodwill. If your use-based application was defective, it can either be amended or refiled, but you have not lost your trademark rights and your priority, which are based on your first use. However, you may find that in preparing your own trademark application, you have not carefully crafted the description of goods to optimize the scope of your exclusive rights. You may also find that you are unable to effectively respond to a USPTO Office Action initially refusing registration. If you can afford to do so, it's best to employ an experienced trademark attorney to confirm that you have selected a good trademark, help you search the same, provide an opinion regarding its availability for use and registration, file a proper application, prosecute the application before the USPTO, and thereafter docket the registration so that you will be reminded when it comes time to file the various declarations and renewals described here.

Any attorney admitted to the bar of any state can represent you or your company before the USPTO in trademark matters. They need not have a technical undergraduate degree and USPTO registration, as is required for all attorneys representing inventors in patent matters before the USPTO. Go to *www.lawyers.com* and do a search to find attorneys in your area that handle trademark matters. Often, patent attorneys also handle trademark matters.

Foreign Trademark Application

If you file a foreign trademark application within six months of the filing date of your U.S. trademark application, you can claim the priority benefit of your U.S. filing date. You can file a Community Trademark (CTM) application that can cover all the countries in the European Community (EC), but, in general, it is necessary to file separate trademark applications in each and every foreign country where you desire to have exclusive rights. In late 2002, the United States enacted legislation implementing the Madrid Protocol. Under this international treaty, U.S. trademark owners can file for registration in various foreign countries by filing a single application in the USPTO. The goal is to provide a uniform international trademark system.

Most foreign countries award the rights to a particular trademark to the first person to file to register it. This leads to a vast amount of trademark piracy. Foreigners monitor trademarks used and filed in the United States and try to file first on the same trademarks overseas so that they can later "sell" the rights back to the U.S. company that first began selling under the trademark when they enter various foreign markets. In some cases, the U.S. owner is able to avoid paying ransom by claiming that they have a famous mark that has been misappropriated, but this can involve drawn out, difficult, expensive, and uncertain legal proceedings in a foreign legal system. The Nike company refused to buy the trademark rights to the Nike trademark for apparel in Spain. I was told that, at one time, both Hertz and Burger King in Australia had no relationship to the U.S. companies that started those car rental and fast-food businesses in the United States. The marks had simply been appropriated and registered in Australia before the U.S. companies ever expanded there. When I started my patent and trademark legal career in San Francisco, California, the law firm where I was employed represented a major supplier of canned fruit. They selected a new trademark in great secrecy and had my law firm simultaneously file trademark applications in more than 100 countries so that trademark pirates could not see the filing in one country and then file on the same mark in another country where my client sold its goods. But, face it, few start-up companies can afford to do this.

One final word of caution about foreign trademark piracy: I have seen cases where the client manufactured the goods and had an exclusive distributor in a particular foreign country. Then, after many years, the client decided to change distributors, only to find out that its existing distributor registered the trademark in the foreign country in question in his own name to prevent the client from selling the goods under that trademark through any other distributor.

CHAPTER 26

Licensing, Policing, and Enforcing Trademark Rights

(T)he assumption in this chapter is that you own valuable trademark rights and that they have been federally registered. Without a federal trademark registration, you will be hamstrung if you try to stop an infringer in the United States. The registration is prima facie evidence of your ownership of the exclusive rights to the mark indicated in the registration for the goods listed. It permits you to sue in federal court where the judge can order the infringer to cease and desist from infringing in all 50 states in one injunction. There is a section of the federal trademark law that allows an injured party to sue for false designation of origin even in the absence of a federal trademark registration, but it is more difficult to win this kind of case.

Licensing

Licensing allows you to permit another party to use your trademark in return for a royalty. In some cases, you may want to license your trademark for goods that you do not manufacture, and as soon as your licensee sells those goods, you should file a federal trademark application to register your mark for those goods. The potential licensee still needs a license to use your mark even if it is not currently registered for the goods it wants to sell under the mark if such a sale would create a likelihood of confusion. For example, if the Nestle company doesn't manufacture coffeemakers, it could license that trademark to an appliance maker so that it could sell coffeemakers under the Nestle trademark. Any trademark license should have a quality control provision to avoid possible invalidation of the trademark. The theory in trademark law that applies to licensing is that the public should be able to rely on the goods manufactured by the licensee as having a certain level of quality controlled by the licensor, which presumably means that the licensed goods have a similar or higher level of quality than those goods already sold by the licensor under the licensed trademark.

If the licensee intends to keep selling the same goods as the licensor, then it may suffice to simply provide in the trademark license agreement that the quality of the goods sold by the licensee shall be at least as high as the goods sold by the licensor (trademark owner) under the trademark. In the coffeemaker example, the quality control provision could be quite specific in providing that the coffeemakers sold by the licensee under the licensed trademark shall be approved by Underwriters Laboratories (UL), shall be made only of high-grade plastic and stainless steel parts, shall include a color LCD display indicating brewing status, and so forth. The quality control provision could require prior approval of any particular coffeemaker by the licensor. You will definitely need the assistance of an experienced trademark attorney to draft a proper trademark license agreement.

Service marks can also be licensed, but a service mark license may be viewed in many states as a franchise agreement. Such agreements are subject to heavy regulation by state and federal laws that require complex registrations and disclosures similar to those required for companies that want to go public and sell stock. It took a great deal of sophisticated (and expensive) legal work to gain governmental approval for marketing the Mail Boxes Etc. franchise outlets that allow customers to send and receive packages and mail, make copies, purchase office supplies, and so forth, all in one convenient location.

Policing a Trademark

Policing a trademark refers to the regular activity of determining whether your trademark is being infringed. Trademark infringement occurs where another party sells goods under a trademark that is so similar in sound, appearance, or meaning to a federally registered mark as to create a likelihood of consumer confusion as to the source and origin of the respective goods. For example, "W-Dee Forty" motor oil would create a likelihood of confusion as to whether it is made by the manufacturer of WD-40 spray lubricant.

Check the Internet and see if goods are being offered for sale with your trademark that were not produced by you or your licensee. Check with your sales representatives to see if they have noticed any knockoffs. Make sure that you are using the (®) symbol next to your trademark if it has been federally registered. This will deter others from using your trademark without your authorization. It will also ensure that you have the right to recover maximum damages should it become necessary to sue for trademark infringement. If infringing goods are being imported, register your trademark with U.S. Customs so that infringing goods don't make it off the dock. Make sure that you only use your trademark as an adjective, not as a noun, to avoid having your trademark invalidated because of genericness. Similarly, only use your service mark as an adverb, not a verb.

Enforcing a Trademark

When it comes to enforcing your trademark rights, make sure your timing is right before you sue an infringer. If your application is pending in the USPTO, wait until the registration is granted before having your attorney send a cease and desist letter. This will lessen the likelihood that you will become involved in a USPTO opposition proceeding. If you have your registration in hand and you sue in federal court, the accused infringer will have a major disadvantage in trying to convince a judge or jury that your trademark rights, as evidenced by a beautiful registration certificate with a handsome gold seal, are invalid or limited. In most trademark infringement lawsuits, you will be trying to obtain injunctive relief; that is, a court order forcing the defendant to quit using the mark it is using, or any other mark that creates a likelihood of confusion. It can be difficult to prove monetary damages because you generally have to show that but for the infringer's sales, you would have gotten the same sales, and that these customers would not have purchased similar goods bearing a different brand.

Federal law permits the trademark owner to sue for dilution, in which case it need not prove that there is a likelihood of confusion in order to get a court order enjoining the defendant from further sales under the trademark in question. Dilution occurs where the distinctiveness of a trademark is being impaired by selling goods under the same trademark or a similar mark, which, while not raising a likelihood of confusion, effectively waters down the trademark. For example, the Kodak trademark is not registered for bicycles, yet the Kodak Company would have no trouble winning a dilution case against a company that tried to sell bicycles under its trademark. Dilution cases can be tough to win if you do not own a well-known trademark.

If there is a finding of infringement of a federally registered trademark, or a finding of false designation of origin, the plaintiff may recover the defendant's profits, any damages sustained by the plaintiff, and the costs of the action. Under certain circumstances, the court can award up to three times the damages found, and reasonable attorney fees.

Counterfeiting is a particularly egregious type of trademark infringement where the pirate duplicates the trademark and the goods with the intent of passing them off as genuine goods. A good example of counterfeiting in the trademark context is the importation of knockoffs of the famous Rolex watch. These counterfeit watches are hawked on street corners, and, more recently, over the Internet. Such infringement can result in seizures by U.S. marshals and criminal penalties for the infringers.

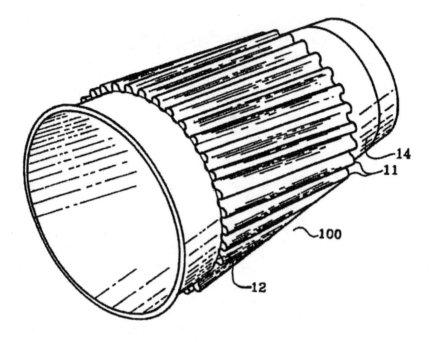

14
11
100
12

FIG. 3

U.S. Patent No. 5,205,473
"Recyclable Corrugated Beverage Container and Holder"
Granted April 27, 1993
(paper coffee cup holder used by Starbucks)

Conclusion

A fter reading this book, the U.S. patent and trademark legal system should no longer be a mystery to you. Hopefully, you have a better idea of the origins and functions of our patent system, what can be patented, the process of getting a patent, what can happen after you get a patent, and whether you should seek patent protection. You should also have a basic understanding of trademark principles, how to select a good trademark, and how to protect it.

I want to reiterate that I am not giving specific legal advice to anyone through this book. Patent law and trademark law are constantly evolving, and, therefore, some of the laws explained in this book may no longer exist or they may have changed since its publication. I sincerely hope that I have not offended anyone with any of my war stories, but they were included to illustrate my points. In the law business, experience is the sum of all of a practitioner's involvements in cases, large and small, good and bad.

If you have an idea for a new product or the name for a new product, go to the official USPTO Website at *www.uspto.gov* and play around with its free patent and trademark database search engines. You will be surprised at the wealth of information that is readily available at your fingertips. The power of information to enlighten and inspire is amazing. If you feel the need, seek out a good registered patent or trademark attorney in your locale. Happy inventing and happy branding!

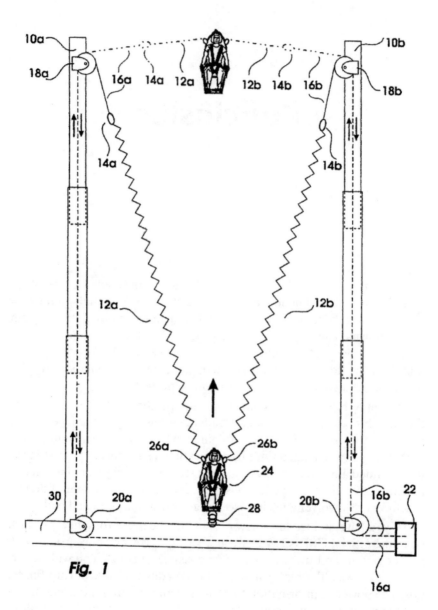

Fig. 1

U.S. Patent No. 5,421,783
"Human Slingshot Machine"
Granted June 6, 1995
(thrill ride developed by Bungee Adventures)

Website Resources

P lease note that some of these Website addresses may have changed since the publication of this book. Use one of the popular Internet search engines, such as the Google search engine, to locate any new Website addresses.

www.access.gpo.gov

Through using this official Website of the United States Government Printing Office, you can order copies of various patent-related publications such as the Manual of Patent Examining Procedure (MPEP), Title 37 of the Code of Federal Regulations, and various informational pamphlets.

www.european-patent-office.org

The official Website of the European Patent Office (EPO).

www.innovationcentre.ca

Founded in 1981, the nonprofit Canadian Innovation Centre has assisted more than 70,000 Canadian inventors and entrepreneurs by providing objective idea assessment services. This Website contains information on how to register for invention assessment services, an online inventors' newsletter, and basic information for inventors and small businesses interested in developing new products.

www.inta.org

The International Trademark Association (INTA) was founded in 1878. According to its Website, INTA is "an international association of trademark owners and professionals dedicated to the support and advancement of trademarks and related intellectual property as elements of fair and effective national and international commerce." The Website contains answers to frequently asked questions about trademarks, useful links, and a trademark checklist.

www.inventnet.com

Another Web portal for individual inventors with access to intellectual property discussion boards.

www.inventorsdigest.com

Inventorsdigest.com is sponsored by the publishers of *Inventors' Digest Magazine*. It allows free access to past articles online on subjects of interest to individual inventors seeking to develop and market their inventions, obtain patent protection, license their discoveries, and take legal action against infringers.

www.ipo.org

The Intellectual Property Owners Association Website contains timely patent-related news written in an understandable format.

web.mit.edu

MIT's Website provides a link to a short handbook created by the Lemelson-MIT Prize Program that addresses independent inventors' and entrepreneurs' most frequently asked questions. Type the words "invention handbook" into the search field of MIT's internal search engine and click on the link to the handbook that comes up second in the list.

www.patentcafe.com

This Web portal contains a plethora of hyperlinks to various other Websites that are helpful to struggling inventors. You can access chat rooms that discuss intellectual property, but beware of bad advice spread by uninformed novice inventors, and don't inadvertently publish your invention.

www.piperpat.co.nz.

This Website contains an excellent listing of patent law firms in foreign countries.

www.sba.gov

The United States Small Business Administration Website provides a helpful guide to federal government assistance in starting a new business to manufacture and sell products embodying your invention.

www.techweb.com/encyclopedia

Techweb.com provides helpful technical explanations of more than 20,000 technical terms. Examples are CMOS, GSM, visor, RAM, Internet, ultraSPARC, and LINUX.

www.thomasregister.com

You can search 168,000 companies to find out which ones manufacture products most similar to your invention.

www.uspto.gov

This is the truly incredible USPTO Website. There are more than 20 pages of information designed to help inventors learn the basics of patents, patent searching, how to evaluate patent costs, and how to flush out unscrupulous invention promoters. Full text and images are available for all U.S. patents granted since 1976. They can be searched at no cost with simple and advanced search engines. Easy-to-understand online searching tutorials are provided. Unfortunately, U.S. patents granted between 1790 and 1976 are searchable only by patent number and current U.S. classifications. You may have to download a free tagged image file format (TIFF) graphic plug in order to view patent drawings. Instructions on how to do this automatically come up if you try to click on the image icon and the drawings are not displayed. If you don't have a cable or DSL Internet connection, and only have a dial-up Internet service provider (ISP), as a practical matter, it will take too long to download patent drawings. The USPTO Website also has an extensive database of more than 2 million trademarks and service marks that have been registered, as well as pending trademark and service mark applications. Simple and more advanced search engines are available with instructions that allow you to determine if your proposed mark might be available for use and registration.

Index

About the Author

(M) ichael H. Jester is registered as a patent attorney with the U.S. Patent and Trademark Office. He holds undergraduate and law degrees from the University of California, and has been in the private practice of patent and trademark law for nearly 30 years. He has prosecuted more than 400 U.S. patent applications for all sizes of businesses and for individual inventors in a broad range of technologies. Mr. Jester has obtained a patent on his own electronic invention, giving him valuable insight into the process from the inventor's viewpoint. He also has extensive patent litigation experience. On the trademark side, Mr. Jester has conducted numerous searches and registered many trademarks and service marks for his clients.